The Miracle of Grace

London reared of Irish parents, Kate Kerrigan worked in London before moving to Ireland in 1990. Her first novel, *Recipes for a Perfect Marriage*, was shortlisted for the Romantic Novelist of the Year Award. She is now a full-time writer and lives in County Mayo with her husband and son.

Praise for *Recipes for a Perfect Marriage*

'A moving portrait of love and marriage through the eyes of two women . . . the author looks closely at love as a romantic ideal and poses the question: Can a woman learn true love?'
Sunday Express S Magazine

'An intelligent, droll and heart-warming read . . . Kerrigan is a lovely writer and her book breaks from the traditional mould of chick-lit'
Sunday Tribune (Ireland)

'This book is one to keep. Anyone who reads it will return to it, time and again, either for the story or to seek out one of the many old recipes'
Ireland on Sunday

'Both wholesome and satisfying'
Heat

Also by Kate Kerrigan

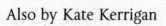

Recipes for a Perfect Marriage

Kate Kerrigan

The Miracle of Grace

MACMILLAN

First published 2007 by Macmillan
an imprint of Pan Macmillan Ltd
Pan Macmillan, 20 New Wharf Road, London N1 9RR
Basingstoke and Oxford
Associated companies throughout the world
www.panmacmillan.com

ISBN 978-0-230-01478-7

Copyright © Kate Kerrigan 2007

The right of Kate Kerrigan to be identified as the
author of this work has been asserted by her in accordance
with the Copyright, Designs and Patents Act 1988.

The quotation on p.ix is from 'Entirely' by Louis MacNeice,
from his *Collected Poems* published by Faber.

1 3 5 7 9 8 6 4 2

A CIP catalogue record for this book is available from
the British Library.

Typeset by Intype London Ltd
Printed and bound in Great Britain by
Mackays of Chatham plc, Chatham, Kent

Visit www.panmacmillan.com to read more about all our books
and to buy them. You will also find features, author interviews and
news of any author events, and you can sign up for e-newsletters
so that you're always first to hear about our new releases.

For my mother, Moira

In memory of Maureen Kelly and Mary Gunn: your legacies live on in the hearts of your daughters.

If we could get the hang of it entirely
It would take too long;
All we know is the splash of words in passing
And falling twigs of song,
And when we try to eavesdrop on the great
Presences it is rarely
That by a stroke of luck we can appropriate
Even a phrase entirely.

from 'Entirely', Louis MacNeice

Prologue

My mother wrote notes. Notes to remind herself to do things: put the rubbish out, feed the cat. Notes of things she had to buy, people she had to telephone, TV programmes she wanted to watch, things she must find. Often, at the top of her day's 'To Do' list was 'Must find "Must Find" list'. While talking on the telephone, Mum would take notes to remind herself exactly what had been said, then refer back to them when telling me about the call. Every time she went out she would leave me a note saying exactly where she was going and what time she would be back, just in case I might call in and wonder where she was.

I put the books down on her kitchen table and searched around for my note. On the shelf by the telephone, there was a memo pad in the shape of a house. It had 'Your Jobs Today' written at the top; down the left margin were numbers one to ten – each one a rung on a teddy bear's ladder. The teddy was on the roof of the house holding a hammer. It was exactly the kind of tasteless tat that my mother felt compelled to buy, then regretted as soon as she got home. I knew that this note was just one of Mum's lists and not written directly for me, but I read it anyway. It would surely contain some interesting titbit she intended to tell me.

1. Tel bill
2. Ring Shirley – return purple top
3. Bathroom floor tiles! Ring Dennis
4. Tell G scented candles, £2 for 50
5. Cashpoint
6. Tesco: bread, milk, eggs, gravy, apples, spread
7. Bins! Bins! Bins!
8. Tell G have ov cancer. Prob term
9. Bins!
10. Chemist: Moisturizer, deodorant, prescription

That would be item eight. Despite the abbreviation, I knew what it meant immediately. I wasn't expecting it. I certainly had never thought about ovarian cancer in relation to my mother and there had been no recent conversations I could recall that might have brought it to the front of my mind. Yet straight away it read to me as a complete sentence: 'Tell Grace I have ovarian cancer and it's probably terminal.'

one

Grace

Amanda Nicolson sat in front of me and bawled her eyes out. She was a thick-set, sensible fourteen-year-old and the last child in St Anne's, the private girls' school where I taught, whom I would have expected to get pregnant. By the state of her, I imagined it was a sentiment that would be shared by her parents, if and when she told them.

'I'm sorry, miss, I'm sorry, I'm sorry, miss . . .'

The students always apologized for getting upset. It was the most heartbreaking aspect of being the school's counsellor, a voluntary position I held in addition to being the deputy head. Most of the other teachers shuddered at the idea of being a sounding board for the girls' problems, but I enjoyed it. Perhaps because I didn't have children of my own the reponsibility of it didn't faze me. It might have been naive of me to take on the position of adviser and confidante to four hundred hormonal teenagers, but I believed someone had to listen to them. I remembered what it felt like to be a teenager myself – confused, pained, isolated, passionate, excitable – and it

3

seemed a shame to me that so many adults generally, and teachers specifically, seemed to have little or no empathy with them.

I talked Amanda through all of her options but she was so distressed she barely took it in. The father was a seventeen-year-old Italian student who had been boarding with her family the previous summer – they had only done 'it' once.

'My dad's gonna kill me, he's gonna k, k—' and she collapsed again.

I knew Dr Nicolson would not kill Amanda. He would be disappointed and concerned. He would make an appointment at a private clinic where his serene manicured wife would take their precious daughter for an abortion. She would be kept home from school for a week, pampered by their housekeeper, then sent back and told to forget all about it. Amanda's education would not be interrupted by a baby, and the respectable, middle-class lives of her parents could not incorporate an unexpected grandchild. It was out of the question. Amanda was too young to make a choice so her parents would make it for her. Along with choosing her university, her career and, if at all possible, her husband. The course of Amanda's life was too important to be left to chance. It was not the pregnancy itself that was the tragedy, but the unexpectedness of it; the loss of control.

In the end, I just leaned forward and put my arms around her. She curled her chubby legs up gratefully on the sofa and put her head on my lap like an infant. I patted and stroked her head and indulged myself by wondering if her perfect mother would do the same when she found out. I knew it wasn't my place to wonder – I was just there to provide temporary relief and solace – but I said a silent prayer that she would be all right. The exchange left me heavy with emotion.

A little of Amanda's pain followed me into the car as I drove over to my mother's house to deliver her some cookery books she had asked me to order off the internet for her.

Although I inherited my moderately left-wing politics and my liberal attitudes from my mother, it seemed that on a day-to-day basis she was the person who most completely challenged my personal belief system – my private ideas about the correct way to do things. If I had to describe myself I would have reluctantly used the label 'new-age liberal', although of course by our very nature we liberals object to putting people in boxes. (Except for 'fascists' and 'racists' and 'conservatives' and 'religious right-wingers' and, in fact, everyone who isn't as 'open-minded' and 'inclusive' as us.) And yet my mother seemed capable of eliciting behaviour from me that was the opposite of liberal. Uptight, irritable and critical just about covers it. Much of it came from just the fact of who she was. I knew that I loved her more than I ever loved anyone and yet she was always the brunt of my careless criticism. We were very different and the only thing that irritated me more than the differences between us were the similarities. I could be kind and comforting towards another person's pregnant teenage daughter, and yet I was rarely as kind to my own mother. A mother gives her child love: endlessly, unconditionally, on demand, constantly, from birth to grave. That's what they do. The more they give you, the deeper they dig a pit which you expect them to fill. The bad news for both of you is the pit is bottomless. The *really* bad news is, knowing that doesn't make it any easier.

I could never be certain if it was my own insecurity or my mother's failing that she never felt like quite enough for me. I knew in my heart that she was a great mother, and yet I always carried around a little resentment towards her.

One of the things that broke my heart about my mother, and also irritated the hell out of me, was her lack of confidence. Mum never grew out of wanting to be slimmer, more fashionable, different from how she was; neither did she mature into one of those refined older women who settle into muted shades of cashmere that complement their beige, grey-peppered bobs. Mum was never happy with the subdued haircuts the hairdressers kept giving her.

'They've made me look like a sixty-year-old suburban shop manager.'

'You are a sixty-year-old suburban shop manager,' I would say.

'I don't care,' she'd snap, 'I want to look "way out" and interesting. I want to look like Judi Dench!'

Mum was always experimenting – trying to find her 'look'. She went through fads and phases. Loud African-print kaftans, then pashminas, then candy-coloured velour tracksuits with chunky training shoes that added an extra two inches to her five-foot-nothing frame. I towered over her, and I often sensed her irritation that I didn't use the advantage of my height and slim build to more glamorous effect. As my mother never grew out of wanting to look 'trendy', I never grew out of being irritated by her lack of self-confidence. 'Be who you are, Mum,' I used to say when she asked me what I thought of a new handbag or haircut. Once she said, 'I don't *know* who I am, Grace.' I assumed she was being flippant; it sounded like a line from a magazine. Despite how much I loved her – or rather because of it – I was compelled to constantly point out to Mum where she was going wrong. I wanted her to be the exception to every rule I knew about human behaviour. Publicly I said she was a great mother but secretly the child in me always believed that there was a better, more enlightened mother living inside her. Some part of me thought that all it would take was a nod from me and this all-knowing person would emerge from the flawed, vulnerable, unhappy mess that in my darkest moments I believed she was. It never occurred to me that perhaps that *was* her truth: she did not know who she was. She was unsure, floundering. She said she was content, that she had achieved all she had ever wanted in her life, but I didn't believe her and that made *me* insecure. She was my mirror. I wanted her to be as good as she could be, so it would reflect well on me. My mother did not compete with me, but sometimes I thought it was only a lack of confidence that was stopping her.

I knew that my mother loved me, but always, even as a small child, I felt there was something missing. A mother's love for her only child is supposed to be absolute. Somehow, my mum's love never felt complete.

*

She had called and asked me to order the books weeks beforehand. She had telephoned at midnight, after sharing a couple of bottles of wine with Shirley, a divorcee who had become her new best friend, since her husband had run off with his secretary six months before. I was astonished that men in our modern age still had secretaries who would run off with them, but then Shirley was a walking cliché. She was, to put it politely, 'dysfunctional'. Neither her son nor her daughter spoke to her any more; she was a chain smoker who rarely made it past lunchtime before cracking open the Chablis. Doubtless as distraction from the sadness of her own life, she had cast herself in the role of my mother's keeper and was instructing Mum in subjects as diverse as diets, hairstyles, animal print and mother–daughter relations. It seemed she had added cookery to the list. The phone call could *not* wait until morning: 'Shirley says the recipe for Thai chicken is superb, and that I simply *must* try it as soon as possible. So please order the book immediately, and sooner if possible. Thank you!'

My mother's assertive tone was for Shirley's benefit. It annoyed me that Mum, at the age of sixty-two, was being so easily led by this grotesque woman; also annoying was the fact that I knew she would forget she ever wanted the books and would blame me for adding to the already substantial pile of unused 'stuff' in her kitchen.

Mum seemed to be in a constant state of low-level self-flagellation; enough to keep her permanently irritated with herself, but not enough to motivate change.

She regretted eating that big dinner, but then she'd have dessert and regret that too. She regretted buying that wool coat that didn't fit her, but it was expensive so she would wear it anyway, then she would buy another one and regret the waste of money. Those orange curtains she had bought in a sale were absolutely vile, she didn't know what had come over her, but they were up now and she would look at them every day thinking, Why, why, *why* did I buy them? 'I'll take them down, Mum, I'll exchange the coat, I'll take this fifty-pence tasteless notepad and throw it right in the bin.' Then she would say, 'No!' It was as if she needed all these minor regrets. The wrong purchases, the half-written letters, the lapsed gym membership. Between them they formed a security blanket for her, a weight to stop her moving too fast. Without it, she might have had to get a computer and order her own books on the internet, or fulfil that ambition to be a stone lighter. The novelty notepad was a symptom of all that. As I picked it up I wished, not for the first time, that I wasn't one of those co-dependent people who look inside other people and see their pain.

After I had been whacked with the initial bombshell, I turned the page over. It was an automatic action, like swearing at a paving stone after you've tripped over your own feet. I wasn't expecting to find anything. Or perhaps part of me was hoping the next page would read 'Only joking! April fool!'

It didn't. It was written in the hurried short-hand scrawl my mother used when recording a phone call.

19th Feb
Dr Feltz – Royal Free Hosp.
Biopsy – Stage IV, MMMT rare sarcona
    (sarco*m*a?)
MMR – tumour 10cm, probably spread – maybe
    liver?
Operation – scheduled next 2 wks
Sponge bag – M&S new range + FIND PURPLE
    SLIPPERS! Grace?

I jumped at the sight of my name. I understood the
other information. I had a basic knowledge of cancer –
I knew it was sarco*m*a, for instance, and that Stage IV
was almost certainly terminal. The information registered but it was so dreadful that my mind did not want
to let it in. It opened the door and looked at it, but then
closed it quickly again. So the terrifying truth of my
mother's cancer remained in the form of a handwritten
list on a novelty notepad she had left lying around. I
figured if my mother was going to distract herself with
purple slippers then I was entitled to sidestep pain with a
bit of well-deserved anger.

I believed that there were no such things as acci-
dents. So I found myself in my mother's kitchen freaking
out *not* because she had Stage IV ovarian cancer, *not*
because this meant that she was almost certainly going
to die sooner rather than later, but because she hadn't
told me in the 'correct' way. In the three seconds (or ten
minutes) that passed with me standing there holding the
revelatory note in my hand, I was aware that I separated
in two. Part one buckled against the fireplace, then
leaned stock still against the cold bricks in a state of

shock. The other, fluid, emotional part of me seemed to float out of my body, then bounce up and down in a state of hysterical fury.

She *had* intended me to find out in this way, I just knew it. She lacked the courage to tell me properly, so she had done it in this throwaway manner to try to make it more manageable, the stupid misguided woman. I mean, *number eight*? Number *eight* on a 'To Do' list is to tell her daughter she is dying? Squashed in between two reminders to put the bins out? Was this a metaphor of some kind – her subconscious saying, 'I am a rubbish mother'? She put telling me below her grocery shopping, below telling me about scented candles on special offer at the pound shop! This was completely wrong, me finding out like this. Part of me was puzzled; why didn't my mother tell me sooner, bring me along with her to the hospital, the doctor – whatever? Why didn't she involve me, lean on me? The hysteric in me was raising her hands up, going, 'This is so, *so* typical of my mother.' I had no siblings to discuss it with; there was nobody else to break this gently to me; no father to share the pain of losing her with. Just me – on my own. The silly woman should have acquired enough wisdom by now to find a better way of telling me, rather than leaving a note on her kitchen table with all the gory facts detailed on the back.

So loudly and insistently was my inner hysteric shouting that I didn't hear my mother come in.

'Oh, I'll take that,' she said, snatching the notebook out of my hand and walking straight past me to the sink, where she proceeded to fill the kettle. 'I have nice ham from the butcher's and a fresh loaf, so if you can wait five minutes for lunch, it's ham sandwiches. And before you start, no, I do *not* have any pesto!'

Was it me, or did all mothers do this: cram so many mixed messages into one short statement that their children need twenty years of therapy just to understand what they're saying?

I was momentarily surprised by the amount of effort it took my body to move away from the fireplace where I was still leaning and face my mother's busy, kettle-filling, sandwich-making back.

'I read the list,' is all I said. I left out the phone-call notes. It would have been too harsh to overload us both with practical details.

There was a moment's silence, which I hoped she was going to fill with the solemn details of her news by sharing it with me properly.

'I hate that pad. I don't know what possessed me to buy it when I have drawers full of lovely notelets that I never use.'

With that, she pointedly flicked open the kitchen bin and hurled the teddy bear and his ten-runged ladder into it.

My mother had a habit of being apologetic over little things, but stubborn and defensive over big things. For example; she deeply regretted making me give up ballet lessons but 'had her reasons' for not telling me why my father left. So, what possessed me to buy that hideous notebook? I was going to tell you about the cancer in my own good time.

Sometime in the next six months, presumably.

Still, the notepad was in the bin now. Problem solved, eh? I let rip. My opening gambit would have been so different if I had held on to myself. It could have been 'There is no need to carry this alone, Mum. I'm here for you.' Or I could have created a comfortable distance by using her name: 'Eileen, I know about the cancer.'

Instead I opened my mouth and out came 'How – *how* – could you put telling me you had cancer below returning a blouse to Shirley? HOW!?'

It could only get worse after that.

'Shirley lent me that blouse over a month ago – it was important.'

'And telling me you had cancer wasn't important?'

'Of course it was – that's why it was on my list.'

'Not as important as Shirley's blouse, though – or going to the cashpoint, or ringing Dennis about the tiles in the bathroom?'

'That's not how it works. It's just a list – the order doesn't mean anything.'

'Of course it means something. Everything fucking *means* something.'

I believed that. That everything meant something. But I shouldn't have said the word 'fucking'. She went tight-lipped and determined.

'How dare you talk about Shirley like that? Shirley is my friend!'

So wrong on so many different levels. Shirley was more of a bad influence than a friend.

'I *do not* want to talk about Shirley. Don't try to side-track me by talking about Shirley.'

'Well – you brought up her name.'

'Only in the context of something else.'

'You've never liked Shirley. I don't know why – she's always saying how nice you are.'

'You're doing it again! Trying to distract me into talking about Shirley!'

'You're the one whose got a problem with her – you're the one who keeps saying Shirley, Shirley, Shirley . . .'

'YOU'VE GOT CANCER!'

'STOP SHOUTING AT ME!'

And I *was* shouting at her. I was towering a full foot over my tiny, frail mother who had cancer and I was yelling at her. I was ashamed of behaving like a bully, but I still did not want to stop, wanted only to pick her up and shake some sense into her, or the cancer out of her.

Mum's lip quivered and from behind my rage I noticed that her hand was shaking, with the butter knife still in it. She looked down on the worktop, fumbled a slice of bread out of its packet and resumed making our sandwiches. Her actions had slowed down; the clipped determination was gone, but I didn't want to see that. She was offering me space now, inviting me to sit and have lunch quietly. She was defusing the anger by busying herself and the air in her cluttered kitchen felt light in anticipation of our talking.

But because it was Eileen offering the space and not vice versa, I couldn't accept it. My pride wouldn't let me, or perhaps I just wasn't ready to hear her say it yet. I knew, even as I turned my back on my mother and walked out of the door, that I was wrong. That I was hurting her, and myself. But then that was one of the disappointing things I had learned during my stint in therapy. Knowing what to do is one thing; doing it is something else.

two

Eileen

It's funny how, when you look back, it is often the small things that are really important. As a child I believed in magic. Then, when I was eleven, a pair of red trousers changed everything and made me start to see the world as it really was.

I was born in 1943 in a terraced cottage in Ballamore, a small town on the west coast of Ireland. Fifteen miles to the east was a flat-topped mountain, and to the west we were five miles inland from the sea – next stop America. At one end of our road was Ballamore Cathedral, tall, grey and grand, and at the other, in its own lush gardens, was the Bishop's Palace. My mother said we lived in the safest place in the world because no matter which way we looked – up or down our street, behind or in front of our house – we were hemmed in by God's greatest achievements. Mountain and sea, church and clergy – they were the outer and inner perimeters of my early life.

My family name was Gardner and my father was Senior Clerk in the town hall, which was considered a very good job, but not so good that we looked down our noses at people. Civil servants were respected without being considered snobbishly middle-class, privileged through education rather than money; it was an enviable position. We were neither looked down upon by the doctors and solicitors nor envied by the poor. I went to school alongside children who had to share shoes and came to school hungry. The poor people lived at the top end of town and sometimes, when my sister and I walked past their houses on our way home from the cinema, they would throw small stones at us and shout, 'Big shots!' When we told our mother she would tell us to thank God we weren't one of them – and we did. I grew up knowing I was lucky to have been born into the family I was.

The house we lived in was on a street called The New Line, on account of the houses being newly built by the town council when my parents had moved there some ten years before. Because of his job, my father was given one of these houses for a peppercorn rent. We had a bathroom upstairs with running water, two bedrooms and a box-room, and downstairs we had a dining room, which was our main living area, a drawing room for entertaining important guests like visiting clergy, and a small scullery, where my mother prepared food and washed the pots and clothes. In the dining room was a range where my mother did all of the baking and cooking. Our house was considered luxurious by my mother's family, who lived out in the country. Once, a coarse man who was married to a cousin of my mother's said, 'You'll get calluses on your arse from sitting down all day.' Her family thought my mother's life was too easy, with water 'inside in the house' and her having a 'contraption' to cook with rather than an open hearth.

But my mother did not sit down all day. I had a younger brother and sister, and between cooking and cleaning for us all, Mum was constantly complaining that we had her 'robbed of every ounce of energy' she ever had. I did what I could to help her. My jobs included cleaning the ashes out of the range every morning and carrying the kettle of hot water up to the bathroom for my father's morning shave, but by far my favourite job was being sent up town to get my mother's 'messages'.

Every Saturday morning, Mam gave me two shillings and sent me up to Mrs Durcan's shop. The money was to pay for my father's newspaper bill plus our comic books and my mother's weekly *Woman*. Durcan's had a bakery out back, so while half of the shop was given over to tobacco and papers, the other comprised a counter weighed down with delicious cakes. The smell was something else, and I soon got into the habit of sneakily spending some of my mother's change on a delicious sugary doughnut. The first time I bought one, Maidy Durcan, who had a stern face and a starchy manner, said, 'Does your mother know you're buying doughnuts, Eileen Gardner?' Like most children, I was shy talking to adults and only blushed in reply, but Maidy took my money anyway. There was no love lost between my mother and Mrs Durcan ('Tell that woman nothing if she asks you!' Mam shouted after me as I left each week), but at the age of eleven I knew that Maidy Durcan wouldn't tell my mother for fear she'd miss the tuppence worth of business. I felt guilty sometimes, because I knew that my mother only went to Durcan's because they were the only shop that supplied English magazines and papers. Mam baked a soda cake every day, but when she had visitors and needed yeast bread to impress them, she made a point of buying it ready-sliced in Carey's grocery shop – even though she knew the bread in Durcan's was superior. My weekly dough-nut was the only purchase given to the Durcan bakery each week and I knew my mother would be furious with me if she found out I was giving Maidy money.

There was also the element of sin to consider. I avoided sinning as much as possible, but for a Catholic child in those days, sinning was a very complicated business. Technically, spending my mother's money without consent was classified as stealing, but unless it was something big like a purse or a cow or a donkey, stealing was only a venial sin, punishable by extra time in purgatory. Purgatory was heaven's waiting room but it wasn't nice, full of flames and horned devils – like hell, we were told. The only real advantage purgatory had over hell was that you knew you weren't going to be there for all eternity so you could console yourself that you *would* get to heaven eventually, once all your earthly sins had been atoned for. The smart Catholic would start this process while they were still alive by saying prayers called indulgences. I had received a book of indulgences for my eleventh birthday and was work-ing my way through it determinedly. I knew that one indulgence prayer said three times in immediate suc-cession would buy me a fortnight off purgatory. It wasn't much when you considered how long eternity was, but I had estimated that one doughnut amounted to about two months in purgatory and reasoned that not even an all-powerful, all-punishing God could justify more than that. So by saying four sets of indulgences (which could be one prayer said twelve times), I was off the hook. It seemed a small price to pay for my delicious, illicit doughnut.

It was during one of my covert doughnut-eating sessions that I first saw the picture of the lady in the red slacks. It was a fine day and I had settled myself down among the ruins of the monastery behind the cathedral. It was a quiet, some said haunted, spot, and one of the few places in the small town where I could be guaranteed privacy. I liked it there because it was close to God's house, the cathedral, and yet it wasn't *in* His house. All through my childhood, I had felt a deep love and devotion to the Blessed Virgin, and God and I enjoyed an easy understanding. I didn't commit any big sins – like murder or sex – and He didn't go too hard on my minor misdemeanours like doughnuts. My favourite expression was 'God moves in mysterious ways', and my best friend Breege and I loved to glamorize everyday coincidences by turning them into 'signs from God'. If we saw three swans on the river together, we knew that it was going to be sunny on Saturday. If there was a crow sitting on the railings by the Blessed Virgin's statue, the number of Hail Marys we could say before it flew away was the number of children we were going to have. Breege would point out the signs, but I was the one who would get the 'spiritual feeling' that determined what the sign meant. We often discussed how I knew all these extraordinary things. I said I didn't know, I just *felt* it.

As if God was inside my head, telling me facts like 'If you step on three pavement cracks you will burn in hell for all eternity,' or 'If the petals fall off that rose in the next week, someone in the town is going to die.' When my mother read the death notices in the paper and pointed to somebody that she knew who had died (which was every week, as she knew everybody in the town), it only strengthened my belief in my own abilities as a prophet. While there was no way of knowing if the pavement-cracks theory was really true, neither of us took any chances. Breege said that if God was talking to me like that it meant that I was really special and would probably become a nun.

As I was settling down to my doughnut, the *Woman* magazine that was on the top of my pile of papers flicked open. It settled on a page that featured Father Peyton, the famous 'Rosary Crusader', standing next to the most beautiful woman I had ever seen. They were in a big park and there seemed to be hundreds of people in the background, but all I could see was the woman. She had blonde hair drawn back into a bun and an enigmatic smile, as if she knew something that nobody else did. It occurred to me that if the Blessed Virgin were alive at the time she would probably have looked like that woman. I felt certain that God was sending me a message. The caption said the woman's name was Grace Kelly, and in the picture she was wearing a cream sweater and a pair of red slacks. Slacks were like men's trousers, except they were worn by ladies in magazines. My mother didn't wear slacks, nor did any of the women in our town. But suddenly I felt an overwhelming desire to own a pair; a pair of red ones just like in the picture. I decided I would go home at once and ask my mother to make them for me.

Five weeks, three days and seven hours later – that was how long it had taken me to persuade my mother to order the pattern from England, buy the red cotton from Foyles's and then actually sew them – I was curling my fingers around the handle on my mother's wardrobe door, tapping it in anticipation, holding off for a few more seconds the glorious moment of seeing myself in her full-length mirror.

I closed my eyes tight, opened the door, took a few steps back and then gradually opened them. In the mirror was a vision. It still looked like me; there were the two thick chestnut curls at the end of my plaits, a face sprinkled with freckles. There was my favourite blouse with the forget-me-not pattern that my aunt had sent home from America. But then – oh then! My lace communion and confirmation dresses had made me feel special in a holy way, like a child bride of Christ, but this was something different altogether. I placed one hand on my waist and pushed my hips one way, then the other. I lifted my left leg and kicked, then my right. I had been worried that I was going to look like a boy, but I didn't at all. I remember trying to think hard about how I felt, and deciding that the best word was 'free'. I knew that this good feeling must mean something, and so I thought it was probably another sign from God.

three

Grace

As I drove around the block after my dramatic exit, I tried to placate my rage with an image of Mum sitting with her head in her hands, regretting, regretting, regretting the thoughtless way in which her only child had discovered her cancer. But before the picture was half formed, I realized I was on to a loser. Terminal cancer definitely gave my mother the edge on me guiltwise. I had to go back and straighten things out. I took a deep breath and told myself it wasn't important that we had fought. I should apologize, because after all what was important was not how I was told, but rather that my mother was terminally ill and we had to shoulder it together.

I had only been gone around five minutes and expected to find Mum more or less where I had left her, in the kitchen, either eating her lunch or mournfully tidying up. I imagined she might be standing by the sink with her back to me and would visibly freeze as she heard me enter. I would then go and place my hand on her shoulders. 'Oh Mum,' I would say. No words needed then; we'd hug, cry – do the things that mothers and daughters do at times like this.

However, when I opened the hall door, I could hear she was upstairs. I followed the happy racket of Christian music radio into her bedroom where I found her, sitting topless except for her bra, blow-drying her hair in front of the dressing-table mirror. She was singing along to a song I had never heard before. Her habit of listening to Christian music as an alternative to easy listening irritated me. I had once asked her if she was intending to become 'born again' and she replied that it was just an easy way of ensuring God was around you without having to go to Mass. It struck me as an idea that was not only ludicrous but completely lacking in any spiritual integrity.

'Jesus, love, I didn't hear you come in,' she said, jumping slightly as she saw my reflection in the mirror. She continued to grab sections of hair in her small rounded brush and tease them back. The mottled flesh at the top of her arms quivered as she let go of each curl. She didn't look angry or upset so my intention to apologize dissipated.

I walked over and put my hands on her bare shoulders. Her skin felt soft and dry, hot from the hair-dryer.

'Mum,' I began. Even I could hear that my voice was leaden with deadly seriousness.

'Oh, you're freezing,' she said, jumping up and moving quickly over to the bed. 'Just let me get dressed.' She picked up a blouse and began to put it on.

The conversation I had been holding on to in my head, the most important conversation of my life, became interrupted then by a small but intensely irritating thought. The blouse was purple.

'Is that Shirley's blouse?'

Mum was clearly delighted. With both the blouse and the fact that I had changed the subject.

'Yes it *is*. She called just after you left and invited me out to lunch.'

'I thought you were giving it back to her?'

I was annoying myself now. My mother had cancer, Shirley's blouse was not important, and yet here I was getting tangled up in the minutiae of her meaningless arrangements.

This was just one of my mother's traits that I seemed to be unwittingly and infuriatingly adopting as I got older. It was as if the supply of energy I had used to rebel against becoming like her had run out when I hit forty. I'd found myself buying a hot-water bottle one day as if I had been genetically programmed. A single woman of forty-three using a hot-water bottle was, I had always believed, offering a negative statement about her sexuality. Despite that conviction, I just couldn't fight the pull of the comforting smell of warm rubber. Ditto my discovering cushioned shoe insoles, neck warmers and pop socks; putting a tea-towel on the draining board for no logical reason; and writing myself lists. After years of my mother frying my head by making me get her to the airport two hours before check-in, I found it impossible to be late for anything, usually arriving half an hour earlier than arranged. I took a book with me everywhere and told myself I was creating extra space in my life for reading. But in fact I was just turning into my mother. Slowly, at times imperceptibly, perhaps in the way I stretched my mouth and raised my chin before I had my photograph taken. I used to be able to make myself look nothing like her, but a declining commitment to fashion and the gentle fleshing out of my features had put paid to that too. I was like a taller, younger version of her now. I could cope with the physical stuff, but the idea that I was, by some alarming spiritual osmosis, acquiring aspects of her character freaked me out. Being distracted from issues of life and death by a question as petty as a borrowed blouse was so not me.

'Oh – the *blouse*.' Mum sucked in her breath, opened her eyes wide, then spread her fingers and parted her hands to indicate that there was an anecdote on its way.

I came to my senses and realized that I was not ready for another Shirley conversation, so I held up my hand with equally dramatic aplomb and said, 'Mum, I don't want to—'

But the train had already left the station. 'Shirley rang and said that what with one thing and another I could keep the blouse for as long as I wanted it. Look, it's designer' – she thrust the label at me – 'so I thought, what better way to thank her than to wear it right now. We're going to Debenhams because they've *just* done up the café. Terracotta walls and a mural with elves; I believe it's gorgeous. Why don't you join us? I'm sure Shirley won't mind.'

She had told Shirley about the cancer. That's why the ghastly woman had given her the blouse, because she knew Mum was going to die in the next six months. My life with my mother – which seemed like my life in its entirety – was summed up in that moment. In all that she wasn't able to say to me and in the way that I so desperately wanted to be close to her. My mother was dying of cancer and she couldn't, or more accurately, didn't feel that she could, talk to me about it. She could talk to Shirley, though, and with the addition of the phrase 'one thing and another' the terrible woman had been saying to my mother, 'You can borrow my blouse until you are dead,' or, 'I am going to make you a gift of that blouse in order to enhance the last few months of your life.'

The point was not Shirley's intentions but rather the fact that her trite, tasteless gesture had succeeded in cheering my mother out of the dark mood she had been in less than ten minutes beforehand. Therefore, for the second time in the first scene of what was supposedly the last act of my mother's life, horrible-new-best-friend-of-less-than-one-month Shirley had played a starring role. Whereas I, her daughter, had yet to be formally told of her illness.

Do we ever really get closure when we fight with family? With lovers, you can have sex afterwards. With friendships, you can either drop the person or draw closer in greater understanding. But with family, when people disagree they seem to really dig their heels in. It is so often a case of suck-it-up or never see that person again for the rest of your life. Often it's over dumb stuff like criticizing their new garden furniture or ownership of their late granny's china dog. Of course, every family fight stems from a childhood grievance, and the reason I had such a problem with Shirley was because I hadn't felt as close to my mother as I would have liked, and I was jealous. After years of therapy and healing meditation weekends I was supposed to have learned all these lessons and yet still, *still* I knew this was all my mother's fault. Why could she talk to Shirley and not me? How *could* she put a tacky blouse ahead of the emotional well-being of her daughter? There were probably reasons why she had chosen to tell Shirley about her cancer first, but they were rubbish reasons and she was a rubbish mother. Suddenly I was behaving like a child again and everything about this whole scenario was wrong, wrong, wrong.

Then the sensible part of me kicked in and drew a picture of what would happen if I opened and closed my mouth around the word 'Shirley' at that particular moment in time. My mother would storm out. I would drive around the block as I had done before, then come back later and have the same argument again. This could go on for days, weeks, months. My mother could die before we would ever resolve the issue of her having not told me about her cancer before Shirley. The important thing was to stop the issue from rolling around and around in my head before it gathered any more momentum. The important thing was to get her to tell me now.

'Mum, sit down.'

'I really don't have time, Grace, I told Shirley that—'

'Please, Mum.' I trained my eyes on hers and pleaded. 'It's important.'

She eyed me defiantly, then sat down. The blouse was unbuttoned and she squeezed her hands between her knees, like a child about to be told off. I pulled the stool over from the dressing table, then sat in front of her and took both of her hands in mine and placed them on my lap.

'Tell me what's going on, Mum.'

She wouldn't meet my eyes, and for a second her cavalier expression dropped. I saw real fear in her face, although I couldn't tell if it was her own fear of dying or simply her fear of telling me about it. Probably a bit of both.

Then it was gone and she smiled a snappy, too-bright smile. She eased her hands out from under mine, gave them a patronizing squeeze and said brightly, 'It's fine, Grace. Nothing for you to worry about. I'm going to be fine. Really.'

Sweeping my hands aside, she stood up and buttoned her blouse. I tried to keep my voice steady and safe. 'Come on, Mum. I read the note. I know you've got a rare sarcoma and that the cancer is at stage four. Have they given you a date for the operation yet? You have to tell me, Mum. We have to sort this out – make plans.'

At this stage Mum was already hurrying out the door. 'I haven't got time for this, Grace.'

I followed her down the stairs saying, 'Mum, please, you'll have to talk about it sooner or later. I need to know what's going on.' My voice came out in a teenage whine. In times of crisis, the child will out.

As will the angry parent. Mum opened the front door to leave, then changed her mind and closed it just enough so the neighbours wouldn't hear her shouting. My mother had rarely asserted herself over me. Even as a small child I occasionally remember her yelling at me over things I knew were important, like disappearing off during shopping trips or playing with the cat litter, but even then it just seemed like empty shouting. I never believed she really meant it. But this time I did.

'I don't *have* to tell you anything, Grace. This is *my* life – and I am fed up with you interfering. I will live and die as I choose, do you hear me? Just mind your own bloody business!'

Then she slammed the front door and went off to meet Shirley for lunch.

four

Eileen

At eleven I was extremely proud of my collection of religious knick-knacks and ornaments. There was the standard stuff – my badge from the Family Rosary and my Legion of Mary uniform, including the beret and a big Miraculous Medal on a thick blue ribbon. A great-aunt of my father's was a nun in London and she used to post me over a regular supply of medals and buttons which I took out often and counted like a banker. I had twenty-five Our Ladys – including five in full colour and seven blue; two St Martin de Porres, one St Anthony, two St Francises, one St Joseph and eleven St Patricks; and a St Christopher medal in real silver which I had inherited from my mother on my tenth birthday and kept in a special box. I didn't count my Sacred Heart medals because they were only made of fabric and paper, but as for rosary beads – I had no less than four sets: two glass ones from my first holy communion, pink and green; one ordinary white plastic one for everyday use; and the one which my aunt had sent me that had been blessed by the Pope. That was my least favourite because it was made of ordinary navy beads. It came in a plain leatherette pouch with A GIFT FROM THE VATICAN stamped on the front of it so I knew it was especially holy, but it annoyed me that things couldn't be holy and pretty at the same time. The glittering exception to this, and the thing which I most longed for in the world, was the Children of Mary cloak.

I was already a member of the Legion of Mary, with my brother and sister. My mother was the secretary of the local branch and we visited old people and generally did good works for the Church and local community. But the Children of Mary was a different organization. It was for women and girls only and was given over entirely to one's personal devotion to the Blessed Virgin. On joining at the age of sixteen you received a medal inscribed with your name, a certificate, a prayer book and the 'uniform' of a simple white dress and the cloak. The cloak was a long sky-blue garment with a floppy hood and could be made of any fabric you wanted as long as it was a certain shade of sky blue. My mother was a Child of Mary, and her cloak was made of wool, but she had promised me that when I was old enough to join I could have my cloak made in heavy silk. Children of Mary wore this costume to important religious events, but you had to look after it as you would be laid out and buried in it when you died. You also got a candle which would be lit beside your coffin and which, if possible, you should hold as you were dying. I was already in the Angels of Mary, the junior version. This meant that the elders could keep an eye on you while you were growing up and make sure you were good and holy enough to become a Child. The blue cloak was the best deterrent to sin that I could imagine, although I knew I would have to wait another five years – a lifetime – before getting one.

I worried sometimes that I might die before I became a Child and got my cloak. I didn't know what happened to mere Angels when they died, and when I asked my mother she told me to 'Stop talking about death, Eileen, it's morbid.' I took to bringing my confirmation candle out with me anywhere I thought I might be likely to die. In the pocket of my coat on fair day, for instance, in case I got run over by a horse and cart, or a cow. I played the scene out in my head sometimes. There I would be, lying in the middle of Bridge Street, having been knocked down by some marauding animal into a bed of hay. People would clear a space all around and my mother would kneel by my side wailing; 'Eileen! Eileen; my only daughter!' (That wasn't true because I had a sister, but at times like these a mother tends to forget everything.) I would then struggle bravely to get my hand in my coat pocket and there would be a collective gasp from the crowd as I took the candle and held it to my chest. Tears streaming down his face, my father would light the candle; 'My daughter, Eileen – my only child!' (My brother would also be temporarily forgotten about.) 'Say something – speak to me!' As I looked up and saw a circle of dismayed, agonized faces staring down at me, I would know instantly what to do: 'Hail Mary, full of grace, the Lord is with thee. Blessed art thou amongst women and blessed is the fruit of they womb, Jesus . . .' Rosary beads would be whipped out of handbags and trouser pockets as the good people of Ballamore sent up decade after decade of the rosary to pray for the soul of this exceptionally brave and devout young girl. In the full-length version, the one I turned to when I was feeling put-upon or upset, I would become encased in a shaft of white light, and anyone who had ever annoyed me would see me being lifted up through the clouds, a shimmering blue cape miraculously appearing around my shoulders as my angelic face of innocent exaltation looked forward to my deliverance directly into the lap of Mary, the Mother of Christ.

In the mean time, I had to content myself with sneakily trying on my mother's cape when she wasn't around. In the run up to Father Peyton's visit, my mother wasn't around a lot.

The Pope had declared 1954 Marian year, but for most people in Ballamore and its surrounding areas it would be remembered as the year that hosted a rally for Father Patrick Peyton, the Rosary Crusader. Father Peyton was described as the Modern Apostle of Family Prayer and, with the help of Hollywood stars like Gregory Peck and Bing Crosby, had led a crusade to bring the rosary into ten million homes across America. He had been born in Attymass, a small farming community in County Mayo, and the return of this local hero was the cause of huge excitement around the town.

My parents were committed Father Peyton followers, and along with most of our neighbours we were members of his worldwide organization Family Rosary, which essentially meant we knelt as a family and said a decade of the rosary after our dinner every evening.

With the news of his trip in June, membership of the Legion of Mary went through the roof. It was everyone's big chance to parade in uniform in front of someone who'd shaken hands with Bing Crosby and Grace Kelly. In the weeks beforehand, my mother was caught up in a frenzy of arrangements. All drapers in the region had run out of uniforms, so berets and medals had to be transported from Dublin; the new statue which had been erected opposite the Bishop's Palace had to be painted; seating in the park had to be rigged up, and benches made; refreshments and tea urns had to be organized, the pecking order of religious groups and schools arranged, plus accommodation for visiting clergy, transport for the sick and elderly, et cetera, et cetera, for ever and ever amen. My mother was so caught up with business that she failed to notice that I was wearing my striking red slacks day and night, and not just on 'appropriate occasions' as designated by her.

Immediately I got home from school, I would run upstairs to my room and pull them on. I had worn them uptown to collect messages, and sitting on the river wall in the evenings talking with Breege; I had even worn them to Sunday Mass. Breege had been uncertain about them at first. She'd never seen a girl wearing trousers before, except in movies. She told me that her mother had commented that she didn't think it was 'befitting' for a young girl to be wearing such attention-drawing clothes about the town, and that she had a mind to speak with my mother about it. I begged her to talk her mother round.

'But are the slacks not a sin, Eileen?'

'Of course they're not a sin. Sure didn't my mammy make them for me, and she's the holiest woman in Ballamore!'

'But the women in Hollywood are the only ones that wear them and my mammy says they're *full* of sin.'

'Not this one, Breege. Not this one.'

I had been carrying the picture of Grace Kelly around with me, and decided it was the right moment to tell Breege my theory about the famous actress being an incarnation of the Virgin Mary.

Breege was sceptical at first, but I persuaded her.

'I mean, just look at the way Father Peyton is gazing at her.' I pointed at the handsome Irish priest's friendly face. 'I mean, he is adoring her, Breege, *adoring* her, and he's a priest, and they're not allowed to adore any woman except the Blessed Virgin.'

Even as I was saying it I was getting a message from God in the form of a very strong idea in my head.

Over the next few days the idea grew and grew until I could barely sleep at night with a mixture of fear and excitement. This was no passing fancy, I was sure of it – but there was only one way to be absolutely certain.

Three days before Father Peyton's rally, my mammy packed my younger brother and sister off in a taxi to stay with my father's family in Ballyhaunis. With my father at work and my mother away up the town, I had the house all to myself.

I pulled the curtains in my parents' room, then put on my red slacks and took out a stool from under the bed so that I could reach through my parents' clothes, up to the high hook at the back of my mother's wardrobe where she hung her cloak. Careful not to disturb any of the clothes, I eased the cloak on to the bed, took off the old sheet which was hung around it for protection and swung the heavy cape over my shoulders. It was far too long – I would have to find a way of holding it up – but before I started fiddling around with safety pins or belts, I had to be absolutely certain that this was not just a silly idea that I had got into my head but was, indeed, a proper message from God.

I stood in front of the mirror on the wardrobe door and looked at myself. I looked good. The red slacks and the blue cape had a kind of crusading, adventurous look about them; like Maid Marian in *Robin Hood*. I closed my eyes then and waited for my message. It started when the light behind my eyelids turned red as a shard of sunlight pierced a tiny gap in the heavy wool curtains. It was a dull day and the curtains were closed, so that was miracle number one. I was so excited that I was almost afraid to open my eyes, and when I did, I could hardly believe the magic that was actually happening. There, dancing across my knees, was a tiny white light, flickering over the cape and the slacks like a fairy. After a few seconds, the light disappeared and I felt drawn over to the window. The Japanese cherry tree that sat outside my parents' window was rustling, and behind it was the final answer I needed: a rainbow. Rainbows were God's way of telling me that I was definitely right. Whenever I doubted my instincts, I would look for a rainbow, and if I saw one I knew I was on God's track. Now, I had seen a rainbow and I hadn't even been looking.

This was it; this was the outfit God wanted me to wear to Father Peyton's rally.

five

Grace

Mum had brought me up as a Catholic but I was never really convinced. When I was thirteen and started to ask questions, the religion thing fell apart on me. It was also around then that I started to get really curious about my dad. He had left home when I was four and I had scant memories of him: being small and sleepy in the curve of his lap; him drying my hair with a towel in front of an electric fire we had. It had plastic coals and a light behind it that cranked around to give the appearance of a flickering flame. That I remember the fire better than him is probably testament to how little he was around. All my mother would say was that he was an alcoholic. He died when I was ten and by then they had lost touch completely. He became a writer, which I thought was really glamorous; Mum had read about his death in the newspapers. I was upset that he had died before I had met him, but was more unsettled by the idea of death itself. It was my first experience of mortality and I must have driven my mother mad with questions. 'What was my dad really like? Why did you let him leave us? Is there a God? If there is, why does He let bad things happen? Why do people die?' In the crucial transition phase from child to young adult, these questions seemed inexorably linked. My mother was not able to supply me with satisfactory answers to either personal or ethical questions, and from that I developed an early disrespect for her 'blind faith'. Even the phrase itself smacked of ignorance. I discovered self-help, spiritual and emotional healing techniques and yoga meditation in my twenties, and they formed the basis of a belief system that was so much more meaningful to me than the parrot-fashion prayers of the Catholic Church.

The Church was a very big part of my childhood, insofar as my mother worked as a housekeeper in the local parish priest's house up until I was about fourteen. He was a good friend to us, Father Price – young at heart and ahead of his time. He rarely wore his official garb, and Mum and I always just called him Frank. I often think Mum was secretly in love with him, because when the new priest who took over from him brought his own housekeeper with him and Mum lost her job, she seemed less upset about that than Frank's going away to the missions. He kept in touch for a while, I think, but Mum's faith in the Church seemed to decline with his leaving. She made an effort to go to Mass most Sunday mornings, but was easily tempted away, often by something as small as a television programme or an offer from me for a late, cooked breakfast.

Her faith seemed to me haphazard and lacking in commitment. I believed her Catholicism had its roots in habit more than belief. While she had never judged me for turning my back on her Church, she had never really appreciated that my journey into healing and meditation was a form of spirituality. I always hoped that one day I could get her to broaden her own spiritual horizons.

In the mid-nineties, there was a moment when I thought that might happen.

In the summer of 1992, Bishop Eamon Casey, charismatic and well-loved Bishop of Galway, was discovered to have fathered a child. The boy's mother, Annie Murphy, 'outed' Casey and his cold treatment of her and her son, but even she could not have imagined the deluge of dissent she was starting. Over the coming few years, there was scandal after scandal. The younger generation were given the perfect excuse to reject a Church that was so old-fashioned they couldn't relate to it anyway. Older people, for whom it was too late to do an about-turn, sided with the party line that the media were simply conspiring against them. But it was the women who were left floundering in their faith. Many of them turned their backs on the Church. Here was an institution that had controlled them as children and curtailed their lives as women, insisting they stay with husbands who abused them and denying them the right to use contraception. Then when they reached late middle age, secure in the knowledge that they had done the right thing in abiding by God's rules all of their lives, the Catholic Church revealed itself to be a corrupt organization full of weak, often evil individuals. Child abuse; Magdalen laundries where girls were made to slave through unplanned pregnancies, then give up their children for adoption; wealthy bishops who had preached family values fathering children then denying paternity. Women like my mother – loyal, rule-abiding Catholic women – felt hurt or betrayed and left the Church in droves.

I was involved in this process because I was running a women's reading group for the Irish City Centre Community Service near the school where I was teaching. The group was called Heal and Read and had a self-help angle, with one of the women reading a chapter from a fashionable tome of the time – *Women Who Run With the Wolves* or *Women Who Love Too Much* – followed by a discussion which usually touched on personal issues: alcoholic husbands, wayward children, distant parents and, after Annie Murphy broke her silence, anger at the Catholic Church. As the weeks passed we all came to know each other intimately, although as the paid facilitator I was obliged to keep a slight distance, and rarely mixed with them outside the meeting itself.

Mary, Bernadette, Finoula, Niamh and Cathleen were a revelation to me because they reminded me so much of my mother. They were all in their fifties, convent-educated, and had spent the sixties and seventies picking rusk crumbs out of their Draylon-covered sofas in the suburbs, cooking big dinners for tired husbands, feeding babies and taking their daughters to Irish dancing classes in chilly church halls. As they were wringing out cloth nappies, thanking God this was the month they had enough saved for a spin-dryer, Joan Baez was singing on their kitchen transistors about revolution. Erica Jong, Germaine Greer, Gloria Steinem, free thinking, free love – it seemed like everyone was free except them. They swallowed it because their paths had been set by a higher authority than politicians or artists. In the mid-nineties, when the Church let them down, these women began to look at all they had missed out on. They could have left their husbands, cut their hair, slept with a woman, joined a band, become an artist. I watched on as this extraordinary group took their anger and harnessed it into something positive. As time passed, they discovered yoga and painting and *You Can Heal Your Life* by Louise Hay. Two of them left their husbands, all five left the Church.

During that time, I felt that these women were giving me insight into my mother's background and what made her tick. Although I tried to approach her on the subject several times, she kept batting me back and refused to discuss with me what was happening to her Church. I sensed that she was struggling with her faith, and it hurt me that she would never talk about it, especially as I was working with women who were in the same situation as her. As had happened so many times in the past, something that should have brought us closer together ended up pushing us further apart. She didn't trust me enough to discuss it with me, but I also suspected that perhaps she thought there was nothing to discuss. That she was, despite what I hoped for her, one of those people who stick with religion because of caution and convention, the cornerstone qualities that the Church used for centuries to keep women in their place.

I didn't hear from my mother after she left me standing speechless on her stairs. The following day, unable to accommodate my feelings of hapless fear, I made an emergency appointment to see Sita.

Sita was my friend and my therapist. That is a contradiction in terms, but our client–therapist relationship had been sullied by social interaction. She had originally been recommended to me by my ex-husband Jack, a therapist himself. After three months of my attending sessions with her, the two of us kept bumping into each other at New Age social events attended by mutual friends – a yoga workshop weekend, a child-naming ceremony – and Sita decided that, given her connection to Jack, it would be unprofessional of her to continue to treat me. However, I had already decided that Sita was the most inspiring person I had ever met and was determined to keep her in my life as a friend. She was ten years older than me and had been a medical doctor with an established Ayurvedic practice before she retrained as a psychotherapist. She had come to England from Calcutta when she was a child and was a committed Buddhist. I admired her hugely, professionally and personally. Sita's skill and insight as a psychotherapist were complemented by a warm, charismatic personality bedrocked in a strong, certain character. The bottom line was that Sita brought the coveted 'all-knowingness' of your average psychotherapist to a different level. To most, I presented myself as a self-assured person; some found me imperious. Sita was able to communicate directly with my inner self and was the only person I had ever met with whom I felt entirely safe being vulnerable. She was certainly the only person I trusted enough to defer to on issues that were so personal that they crossed over into the spiritual.

Sita kept herself slightly apart from the real world. She lived in a large house overlooking the sea and spent most of her time there, meditating, reading and seeing clients. I had never heard her bitch about anyone, or raise her voice, never seen her be anything other than serene and loving.

As the years passed, Sita became a mentor; if I was not so afraid of being labelled a crank, I would have described her as my 'guru'. I rang her any time I needed, spent an hour talking then made a donation to charity instead of paying her. Sita was the one person in the world I felt completely safe with. I respected her judgement, and believed in her friendship for me. On that day I felt grateful that I had somebody like her to confide in.

I drove south and arrived in the early afternoon. It was a dull day, a flat grey sky blurring the horizon, no pretty landscape to distract me from my depression. I had explained briefly on the phone, so Sita was ready for me with a pot of green tea and a hug, although we both knew there would be little real comfort to be gained from either. We followed our usual routine: tea and small talk for ten minutes, then she led me into her consulting room. She had laid a bowl of jasmine out on the low, Mexican coffee table and had an aromatherapy blend burning. I didn't ask what was in it but I detected lavender. She sat opposite and pulled her chair in closer so that our knees were almost touching. Sita opened her palms out to me, indicating I should talk, then folded them into a prayer cup and held them to her closed lips to indicate she was listening. She closed her eyes to hear me all the better. As she did, I felt a rush of sadness that I knew this woman intimately enough that her physical actions spoke to me, yet I could not communicate adequately with my own mother. It came out in an untidy stream: the list, the blouse, Shirley, death, fear, grief, confusion, anger – crying, shouting. Mostly shouting. Once I started shouting, I became afraid that I would not be able to stop and that the force of my anger might be too strong; I was worried that it might even demolish Sita's eminently tranquil countenance. So I made myself fall suddenly silent and Sita asked gently if I was sure that I was 'finished'. I said yes, but I was lying. I could have happily sat there all night effing and blinding my mother into oblivion, with the result that, as Sita gave her advice, I could hear her but I wasn't really taking it in. My face wore an expression of attentive listening but my body was tingling with stress and panic.

As I was leaving, I thanked Sita for the warm, peaceful calm I pretended I was feeling. As soon as her house was out of sight, I stopped the car and scrabbled in my handbag for something I could write a list on. I could have cried at my inability to hold Sita's wisdom in my head, but I knew I would forget everything she had told me if I didn't write it down. I found a biro in the glove compartment and on the back of a parking ticket I hurriedly wrote the essence of Sita's advice to me.

* Death/God – respect other's faith
* Give Mum space to be herself

Lastly, and with a feeling of deep reluctance I wrote

* Make peace with Shirley

Despite how I was feeling, I knew I would have to follow her suggestions. That was the deal, and besides, it was all I had to hold on to. Somehow, in the shock of the last couple of days, I had lost my faith in my own judgement of what was 'right'. And like my mother, I needed to turn to a list.

six

Eileen

My mother had to get to the rally early to help set things up, so she arranged for me to go with Breege and her mam, Mrs Feeney. They were both looking at me strangely as we walked up to the park together. The cloak underneath my coat did make me look bulky, although I had tied the belt of my macintosh tightly around my waist to try to make myself look a more normal shape. At the last minute I realized that I'd forgotten to conceal my red trousers, so I quickly rolled them up to my knees and fastened them roughly in place with some dressmaking pins I grabbed from my mother's sewing box. The pins scratched my knees badly as I walked, and in fact the whole ensemble was extremely hot and uncomfortable. I guessed that this was what God meant when He said, 'Suffer little children to come unto me.'

The crowd thickened the closer we got to the park, and by the time we reached the top of St Patrick's Hill I could tell that Mrs Feeney was so busy trying to keep track of us that she had all but forgotten her curiosity about what was under my coat. She gripped us both by the hand and dragged us head-first through the crowd until we reached the Legion of Mary section, directly behind where the religious were sitting.

I had never seen such a sight in my life. The park was normally used for football matches and I had been to a few with my father. The chaotic crowds of shouting men had been replaced by the orderly arrangement of what seemed to me to be millions of people, organized according to religious rank and uniform. Sitting in the very front row were a handful of bishops and monsignors. Behind them were two horizontal rows of black, which were the nuns and priests, followed by a thick stripe of Sisters of Charity in white, then there were the Christian Brothers in their brown, belted robes. In vertical lines behind them were the other uniformed organizations: Legion of Mary in their berets and medals, convent girls in navy-blue skirts with starched collars and neck-ties, then nurses and military. In a dense rectangle on top of the hill stood the Children of Mary in their hooded robes. The sky blue of their outfits formed a mass of colour against the threatening clouds, as if they had sucked the very colour out of the sky. As I was pushed into line behind Breege, a very bad feeling gripped my stomach. Most of the other girls were holding their raincoats, neatly folded over their forearms, although some still kept theirs on. I gripped the closed buttons of my coat and began to pray for rain. With the same certainty with which I had believed a miracle was going to happen today I now knew, without a shadow of a doubt, that I had made a very big mistake.

Then the Children of Mary became lit up from

behind as the sun appeared. At first it was just a glimmering threat, but within seconds glorious shafts of sunlight beat down on them, threatening to lift them clean up to heaven. The crowd murmured in unison; it was a miracle – the sun was going to shine for Father Peyton after all. As the last of the sceptics removed their raincoats to reveal their full uniforms, I wanted to run – out of the park, away from the crowds, to just sit at the back of the cathedral and have a good talk to God about what was going on. How had I got it so, so wrong? The change in weather had been the miracle God had meant for today and I had turned it into something else. I was about to think of an excuse – a headache, I was going to be sick – when I felt the firm hand of Mrs Feeney tug at my belt and reach for my buttons. I shouted a terrified 'NO!' and everyone turned to look at the girl who wouldn't take her coat off. Mrs Feeney did not like to be defied, and short of pulling her hair or hitting her hard in the face, which I felt very much like doing but didn't, there was nothing I could do. She had most of the buttons undone before I could wrestle myself away.

'Holy Mary, mother of God,' Mrs Feeney said, blessing herself as she stumbled back from the shock of seeing what was under my coat. She held one hand up to her face while the other pointed at me as if I were Satan himself. I put my hands over my face and started to cry. I didn't know why I felt as ashamed as I did; it didn't make sense, it had just been a simple mistake. But with everyone looking at me, and with everything being so very different from what I had been expecting, I just couldn't help it. Patrick Lowny, the group leader, came over to see what the fuss was about and asked Mrs

Feeney to take me home. He would explain to my mother, he said. He gave me a kind look, but it didn't make me feel any better.

Mrs Feeney marched me back to my house in complete silence, making my keep my coat shut and pulling me roughly by the arm across the roads. I knew that Mrs Feeney wasn't angry with me because of what I had done, but because Patrick's request meant that she would miss some of Father Peyton's rally. Mrs Feeney was one of those women, like Maidy Durcan, who quite liked it when things went wrong for other people. That was what my mother said. As Mrs Feeney pushed me into the back door of the house and said, 'Now you sit down, Eileen Gardner, and think about how you have disgraced yourself,' the full horror of what I had done hit me. I had upset my mother, my father, my best friend; worse still, I realized that I had probably upset the most important person of all – God.

seven

Grace

My conversation with Shirley was what we therapy junkies call a 'learning experience'.

I found her number in the local phone book, although I felt guilty for contacting her behind my mother's back.

Sita's instructions had been characteristically vague and open to personal interpretation. Having decided that 'Make peace with Shirley' meant make her a subject of my daily meditation, I conjured up an image of her grotesquely made-up face and offered her up to the universe. What the universe sent back to me was 'Ring Shirley and find out what the story is with Mum's cancer.' I guess I was playing around with the spiritual ideal of unconditional forgiveness, but then I was desperate, and in my book sometimes that *is* an excuse.

'Hello, Shirley?'

'Who's this?' Right away a candidate for phone-charm classes.

'Shirley, it's Grace.'

'Who?'

'Grace. Grace Blake? Eileen Blake's daughter?'

'Whose daughter?'

My eyes idly surveyed my kitchen clock. Four in the afternoon. Happy hour. Or not, as the case may be.

'Eileen Blake? Your friend? I'm her daughter Grace.'

Heavy breathing. I think she was lighting a cigarette. This was clearly not going to happen over the phone.

'I was wondering if we could meet up? I wanted to have a chat with you about Mum?' My face caught itself up in an excruciated grimace. 'I thought if you were free I could take you for tea in Debenhams? I believe they have just done the place up and . . .'

'I'll meet you in Morton's wine bar, next to the station – know it?'

As it happened I did know the place and agreed to meet her there, although I had to negotiate an extra twenty minutes for my journey as she seemed keen to get there as soon as possible.

When I arrived Shirley was sitting up at the bar chatting to a bloated drunk in a business suit. They were clearly having an Alcoholics Anonymous meeting without the anonymity. She was one of those women who display an impressive ability to balance when perched cross-legged on a bar-stool, the problems only starting when they try to dismount. There was no point in my being coy, so after the briefest of hellos I ordered a bottle of Chardonnay.

It didn't take much to get rid of the man. I had become adept at offering withering looks to undesirable middle-aged suitors after I hit forty and started to attract more than my fair share of them.

The next hour was a blur of confused communication and hateful emotion. Getting information out of an emotionally incontinent alcoholic was harder than I could ever have imagined possible. Details of my mother's illness emerged through a fog of Shirley sniffing and sobbing with the uninhibited grief of a woman about to lose her closest friend in the world.

'She is a wonderful woman, Karen.'

'Grace.'

'Yes – your mother is a wonderful woman, a wonderful, wonderful woman. I can't bear it, Karen. I can't bear that she's going to DIE!'

Between the hyperbolic outbursts, Shirley's story flung facts at me like knives: 'Stage Four', 'hospital', 'I was the only person she could talk to'. I was grateful for the information, but also felt pushed even further into this terrifying, unfamiliar world where my mother was not only extremely ill, probably dying, but had certainly deceived me about it. This woman who wrote me notes to inform me of changes of management in her local shop, who rang me every day (except for those days when she was in hospital – I did a quick calculation and placed the date almost exactly) to tell me every boring detail of her life, had managed to hide all of this from me. Like a wife whose marriage is struggling, but is still shocked to discover her husband has been having an affair. My relationship with Mum was far from ideal, but I thought the dissatisfaction had been all on my side. It shocked me that she had not felt we were close enough to tell me what was going on.

Mum had Stage IV ovarian cancer, that I knew. Without Shirley, she would almost certainly never have been diagnosed.

She had been complaining that previous year of persistent tiredness and vague stomach pains, but these minor maladies got swallowed up in our mutual grumbling: badly chosen curtains, forgotten dry-cleaning, running out of tomato purée. Somehow my mother's symptoms got lost in the must-ring, must-do, must-remember of our daily conversations. We were mother and daughter – we didn't need to entertain each other, all we ever did was have a good old moan. She had stomach pains; I had period cramps. She was tired; I'd been up all night marking exam papers.

Her doctor hadn't noticed either. Typical of women of her age and background, my mother approached doctors and downplayed what was wrong with her as if she were worried about causing them too much trouble. She had been told by her GP that the bloated tummy she had been complaining about was just middle-age spread. Tiredness and mild stomach pains were old age and trapped wind – which could be surprisingly painful. She had been told that if the pain persisted she should go back and have tests for irritable bowel syndrome. She hadn't liked the sound of that and so never went back. At my suggestion, Mum had joined Curves gym to try to give herself more energy and get fitter generally. It was there that she had met Shirley, and while she was complaining to her over coffee about her 'big belly', Shirley – probably more for dramatic effect than anything else – alerted Mum to an article about ovarian cancer she had read in the local paper, highlighting bloating as one of the symptoms. They had an information day coming up at the hospital and were screening post-menopausal women as part of their campaign to increase awareness of this 'silent' cancer. Why didn't the two of them go along? It would be a bit of an outing. They could have lunch afterwards in the new café in Debenhams, it had just been done up.

They both filled out a form; it was quite fun – like one of those magazine quizzes. Mum ticked nearly all the boxes but they didn't think anything of it. In fact, Shirley remembered being quite impressed. They handed the forms in, then they had tea and biscuits and listened to a talk (which was a bit depressing). When the talk was over, a few women were asked to stay on for an ultrasound scan and a blood test. It would take half an hour, forty-five minutes at most, and didn't mean anything was necessarily wrong, it was just a precaution-ary measure. Eileen didn't like the idea of the blood test, but Shirley said she should go anyway to put her mind at rest. Shirley went off shopping and bought a pure-wool Windsmoor coat in the nearly-new shop across the road for a mere £15. When she got back to pick Mum up, Eileen was in a state of shock. They had found some-thing ominous on the ultrasound scan. When she asked her what it was, Mum had started crying, then Shirley had started crying and that was more or less the end of the story. She took Mum to the nearest pub, where they spent the afternoon getting thrashed. Shirley thinks Mum went back again after that for some more 'tests', but she had found the whole thing so upsetting that she had asked Mum not to tell her any more about it. She had elected herself the 'entertainments and cheering-up com-mittee. I'm an upbeat happy-go-lucky type lady, Karen – know what I mean?' She turned her mascara-leaking eyes into hopeful slits as she focused on me. 'I'm a very *sensitive* person; I get very upset about death and things like that. Can't handle it – you know?'

I said I did know and she smiled at me and said she was glad I knew about it now as it had been a terrible responsibility carrying it all around with her and Eileen had been scared to tell me on account of my being a judgemental know-it-all.

I managed to persuade Shirley to let me drive her home, during which time she appeared to have sobered up sufficiently to remember my name. As she swung her legs awkwardly out of the car she turned to me and said, 'You're a good girl, Grace, Eileen is lucky to have you.'

It was, despite her drunken state, a tender moment. I felt momentarily grateful for it, and sorry then for the loneliness in this woman's eyes and for the way I had judged her.

'Thanks, Shirley. We'll meet again soon. I'll take you and Mum for lunch next week.'

'I'd like that,' she said – then stumbled on her way out of the car. I had to find her house keys and open the front door for her.

I drove straight round to my mother's house. I didn't want time to gather my thoughts, or process what I was feeling; I just needed to see her. I gave two short rings on the bell to indicate it was me, then used my keys and walked straight through to the kitchen. My heart was thumping.

She was standing by the sink with her back to me. Although she had a dishwasher, Mum still washed most of her dishes by hand. Dipping her hands in and out of the hot water, her fingers an angry red, veins raised by the heat, stacking the soapy plates on the cheap plastic drainer that she hated but had never got around to replacing. When I remembered my mother, that was always the way I saw her. Framed by the window, looking straight ahead out to her garden, her hands automatically performing the humdrum task of cleaning dishes or hand-washing delicates. She called it 'therapy'. It seemed significant that in the most familiar image I had of my mother, I could not see her face. My mother's features were fine, almost elfin, and she had soft, pale skin. With the right light, and in the right mood, she could be strikingly pretty. From the back, though, she was always small and plump and ordinary. Which, cruelly, is how I always preferred to see her.

I went over and took a tea-towel from the worktop and started to dry the plates, absent-mindedly noting that she still wasn't rinsing them after washing. '*Detergent contains carcinogens,*' I had warned her once; '*you'll get cancer if you don't rinse . . .*'

From the side I could see that her face was set and stoic.

'I spoke to Shirley, Mum.'

'Oh yes?'

She forced the words out in a tight snap. She had thin lips, which I had inherited from her and disliked in us both. Our mean lips sometimes made our faces appear more forbidding and stern than we felt. It was an injustice that I understood and pitied in her, perhaps because I shared it.

'She told me everything.'

She rummaged in the bottom of the basin and found that she was finished. No more dishes to wash, the drying in somebody else's hands. No more distractions, no more therapy today.

When she didn't move away from the sink, I said: 'I'm sorry, Mum.'

'Sorry for what?'

She still didn't look at me but reached for the hand cream on the windowsill and tried to turn the lid with her wet hands. I took it from her gently and handed her the tea-towel so she could dry them.

'I'm sorry that I went to Shirley behind your back. I just wanted to know what was going on.'

She gripped the side of the sink, dropping the ends of the towel in the water. She tightened her jaw as it sharted to shake and her eyes filled with tears: blue beach stones behind a veil of age and fear.

'I'm sorry that I'm a judgemental know-it-all and that you didn't feel you could tell me first.'

I wasn't being facetious; I meant it, and she heard that.

'I wanted you to know everything, Grace. I just couldn't tell you.'

I suppose I had known that all along. I put my arms around her to give her a hug, and for the first time in our lives she responded, placing her arms around my waist and pressing herself on to me. I felt her heave quietly against my chest in a demure, quiet sobbing. The suddenness and strangeness of being physically close to my mother made me unable to cry. So I held on to her as best I could: her small bony hands gripped the small of my back, her hair smelled of fruit shampoo and cigarettes; the matronly belly that had carried me was hard and bloated and full of cancer.

After a few moments, she moved away from me and gave me an assertive smile while drying her eyes on the soaking tea-towel. I could almost hear her brain saying, 'Right. That's that over and done with.'

I was alarmed at how relieved I felt. Had that been our intimate mother-and-daughter moment? Was that it? And why hadn't I been the one sobbing and emoting all over the place? I was the one who was supposed to be 'in touch' with my feelings, and yet my mother seemed to have been able to cry on cue.

Mum looked out of the window. 'There's a rainbow,' she said.

I feigned interest and followed her eyes to a dash of colour wavering uncertainly above the trees, vague and watery – a trick of light on polluted, oily air.

'I thought I could take you and Shirley to lunch next week?' I said.

'Oh no,' said Mum. 'I've gone right off Shirley – been avoiding her all week. Between you and me, Grace, I think she's got a bit of a drink problem.'

eight

Eileen

I knew God was really angry with me because He sent me to confession with Father Butler.

None of us girls liked going to Father Butler because he could keep you in the confessional box for ages. After you had finished confessing your sins – not doing your homework, disobeying your parents or whatever – sometimes he would just let you go with a penance, but sometimes he would ask you if you had had any 'bad thoughts'. If you said no, he would go on and on:

'Are you sure you have not had any bad thoughts at all?'

'No, father.'

'No thoughts about boys?'

'No, father.'

'No thinking about what they might do to you?'

'No, father.'

If you were firm and kept saying no you were usually dismissed with a horrendous penance – five decades and ten Our Fathers I once got, for breaking a china cup. But if you admitted to any bad thoughts at all, he would

60

drag every embarrassing little detail out of you. Some of the girls worked out that if you did confess your bad thoughts to Father Butler, he would hardly give you any penance at all. Ciara Murphy was twelve and told us that she once told Father Butler that she had touched herself inside her pants. She said he told her that she was only experiencing natural feelings. He gave her two Hail Marys and a Glory Be and told her to go back the following week and tell him if she had done it again. Ciara said he was a 'dirty old bastard'. I thought that was a terrible thing to say, and told Ciara that she would go straight to hell for making up something so awful about a priest. But I was still nervous when I saw that he was taking confession the afternoon I went up to the cathedral to confess about the red slacks.

There were two weekly confessions in Ballamore. The popular choice was Saturday afternoon. That was when the young people went on their own in small groups. Us girls would be looking over at the gangs of boys, giggling while they smoked cigarettes stolen from their fathers, leaning against the old monastery walls at the back, trying to look moody and cool like James Dean. These were our last-minute sins before our souls were wiped clean for Sunday Mass and communion. Old people went to confession on Friday afternoons. This was, I knew, because old people didn't commit enough sins. They didn't have parents to break cups on or teachers to backchat, and the only other sins were to do with looking at boys, having more than two buttons open on your blouse or – if you were off the rails altogether – wearing lipstick or painting a stocking seam up the backs of your legs. Men's and boys' sins, like smoking and swearing and drinking, didn't really count for much. That was because women were descended from Eve, who was a wicked temptress, whereas poor Adam couldn't help himself. Men's sins were just silly, but women's sins were very bad. The worst were the ones that were to do with 'tempting'. I always did up the top button of my blouse, even in the summer, as a precaution against being tempting like Eve.

I didn't like going to confession when there were old women in the church because I was convinced that they had some special ability to hear what I was saying in the confessional. So when my mother told me she would take me to the quieter Friday confession, I was upset. I didn't say anything because since the Father Peyton rally I had decided to do everything my mother told me.

The long wooden pews and the ornate beams on the arched ceilings of the cathedral held the scent of a century's candlewax and incense. I loved the way the cathedral smelled, and I loved the silence. It was as if all the prayers ever said there made the air thicker than outside. There were a few old ladies kneeling in the back pews, but none in the confessional queue. The door was ajar to indicate that the priest was free.

Through the brass mesh window I could just make out the downturned profile of Father Butler. He mumbled out his opening prayer, then raised his hand. I dropped my chin to my chest and blurted out a list of the worst sins I could think of, most of them made up.

'Bless me, father, for I have sinned; it has been two weeks since my last confession. In that time I have bought a doughnut from my mother's grocery change without her permission, I called Conor Flannery a bastard, I used the Lord's name in vain seven times and said, 'Jesus, Mary and Joseph!' a lot, I stole a shilling from my sister's communion money, I disobeyed my father, I told a lie to my mother and I wore red trousers and my mother's Children of Mary cloak to the Father Peyton rally.'

I made the list as long as I could, putting lots of bad things at the beginning so that Father Butler might lose interest and miss the end part about the cloak.

Father Butler was silent for such a long time that I thought I might have succeeded and put him to sleep. I raised my head slowly and peered through the screen. The priest was looking straight ahead although his eyes were invisible to me: dull and dark like the beads on my papal rosary.

'Tell me about the red trousers, my child.'

I didn't like the way Father Butler said 'my child'.

'They're my favourite, which I suppose is why I—'

'Why are they your favourite?'

It wasn't usual for a priest to interrupt you when you were confessing so I just carried on.

'. . . wore them to the rally. I need to explain really about the Blessed Virgin and about the magazine. You see, on a Saturday morning my mam sends me up town to Durcan's, where . . .'

'I want to hear about your red trousers, my child. I want to know why you like them so much.'

'Well you see, father, it's not really fair if you don't know the whole story about how I got them because it all ties in then and it's to do with God and the Blessed Virgin and Father Peyton . . .'

Father Butler interrupted me again. His voice was soft now, but determined.

'My child, tell me why you like wearing trousers. How do they make you feel, how do they feel . . .?'

In a sudden, shocking blush, I understood. 'Do you mean do they give me bad thoughts, father?'

'Yes – yes – yes, my child. Yes, that's exactly what I mean. Exactly. Do they give you bad thoughts?'

I thought about it for a minute, thought about making something up just so I could get off with two Hail Marys and a Glory Be. But as I was trying to work it all out, my thoughts were interrupted by Father Butler breathing; heavy, anticipating breaths.

'No, father,' I said, and then, as loudly as I dared so that my mother and the old women outside might hear, 'no bad thoughts at all, father.'

I knew my refusal to co-operate in his bad-thoughts routine would annoy him into giving me a heavier penance, but I could not have expected what came next. His words came out in a stream that didn't make sense, the voice low and nasal but sharp – as if he were stifling a shout.

'You are a sinful, sinful girl, tempting men and boys with your wanton trousers, rubbing against your thighs, boy-girl child temptress, you disgust me, God is angry, very angry, and He will punish you, He will . . .'

I started to cry then, I couldn't help it. I realized as Father Butler was saying all those terrible things that they were true: I *had* liked the way the trousers rubbed against my legs, and they *had* made me feel special and free – I thought I should have confessed all of that to him so that God would forgive me but now it was too late.

I didn't wait for him to finish before I repeated over and over again, 'Oh my God, I am heartily sorry for having offended thee and with help of Your holy grace I will not sin again, Oh my God, I am heartily sorry for having offended thee and with the help of Your holy grace . . .'

Father Butler absolved me more speedily than usual and gave me a light penance. I was still so upset when I left the confessional box that I forgot what it was.

The world seemed a very different place to me after that. I knew it was the same, but it looked different. For a few days I watched for signs but in my heart I knew there would not be any. As the weeks passed I realized that I had made a lot of the stuff about miracles up in my own head. It hadn't been God at all telling me about crows on statues and people dying, it had just been my own imagination. Rainbows were just rainbows and the light played tricks through curtains and trees and made things sparkle like they were special, when they weren't special at all. Like the red trousers. Like me. I felt stupid sometimes when I thought of how I had been before, but then people seemed to like me better after I let go of being so devout. I even told Ciara Murphy about Father Butler calling me a 'sinful girl' in confession and when she called him a 'dirty bastard' again, I laughed this time. My mother seemed happy when I refused to go to the weekly novenas and wanted to stay out and play with my friends. I overheard my mother tell my father one night that she was glad I was 'over that nonsense'.

It wasn't like very much had changed on the outside. I still went to the Legion of Mary and prayed every day, but it was just ordinary now. 'Hail Mary, full of grace, the Lord is with thee.' They were just words said over and over again. No special meaning especially for me. I was just the same as everyone else.

I still believed in God and the Blessed Virgin and all the other things that the Catholic Church taught me, but my faith had changed. Where I had believed in so much that it was bursting out of me, now I had just enough.

Everyone seemed to agree it was better that way.

nine

Grace

I had never aspired to being married. My mother's 'failed marriage' status made her cynical about the institution of marriage generally and bitterly determined to make me 'stand on my own two feet'. Long before boys, never mind husbands, ever entered my head, Mum would tell me that there was no need to get married 'in this day and age', that it was perfectly acceptable to live 'in sin' but more important to have your own career and earn your own money. It always seemed strange to me that she would think I could aspire to live any other way, but then we were victims of the parent–child estrangement that emigration creates. Mum was reared as a devout Catholic in a small, rural town on the west coast of Ireland, while I was the daughter of a single parent reared in a large, anonymous city. She brought me up in a liberal world where women were no longer bound by convention and could 'have it all'. Her own history became little more than a cautionary tale: the stigma of never having studied; the lost opportunity of no career; the waste of marrying young.

For Mum's generation, marriage was a way of life, a vocation. My mother did however have a great romantic love with my father. A dark-haired, blue-eyed, handsome young Protestant; a writer, a poet, a 'dashing' unreliable charmer – he was the kind of guy you fell in love with. As Mum discovered later, he was not the kind of guy you should marry. He turned out to be an alcoholic womanizer and spent all of her hard-earned money on drink and other women. It was the failure of her marriage and the subsequent pain of growing up not knowing my father that made me resistant to the idea of marriage, more than any of her warnings. The way my mother ranted against the institution made me think she had never made that connection between the political and the personal. More likely is that she was testing me; fishing for reasssurance that I had escaped emotionally unscathed by their separation.

I didn't believe I had, which is how I met Jack, my ex-husband and soulmate.

I had been engaged in various kinds of therapy since my early twenties. A friend whose father was also an alcoholic had introduced me to the self-help group Adult Children of Alcoholics in my early twenties. Although I could hardly remember that part of my childhood, my friend assured me that my father's drinking had affected me, I just didn't know it yet. It was at these meetings that I became focused on looking for answers, and I hooked up with a bunch of women whom I could relate to: a grief counsellor in her late thirties, a lesbian social worker, a fellow teacher, a middle-aged housewife who was training in aromatherapy. Our regular Sunday-morning tea-and-tears confessionals convinced me that

I was dysfunctional enough to warrant one-to-one coun-selling and I found that, even from those emotionally charged early sessions, I was excited by the therapeutic process.

Self-discovery was a revelation to me – in providing answers, yes, but also in providing an alternative life path. I became a 'seeker', one of those people who was not afraid to take 'the road less travelled'. We were an enlightened, emotional elite; we hung out in self-help groups and wore our dysfunctions as badges of survival. I was an adult child of an alcoholic, which was fairly tame considering that most of the group were also incest survivors or alcoholics or compulsive overeaters or had what were fashionably known as 'addictive personali-ties', problems that would eventually earn them mem-bership into any of the many anonymous groups that were springing up at that time. Alcoholism being a family illness, and confident that I had my father's wild addictive genes running in my bloodstream, I myself attended Smokers Anonymous, Love Addicts Anony-mous and Overeaters Anonymous before finally conced-ing that five cigarettes a week, a rebound relationship and an extra half-stone, however unwelcome, did not make me an addict. What was important was the feeling of belonging and safety that these groups gave me, and I think it was the same for many of the friends I made during that time. Insecurity was the main symptom of unhappiness my childhood had left me with: a fear of being out of control. I had become a teacher at least partly for the job security, and while my college friends and young work contemporaries were chasing around the city getting drunk and looking for sex, I was sitting in the kitchen of a fifty-year-old divorcee with a bunch of recovering love/cigarette/dope addicts, drinking tea and talking about my feelings.

Jack Green was my third therapist. My previous two had helped me deal with a lot of the basic stuff: looking at my childhood, facing up to its hurts and losses, getting to know how to nurture my inner child. By my mid-twenties, I had done a lot of work on myself and was very together – even if I was inappropriately mature for my years. Jan, my second therapist, had let me go saying she had done all she could for me and that, frankly, after two years I had come as far as anyone could. Did I feel I had achieved what I had come to her for, she asked in our last session. I said yes because I knew she was fishing for closure, but in truth I was aggrieved that she had drawn our time to an end. I did not want to let go of my weekly sessions. There was a gap inside me that had not yet been filled; a feeling of incompleteness. What I didn't realize then was that I was suffering from no more than the human condition: the general dissatisfaction and *ennui* that is part of being alive. The addict treats the empty feeling with drink or drugs or food or sex; the go-getter fills it with work, the intellectual with reading, the yogi will dive in and swim about in it until it turns into something else. Me, I treated it with psychotherapy. I picked apart my fundamental human condition and applied meaning to it. You could say it was a waste of time, as there was nothing terribly wrong with me in the first place, but my interest in therapy did eventually help me find Jack.

I had always believed in the concept of a soulmate, one person with whom you have a strong, almost spiritual connection, when the attraction is so powerful it defies definition. You just know, without rhyme or reason, analysis or explanation, that this is the person you were destined to spend your life with. Boyfriends up to then had been carefully chosen and inevitably dropped because they were missing that elusive 'rightness' that defines the perfect soulmate. I was twenty-five, focused on my career and my 'recovery'. I was still young and gorgeous enough to believe that there was one man out there who would be the perfect soul-fit for me, and that when the time was right I would meet him.

I found Jack through a leaflet he had left in my local café for a series of 'Gestalt' workshops he was doing – a form of holistic therapy. It read: 'Unite all aspects of your personality to become truly whole!' I ran home immediately and booked myself in for the six-session group-therapy workshops, which were on the other side of the city on consecutive Saturday afternoons. The voice on the other end of the phone had been a low baritone. He introduced himself as Jack Green and when he had used my name – 'I look forward to meeting you on Saturday week, Grace' – I had felt a little tingle.

The following evening, the guest speaker at my ACoA meeting was a man I had never seen before. He opened with: 'Hi, my name is Jack and I am the adult child of an alcoholic,' in the same deep voice. He was brilliantly honest and insightful in his speaking. Physically, he was an unremarkable-looking man, small and slim with the long, thinning hair of the reluctantly ageing hippy, but I thought from that first sight of him, sitting in that church hall with the Twelve Steps poster framing his face, that he had an air of 'knowingness' that I coveted. In that sense I was immediately taken with him, but when I went to approach him after the meeting ended he was surrounded by people and I had to leave. I figured if I was meant to see him again, I would.

When I arrived late to my first Gestalt workshop the following week and saw him sitting in the circle of chairs, my stomach lurched and my knees buckled. It felt like an extraordinary coincidence and made me certain that our souls had been flung together by some higher power.

Some people never meet their soulmate, and spend a lifetime looking. A very lucky, very tiny minority meet their soulmate early in life and live happily ever after. That was me and Jack. We were a golden couple. He was enlightened, confident and mature. I was twenty-five, unsure and impressionable. He adored me for my youth and beauty and I respected him. It was the perfect father–daughter dynamic but it worked for us, and over the coming eight years it seemed to transmogrify into a healthy, if slightly textbook perfect, relationship.

I moved into his grand, rent-controlled flat almost immediately and we did all the things that couples did in the early to mid-nineties: we held large Sunday brunch parties, we went on yoga holidays, we godparented our friends' children. We got married in a simple civil service followed by a Native American blessing in our back garden, attended by a handful of friends and both our mothers, each of whom viewed their child's partner and the whole event with obvious scepticism. Jack and I were both only children. His mother, Elsbeth, a sixties veteran, was a yoga master. Apart from waist-length white hair, she looked thirty and could cotton-bud her ears with her big toe. Jack was a 'free love' child and she had plans to turn him into the next Dalai Lama. Those plans did not include him marrying a suburban schoolteacher, an 'ordinary' person like me. My own mother, ignoring my warnings about the wedding being off-beat, wore a traditional mother-of-the-bride ensemble. Unable to resist the allure of matching bag, hat and shoes, she spent the afternoon receiving exuberant compliments from people about her flouncy peach-floral garb. Elsbeth, in an understated Ghost shift dress, flowing hair and bare feet, did not help by throwing Mum a look of pained disbelief across the 'circle of love' just before the service began. I had told Mum to take her shoes off beforehand and the last thing I saw before I closed my eyes to affirm my lifetime commitment to Jack was my mother's toes curling and twitching with discomfort inside her twenty-denier American-tan tights.

Our mothers' lack of confidence in us as a couple only brought us closer together. We began our marriage with a couples counselling course. I wasn't sure why, but Jack said I needed to learn how to 'listen'.

'That's not a criticism, Grace. It's just that there is a right way to listen and, as a therapist, I have learned how to do it. It would really help me if you could learn to do it too.'

So I did, and every week for the seven years we were married Friday night was 'listening' night. After dinner we would light candles; sometimes, if we were feeling good, we would have a bath together. Holding hands, we would look into each other's eyes and one of us would talk for ten whole minutes while the other person 'listened'. We both knew that communication was the key to everything. There was no problem that could not be sorted out through healthy, open discussion. Talking and listening, that was what relationships were all about.

Then one Friday night Jack ran us both a bath and lit candles all around the bathroom. Tonight, he said, he had something special to tell me. Was I ready to accept his exciting realization, he wondered? We had talked of children before and both decided that our life together was fulfilling enough, but now that I was marching through my thirties it was becoming a concern for me. Perhaps, I hoped, it was coming up for both of us at the same time. Could this be another mutual spiritual awakening?

We sat in the warm bath and as Jack took my hands I noticed that he seemed to be holding them tighter than usual.

'I have been offered a job in Byron Bay, Australia. It starts in two weeks' time.'

He didn't stop there, but continued for his allocated ten minutes. I started to turn over the possibilities. It was a big move. Byron Bay was a New Age haven, a psychotherapist's dream; surely my teaching qualification would transfer over there? We could sub-let the flat in case we wanted to come back, Mum could come over on holidays, property was cheap, maybe she could re-locate there as well. Hell, it could turn out to be fun!

'Are you listening, Grace? I said this is something I need to do alone. Without you.'

The water went cold around me. Jack was still gripping my hands, looking at me, waiting for me to give him my feedback.

I wanted to jump out of the bath, hit him with a wet

towel across the face, call him a selfish, narcissistic shitbag. In the years that followed, there were many times I dearly wished I had. I sometimes wondered what would have happened if I had confronted him then. Might he have stayed and subjugated some of his self-righteous ego to the genuine 'goodness' he so dearly believed he possessed?

But I didn't have the confidence back then. Instead, I nodded, affirmed his decision and gave him my blessing.

It was in his heart to go, and in my heart I believed he would come back. I always believed it was important to follow one's heart.

ten

Eileen

There were three career options open to smart young women back then: nun, teacher, nurse. I had always thought I would be called to teaching – but then I fell short by two marks in my Leaving Certificate maths exam. My parents wanted me to resit my exams a year later, but that would have meant staying in school. A year seemed like such a long time to me, and I could not face the humiliation of being put in a class with girls who had been in the year below me. Much as I wanted to be a teacher, I wanted to be out in the world more.

In September my mother enrolled me on a commercial course in Dublin and found lodgings for me in a reputable Catholic ladies' hostel in the city centre. We travelled up to the capital on the bus together. The night before, as I packed my dance dress and silk stockings, my body was bristling in anticipation of the adventure. I scrunched my tulle petticoat into a firm ball so that it would fit into a corner in my father's old cardboard case, leaving room for my stiletto shoes. On the journey the next day, though, I dressed like a novice in my navy school coat, so as not to upset my mother. I knew she was worried. She was only letting me go to Dublin because the hostel was run by nuns and had a strict evening curfew of ten o'clock. There were no men allowed in the rooms under any circumstances, and two years previously a respectable neighbour of ours, the eldest Molloy girl, had done the same course and had come back to a good job in a local auctioneer's office. My mother knew I was sensible, and expected that I would be back home by the following summer.

From the time the bus left behind the mottled, leathery landscape of the far west, and as it lurched through the ordered green boundaries of the Irish midlands and finally hit the flat farmlands that skimmed Dublin city's edge, I was aware of my mother's disquiet. As she drummed her fingers nervously on the arm of her seat, I thought perhaps she was wondering if there was any advice she needed to give me. I was her first-born and, whilst she depended on me to help her, she still viewed me very much as a child. My mother had never talked to me about boys or men, the desires and the dangers of falling in love. Even if she had wanted to talk to me about such things, as a devout woman she probably did not have the language. There was no way of describing desire outside the context of sin; the word 'sex' was never used.

When my mother said goodbye to me on the steps of the Catholic Ladies' Hostel on Henrietta Street, she grasped both my small, bare hands in her own gloved ones and said, 'Be careful.' It sounded like both a warning and a declaration of love.

I loved everything about Dublin. It was full of life and noise and excitement. I loved the city-centre pavements with so many people crammed on to them that they spilled on to the busy roads, buses beeping, men in fancy cars waving at pretty girls, shops on your doorstep selling every colour and class of outfit or foodstuff. I saw things I had never seen before: women dressed in daringly short skirts, rows and rows of televisions in a shop window, a man in a long black coat who stood on a box outside Bewley's coffee house and read poetry aloud. You only had to walk down the street to be entertained. Once I almost bumped into not one but two black men walking together down Grafton Street on a Saturday afternoon and had to stop myself from just standing and staring after them. I had not realized that black people existed outside Africa or the world I knew from American movies like *Gone with the Wind*. Seeing them was proof to me that city life was more exotic than I had imagined. I was part of the great adventure I had always known existed beyond the perimeters of my small town. The foreigners, the fashions. Just being in the city made me feel I was no longer watching the movie but taking part in it.

I made friends quickly. The hostel slept six in a small dormitory and all of the others in my room were country girls. There were two sisters from Mayo, a girl from Donegal and two cousins from neighbouring towns in Kerry. We made friends instantly, country refugees anxious to adopt and enjoy the sophistications of city life, and we had a ball. We dressed up in twinsets and took tea in the Gresham like big-shots; we went to dances in the National on Mountjoy Square, or the upstairs ballroom in Clery's, arriving early so we would get in two hours of flirting and dancing and free minerals before we got back to the hostel for our curfew at ten. On Saturday afternoons we wandered in and out of the laneways and coffee shops off Grafton Street wearing polo-necks and pedal pushers, looking for poets and playwrights. I was a voracious reader and was in awe of the intellect and style of the writers who were hanging around Dublin at the time. Brendan Behan, Patrick Kavanagh – they were more attractive to me than any film star, and I would peer into the infamous Bartley Dunne's or McDaid's pubs – too self-conscious to enter such establishments myself – to catch sight of one or the other pontificating drunkenly to the audience of adoring Trinity students who hung around them.

This was where I wanted to stay, so just before my commercial course was finished I sent away a job application to Aer Lingus, the national airline, who were recruiting for reservations staff in their O'Connell Street office. Along with the form I had to send in a full-length photograph of myself. My mother had sent me money to buy an interview suit, and I had chosen a mossy-green tweed two-piece, with a knee-length pencil skirt and a short fitted jacket. I had the sleeves altered so that they were the perfect length, and a button detail put in at the back to nip the waist in even further. I had never owned such a sophisticated ensemble, and as I walked the length of O'Connell Street towards the photographer's studio I truly felt as if I were on show. Steady in my needle-thin stiletto heels, I felt the thrill of my stocking tops chafing against each other as my buttocks negotiated each step under my tight skirt. I knew people were watching me – women admiring my style and men simply admiring me – and I thought to myself that this was what it felt like to be a woman.

The photographer was a friendly man in his early thirties. He put me at my ease and offered me a cup of tea before standing me in front of a black curtain and training his lights on me.

'Now, Eileen, you look lovely, dear. Just cross one foot in front of the other like a good girl and give me a lovely pretty smile.'

I felt like a fashion model – a peculiar feeling, as if I were entirely aware of my whole body and was infatuated by my own beauty.

'Now hold your chin up, Eileen my love. What a pretty smile. Back straight, good girl yourself. That's just perfect.'

I posed and pouted, and for the ten minutes it took for the session to be completed I was in seventh heaven.

'Lovely. I'll have the prints for you tomorrow.'

As the photographer snapped off his lights I became aware there was someone else in the room. I saw the outline of a man, standing in a corner behind the photographer. From the relaxed pose of his shadow, I gathered he had been watching me the whole time. I blushed with embarrassment, but an unfamiliar thread of wordly confidence made me stay where I was. The man lit a cigarette and as the small orange glow flashed across his features I saw a thick mop of dark hair and a black polo-neck jumper: beatnik camouflage. The cigarette smoke, the mysterious stranger, the glamour of my suit and having my photograph taken took hold of my thread of confidence and pulled me across the room. I stood in front of my Bogart and said: 'Got a cigarette?'

He flipped open his cigarette box and I took one without dropping it; the match lit on the first strike and as I inhaled the pocket of smoke he shook the flame and flicked the dead stick away. The moment was perfect, and so was he: film-star handsome, brooding dark eyes, pouting, petulant lips. I could tell from his 'look' that he was an intellectual of some kind. Writer, poet, student, Dubliner certainly, and possibly even that most exclusive and forbidden of specimens – a Protestant. From that first moment, I knew he was the kind of man a country girl like me could hardly dare aspire to fall in love with.

'Thanks,' I said as breathlessly as I could and walked away, swaying my hips slowly like Marilyn Monroe in *Some Like It Hot*.

Although he didn't follow me out of the studio, I felt the intoxicating power of knowing that he would find me again.

In that glorious moment I knew I had finally grown up.

eleven

Grace

Jack and I corresponded for a year. I tried to keep my letters upbeat as I entertained him with stories of our friends and my students. I sent pictures to remind him of life back home, and was comforted when he acknowledged them and said how much he missed England and me. His letters were long, self-examinatory tomes describing in detail all the treatments and tinctures he was trying. Finding himself, he assured me, was a process he would never tire of. The journey was what mattered, he said. He missed home, but was learning that home was what was in your heart, not your hearth. He loved me, but loving someone was letting them spread their wings and find their own way in the universe. Didn't I agree? I didn't, actually, but I assumed he was talking about me letting him go to Australia so I said yes.

That first year I suffered more than I had imagined possible. After seven years of being a couple, I could not adapt to being on my own again. I had become entrenched in the mutuality of marriage: eating, sleeping, living together, the luxury of having twenty-four-hour access to another human being. Like room service – you don't always use it but you're glad it's there. I stopped cooking an evening meal and put on weight from eating take-aways. The TV, which I had never bothered with, became my friend. I couldn't sleep and it took a short spell on Xanax to sort my body clock out. I had never taken drugs before, and it was a blow to my pride to have to resort to 'chemicals'.

Problems aside, it was busy year as I got my first major promotion to deputy head in a large, reputable inner-city school. I missed not being able to properly share this success with Jack, but it also gave me the confidence to phone and ask my husband when he was coming home.

Of course, he wasn't coming home.

'Grace – I'm sorry, baby, I thought you understood. I thought I'd said this was where I need to be. I'm sorry. I should have been clearer. God, I feel really terrible.'

'No, no – it's okay. Of course, of course you're staying there. I just needed it confirmed, that's all.'

'Of course' – the ultimate two words of self-protection.

Of course. I knew that. I knew he wasn't coming back, I told myself, knowing I was in denial. The alternative was just too humiliating, so I took the fact of my separation, wrapped it up and locked it in a drawer at the back of my mind. After a couple of years, it calcified into spikes, and when those spikes started tapping, they were long and nasty and they hurt all the more for having been left so long ignored and unattended.

I got over it – but only with a very expensive anger-management practitioner, and only partly. Over six sessions, I made ribbons of several rubber pipes, a mattress and my lower back. I learned a few life lessons out of the break-up of my marriage; some of them came under the heading Good Basics, some of them under Twisted. The first was: don't pretend to be calm when you're not because – news flash! – bad stuff will stew away happily in there until it is outed. Also, the phrase 'Follow your heart' is an excuse for doing reckless, thoughtless, irresponsible things which hurt others. Finally, I learned that the definition of cynicism is what you feel when you find your one true soulmate then he pisses on you and tells you it's raining.

Most of the time life lessons are important, learning experiences; pain can help the spirit grow. But sometimes life lessons are just shit things that happen which leave you feeling angry and hurt. My belief after Jack left, that men were all selfish, self-aggrandizing arse-holes, would certainly have fallen into the latter category. But my cynicism felt like enlightenment, and I clung to it because it seemed to give me answers. I knew my attitude was corrosive and destructive; I knew it was stopping me from meeting anybody else – and in that lay the true answer: I didn't want to meet anybody else. Jack had been and would always be my soulmate. It was easier to think of him as a conniving bastard than face the real truth, which was the tragic loss of love. First my father walking out on me, followed by Jack, the great love of my life. Father and soulmate, two relationships that were supposed to be absolute. Two vital people who had said they loved me and yet managed to leave me. Not a great boost to the self-worth. So it was either face that pain or put relationships with men in the 'too hard' box, along with my ambitions to do ballet and maintain natural-looking blonde highlights over a dark base.

Once I had decided that men weren't for me, I found a great freedom in being around them. I had plenty of male friends, gay, straight and married. My married girlfriends never saw me as a threat because I had developed a pragmatic, no-nonsense personality that desexualized me, so they gladly released their husbands to me if I needed a date for a work function or somebody to put up shelves. I built a life for myself post-Jack that meant I was never lonely. I had a handful of very close friends with whom I could share intimacies; they included a pleasant man that I developed a comfortable, physical relationship with. His life was too complicated and mine too simple for 'falling in love', so we met every few weeks and had sex. It wasn't as cold as it sounded but a very nourishing and mutual relationship that involved lots of cuddling and often an outing and a meal. Closeness aside, I had a successful and enriching working life and a healthy network of friendships for cinema dates, evening classes, salsa clubs and the gym. I was a lover, a godmother, a mentor and a good friend. I was also a daughter; for family I had Mum and she became enough for me; one parent was about all I could manage in terms of commitment. As time passed I actually became glad and relieved that Jack had left, and more certain that my career and lifestyle would never have been allowed to develop in such an enriching, successful way had we stayed married.

One week after I learned of my mother's cancer, Jack showed up on my doorstep.

At first I didn't recognize him. I looked out of my office window to check who had rung the bell and saw a very attractive man with a golden tan and a shaven head which shimmered with a few days' growth. He was wearing worn jeans and a casual but expensive-looking linen jacket. I wasn't entirely immune to the fantasy of some Mr Wonderful literally turning up on my doorstep, so I checked myself in the hall mirror and it's possible that I hurriedly applied some lip-gloss. I smiled widely as I opened the door.

'Grace! You look fantastic!'

I knew it was him as soon as he spoke, and the smile atrophied on my face. I was instantly weakened by shock, afraid I would crumble. It was so like him to disarm me like that, so like him to—

'I should have called – I am so sorry!'

Do something shitty then apologize it away after he had all the power, after the damage was done.

I kept it together. 'Jack! What a lovely surprise.' But I was fooling nobody. He knew I was unsettled. Vulnerable.

He came in and we politely pretended to small-talk for half an hour or so. He was 'doing good' in Australia, my work was thriving; he had kept in touch with this person, I had lost touch with others. I didn't tell him about Mum. It was still too new and I was too vulnerable and anyway it was none of his business any more. In the middle of a humdrum sentence about – property prices, I think – he suddenly blurted out, 'Grace. I've met somebody else.'

A short laugh escaped me. He had said it with almost comical urgency, as if I would be devastated. As if it mattered.

'I'd be worried if you hadn't.'

'She's pregnant . . .'

That hurt a bit. 'Great, that's great!'

'. . . and we want to get married. Grace.'

Ouch!

Then, in a seriously patronizing tone, 'I want a divorce.'

Not, 'I need a divorce' but 'I *want* a divorce.' Why did I notice that small cruelty? Why did I care?

'Of course, of course, Jack. It's time.'

And as soon as I said it out loud every inch of me began to scream, 'Divorce! No!' Separation is softer. It sounds less serious, a gentle, civilized arrangement. Separation is reversible, and while I had not consciously imagined Jack and myself getting back together after all these years, I was suddenly hit with the finality of it. Divorce: the last cruel punctuation on what was once love. A sick, empty dread washed over me.

Jack had a big grin splashed all over his face. 'Great! I'll bring the papers over tomorrow.'

The insensitive shit had the papers drawn up already.

I must have let out a noise because next thing he took my hands, squeezed them and said, 'Grace – are you OK?'

I looked up into his eyes and there was the old Jack,

the man I fell in love with – warm and concerned and wise. I knew it was crazy, that we had both changed, but in the moment that I was being asked to finally let him go, I wanted him back. I wanted the passion and the belief I had had in our love, the certainty and the possibility and the day-to-day miracle of our shared beliefs and understanding. Even though I had had eight years of being without him, I suddenly knew that I didn't want to be alone any more. So I said, 'Jack, I've got a lot going on with Mum right now. She's got cancer and we don't know how long she's got to live.'

'Jesus, Grace, I'm sorry. I . . .'

'So I think it's best if we just leave all this for today? Will you be around for a while?'

'Of course. Jesus, Grace – do you want to talk about it?'

I gave him a cursory five minutes talking about what had happened with Mum. He was gagging to give me his feedback but I didn't want to hear it. He left the phone number of the place he was staying and said he would be away for a few days the following week but was available on his girlfriend's cellphone number – which he left. He hesitated over the word 'girlfriend', which made me feel curiously powerful.

After he left the flat felt hollow and empty and so did I. I cried for twenty minutes or so and then I rang Sita.

twelve

Eileen

When I went back to collect my photos, John Blake was waiting for me.

After recounting the adventure to my friends and being whizzed along on a frenzied rollercoaster of anticipation and opportunity, my confidence had disappeared overnight. Supposing he didn't turn up because he hadn't picked up on the signs; men were awful like that. Supposing he did turn up and the two of us got together; I didn't really know anything about him.

As I turned the corner I saw him a few hundred yards away, standing outside the photography shop, smoking. He watched me walk, blatantly waiting. For an instant I felt disappointed, as if he were just like one of the common shop boys back home, eyeing me up, planning to take his chance with a rude comment as I passed. He looked different now he was out of the shadows. Daylight made him more ordinary: his face was younger, whiter, and the polo-neck had been replaced by a white shirt. As he drew nearer, I deliberately recalled the frisson I had felt the day before, reminding myself that I could be at the beginnings of the biggest adventure of my life. I was nearly eighteen, and could not have known that innocence would mould my future out of that perfect first moment: love at first sight.

The next six months passed in a glittering haze. I got the job at Aer Lingus and with it a whole new set of glamorous big-shot friends, a room in a flat on Dawson Street and a salary to pay for my records and smart clothes. Best of all was being with John. He was twenty-two and an English student at Trinity, although when drunk he sometimes referred to himself as an 'author' as he had already written the first draft of a novel. After work, I would meet him in Buswell's Hotel, where he would already have been drinking with his Trinity friends for an hour or so. They drank a lot.

I had never touched alcohol before I met John: it was not available in the dance halls where I had socialized up to then, and my father was a Pioneer and considered drink to be a sin against God. It was most certainly never considered a feminine pursuit. John ran with a cosmopolitan, arty crowd who drank in pubs alongside poets, politicians and businessmen. The girls all drank too and, eager to fit in, I accepted my first glass of Guinness with a confident smile that said I had been drinking all my life. It was revolting, but I quickly found things that I did like: vodka and lime, whisky and red, Babycham. I learned to enjoy them enough to keep up with the gang.

The sixties hadn't quite begun to swing in Ireland yet, but there was just enough *dolce vita* to make us all feel as if we were truly living. Mostly we just drank in pubs and went to house parties. Those who didn't work slept all day – which is what I did at the weekends. During the week, I struggled with the late nights and sometimes tried to persuade John to go somewhere other than the pub. But he didn't like the cinema or the theatre because, he said, as a writer himself, he didn't want to become subconsciously tainted by other writers' work. Reading was different, he said, because he read with his 'conscious mind'. I did not have the first idea what he was talking about and as far as I could see John didn't have much time for reading either. I didn't mind that because I worried that if he got any cleverer he might see how ordinary I was and swap me for one of the bright-spark blue-stocking Trinity girls he was friends with.

Sometimes when we were out John would call me 'my country-Catholic colleen – just look at those innocent blue eyes'. I didn't like it when he spoke about me like that to other people, but I didn't say anything. I was on John's turf now, and I was having such a good time that I could afford to shrug off the occasional trite comment. Besides, I was able to take his ribbing for what it was, which was sour grapes at the fact that I wouldn't let him make love to me.

I had been kissed plenty of times; while being walked home from dances, in the kitchen of the town hall during ceilidhs and in the back row of the movies. I did not consider myself innocent. The fear of sin was still there, but had been considerably demoted from the priority positioning it had held for me as a child. Sin was about guilt, which, as far as I could surmise, was just something you had to live with if you wanted to enjoy yourself in any way at all. However, losing your virginity was in a completely different league. You had to be really sure about a man before you gave him your body. If you gave it away and, God forbid, things didn't work out, then your whole life would be ruined. You would be left with a reputation for being 'loose' and no man would ever take you seriously enough to want to marry you. There were no second chances with your virginity. Once it was gone, it was gone. Kissing and touching were nice but when it came to 'the other thing' I knew that there was blood and pain and general unpleasantness involved. With the logistics of anatomy, how could it possibly be any other way? I guessed more than knew that somewhere along the line it was supposed to be enjoyable, but I also suspected that was just a myth that men employed to try to persuade you to let them have their way. No matter how many of John's liberal ideas I agreed with, my belief was that it really was best to wait until you were married before you started messing around 'downstairs'. Then there was the question of love. And I was not entirely certain I *was* in love with John Blake. Or perhaps, I thought, I was so much in love with him that I was keeping part of myself in reserve because of the unlikeliness of our match. What I was certain of was that John was special and different and that he had chosen me. Also that he was from the upper class.

The Blakes were a respected well-off south-Dublin family, and whilst my family were respectable people, there was a huge difference in our backgrounds. John teased me gently about being a 'culchie' but I knew it made no difference to him if my father was a poor farmer and his a judge. It made a difference to *me*. I couldn't even tell my parents that I was 'walking out' with a rich Protestant. Such a notion was not within the realms of their reality. I tried to paint a picture of our future together, but it looked strange and unnatural to me. The simple Catholic country girl and the rich city Protestant: it was pure fantasy, a romantic fiction. In my dream, our success hinged on his family accepting me, and my parents gratefully complying with the wishes of a more educated, urbane upper class. Considering that my father was an ardent republican who loathed the English, it seemed an unlikely scenario.

When, three months after we first met, John said in a casual way, 'My uncle is having a house party at the weekend and my parents have asked if you'd like to join us?', I was nervous and excited. I called in sick to work on the Friday so that I could spend the whole day shopping and packing.

I did not have much of an idea what to expect and therefore what to bring, but I didn't like to ask in case John accused me of being 'bourgeois', as he did every time I tried to ask him about his family. All I knew at that stage was that his parents were 'well off', that he had two sisters and that his father was a barrister. When I tried to quantify 'well off' by subtly bringing a subject around to, say, how many rooms were in his parents' house, John would immediately catch me out. He was an intellectual and didn't think these things were import-ant. Either that or, I worried, they were *so* important that he couldn't discuss them with me.

We took the train to Gormanston from Connolly Station on the Friday evening. As John read, I sat opposite him reattaching my scarf to my lapel with a brooch, snapping open my compact to powder my nose and check my lipstick, clicking my handbag clasp open and shut and mouthing the contents to myself: handkerchiefs, lipstick, money, blush, stockings, gloves, earrings, lighter – although I didn't smoke I always carried one. I was a bag of nerves. I didn't feel I was 'good enough'.

'Stop fiddling, woman!'

I looked across at John, shocked. Without looking up from his book, my boyfriend's face broadened into a wide smile. He was joking: mocking us both for being like an old married couple. It was his way of telling me not to be nervous or afraid; a moment of intimacy – hidden perhaps, but I knew how it was meant. In his teasing me in that cosy way, John had given me all the permission I needed to love him.

From the moment we stepped off the train, I felt as if I was in another world, a hybrid of Ireland and rural England – a place I recognized from Agatha Christie books and films starring Alastair Sim. We were picked up at the station by a young man called Liam who was driving a silver Rolls-Royce. Without even noticing it, I must have let out a squeal of delight because John said, 'Settle down, old girl,' in a false English accent: 'Haven't you ever seen a Roller before?' Even the scenery, pretty green fields with trimmed hedges and quaint, well-kept stone cottages, seemed more sedate and cultivated than my own 'wild west'. John took my hand and squeezed it warmly. It was a paternal act and I could sense that he understood that I was in awe of his world and would protect me from making a fool of myself.

John took my virginity on the Saturday evening before supper.

There was no scene-setting, no romantic build-up. We had gathered after breakfast at the stables and John had elegantly distracted his family from the fact that I could not ride by taking me off for a long walk. 'I want this one to myself for the day – she deserves better company than horses and hounds!'

'No greater hound than you, young man!' his uncle teased him.

I had been feeling daunted up to then, as if I had been placed inside a posh English novel. The four-poster bed; the freezing, creaking, rambling house; dressing for a dinner that had been cooked by servants – well, a housekeeper anyway; John's distant, distinguished father; his astonishingly beautiful mother in a blood-red dress pulling a moth-eaten cardigan over her white, slender arms as she held her glass out for more wine after dinner. The permissive Protestant conversation on sex and art and British politics and the cost of foreign travel. I made one small contribution, at John's invitation, on the price of flights to New York, then collapsed with gratitude when he artfully steered me away from revealing that I had never actually flown anywhere.

We walked for miles, racing across fields, picking blackberries from wild, heavy hedgerows, taking shelter from the rain under ancient mossy trees – kissing ourselves warm in the damp air, colouring the grey day with the garish red of my mod coat. We returned to the house in the late afternoon, starving and exhausted. John chased me upstairs, into my room and on to the bed. Our faces were wet with rain and perspiration and our limbs stinging with the blush of exercise.

It was over before I was fully aware it had begun. I

was so lost in the passionate petting and the temperature change of being indoors that by the time I composed myself to object the pushing was over. I was wet and John had collapsed his head into my neck; I felt his downturned face stretch into a smile against my skin. I reached up my hand and stroked his hair. He purred gratefully but from that moment I could feel that his satisfaction was distancing him from me.

Two days after we got back, John told me he was going to spend the summer in Paris. He talked about needing to connect with French philosophy in a more meaningful way, and how his mother had French ancestry that he was keen to investigate for his next book. He talked about coming back in September.

I saw him only a little over the next few weeks. I had sex with him one more time but kept myself cold and loveless so he would know he had made me feel cheap and betrayed. Afterwards I felt like an idiot for having tried to punish him with my martyrdom.

Over the summer, the emotional upset of losing John seemed to progress rather than dissipate, taking on physical symptoms such as nausea, bloating, sudden outbursts of temper and tears. That September, when he was due to come home, I met an air hostess, a mutual friend, who said she had bumped into him in Paris. He had given up his place in Trinity and was living with a fashion model in the sixth *arrondissement*. He was unlikely to be returning to Dublin any time soon.

It was six weeks after I got that news that I finally admitted to myself that I was pregnant. By which time the tree-lined paths of St Stephen's Green were covered with autumn's golden debris and I was over five months gone.

thirteen

Grace

I sat in Sita's consulting room and bawled out my anger and confusion and hurt over Jack. She made comforting noises and over the next hour she calmly patted my hysteria away, mostly by just affirming that all the messy feelings I had were natural emotions to be experiencing under the circumstances. Normally my situation would not have qualified me for the level of upset I was experiencing. Separated for eight years and husband wants a divorce? Get over it. But then that's one of the wonderful things about a really good holistic therapist. They validate your pain because they understand that it doesn't really matter where the pain comes from: a death in the family or a broken teapot, depending on the individual it can all hurt the same.

I always hated emotional pain. Who doesn't? – but some people are better at dealing with it than others. I once read that the strongest people, mentally, emotionally and spiritually, are those who have faced their demons, walked through the pain and come out the other side. But for all the self-enlightenment I sought, pain never felt normal to me. It always felt like an injustice; bigger and worse than I was expecting.

'I think I need a break,' I said, indicating that I had finished sharing my feelings and was ready to move on.

I looked out of a window behind her face; a grey sky made the horizon blurred and vague. It was an unremarkable day but the vastness of the sea made every day seem significant in that view. With a pang of vulnerability, I realized that I wanted to stay there, with Sita. I wanted to have more time to gaze out of her window, and have my mentor and adviser on hand to comfort me for a few days. I felt like a sick child who wants to be looked after. Except that I wasn't a sick child. I was a grown woman who was experiencing irrational emotions over a marriage that was well and truly over. 'I have an idea,' she said.

For an instant I thought she was going to ask me to stay with her, but she got up and left the room for a moment and returned with a blue photocopied pamphlet which she handed to me. The title read: *Breathe Into Your Spirit.*

'It's an amazing yoga workshop – and it's on this weekend at a beautiful, remote island off the north coast. Maybe you should go.'

'Thanks, Sita – it looks like a really great idea. Maybe I will.'

As I was leaving we hugged, and, although she was smaller and frailer than me, I wanted to keep holding on to her. I needed an anchor, someone to keep me safe – although from what I didn't know. I felt sad that I was here with a person I could share my secrets with, embrace warmly, yet whom I did not feel comfortable enough to ask anything more than an hour's time from.

I decided to go on the weekend yoga course. I didn't want to talk to anybody about Jack, especially Mum. The one good thing about Jack's return was that it had dwarfed Mum's cancer, and I had a compulsion to keep it that way, for a while at least. I suppose I was enjoying having a 'problem' that was all about me. My love life had been so utterly uncaptivating that I was almost welcoming the drama of a divorce. Living through the epilogue of a marriage is not exactly fun, but as grief goes it is marginally better than a parent dying of a terminal illness. Although, frankly, so is everything.

The island on which the course was being held was only accessible by boat. According to the brochure, the village from which you caught the boat was a taxi ride from the nearest town, which was a minibus ride from the nearest train/coach station, which was a taxi ride from the nearest airport. It was remote. *The journey to this beautiful island*, the blurb said, *is very much a part of the exciting spiritual adventure on which you are about to embark. Enjoy it!*

My journey began with my not being able to get a flight and having to get an overnight train across the length of the entire country with no sleeper. About five hours into the night, buffet car closed, novel finished, cruised by at least three drunken 'undesirables' and with every bit of knitwear I had with me piled on to my freezing bones, I was struggling to find the spiritual dimension in all this. Neither did it emerge when I disembarked at 6 a.m. to discover there were no taxis in operation before nine – a fact which became clear only to myself and my fellow 'spiritual explorers' (we being the only people who were not picked up by private car) after a three-hour stint in an unheated waiting room. During those three hours, I got to know some of my fellow yoga enthusiasts. As both travelling companions and fellow weekenders, I found them unappealing; lack of sleep, food and comfort had made me bitchy and I pegged them instantly as needy, nearly-middle-aged, lonely women in search of answers to problems they didn't really have. What galled me, of course, was the fact that I was one of them. Also, I have one of those faces that make complete strangers feel duty-bound to open up and tell me their life histories. In any case, I had plenty more time after our three-hour wait to hear every last detail of their lives as we were squashed together in a taxi for forty minutes, then spent half an hour on a very scenic but cold ferry journey, before being picked up by a beautiful young Australian woman in a deliciously warm seven-seater Jeep.

Our saviour turned out to be our instructor for the weekend, Leonora, and she had that kind of gentle, clean beauty that has the power to lift even the most sodden, grumpy mood. By the time we got to our destination, an austere building in a place so remote it redefined 'middle of nowhere' and whose grey walls instantly implied we had entered the dry-bread-and-no-mattress school of living favoured by vegan extremists, Leonora had charmed us into believing that perhaps our journey was not a wasted one. She talked about breathing and yoga and 'splendid isolation', but whilst she spoke with enthusiasm, she did not take herself too seriously. She must have been over thirty but her fresh face suggested younger and she exuded a natural kind of serenity which I had once envied but now simply aspired to. I liked Leonora a lot and felt I might learn something worthwhile from her.

Dinner was decent vegetarian fare and I had managed to bag a single room which contained a bed with a mattress and fresh linen sheets in which I slept well. There was freshly baked bread and fresh fruit for breakfast and then our first yoga session. It was amazing. Leonora was sympathetic and encouraging and the breathing techniques were accessible and effective. I came out floating.

After lunch I decided to take a long walk. I power-marched down the drive and turned left along the narrow road until I saw a dirt path leading up into the centre of a bog. I walked until I could see no evidence of civilization. No roads, no houses, no telephone wires or cables, just flat black and gold bog with a frayed hem of scattered forestation. I stood and listened. Silence. There was a whisper of wind and birdsong but it was vague, absorbed into the mossy land-mass. Quite unthinkingly, as if driven by some primal instinct, I opened my mouth and let out a scream. It felt like somebody else was doing it, but my God, it felt good. I didn't recognize the noise that came out but then, I thought, how often does one get to hear oneself screaming? At a funfair? During a row? Jack and I didn't fight. We had never, in all our years together, had a really good screaming match. We were far too civilized for that. Far too 'well balanced'. If we'd spent a bit less time 'listening' sympathetically to each other and a bit more time screaming, perhaps we would have – what? Stayed together?

Then, with sudden and absolute clarity, I saw that my marriage would never have survived even if Jack had stayed. Jack had married a timid girl and then left me as I had started to blossom into a strong and assertive woman. My husband would never have adapted to the self-possessed, successful me. His need to be admired was so strong that as soon as my level of self-knowledge matched his, he ran. As powerfully as I had recognized him as The One, I now knew he had left my life for a reason. I had flourished as a person *because* he had left me, not despite the fact. Finally, I was free.

'Yes!' I shouted out into the huge emptiness, 'yes! Yes! YES!' but each time my 'yes' landed with a dull thud and got swallowed into the damp ground. This was a victory cry that needed to be heard. It needed an echo, a magnificient, mountainous landscape to carry it across villages and continents to tell the world: 'I was right and he was wro-ooong!'

This was the kind of glorious revelation that should be shared. So I started to walk quickly back to 'base camp'. I was bursting to tell someone. Leonora: there had been an instant bonding there. I would find her and tell her, but first, first I would ring Jack. I was in charge now. Utterly in charge of my own destiny. Sita had been right, as usual. Getting away had cleared my head for long enough for the answers to come. The space, the silence, the breathing, even the terrible journey, it had all brought me to a place of completion. A place of letting go.

I seemed to get back to the house in minutes. I must have been running. I went up to my room, grabbed my mobile and switched it on while I rummaged in my purse for the piece of paper with Jack's numbers. He had said he was away that weekend so I took a deep breath and punched in the girlfriend's cellphone digits. No ringtone. No signal. Damn. I walked around the room – no signal. Went out into the hallway. Nothing. So I wandered around the chilly corridors, in and out of empty rooms until finally, in the yoga room, I got a nice long signal and punched in the number again before I had time to think too much about it. I tapped my knees as two, three seconds passed before it started to ring. At the same time, something really weird happened. I could hear a bird singing, really loudly, as if it were in the room. I hung up my mobile and looked around but the birdsong had gone. Peculiar, I thought – it must have been an echo or something. I rang the number again and within seconds could hear the birdsong again. To affirm my own sanity more than anything else, I walked around the room until I located the noise. It was coming from a handbag behind the door. I quickly surmised it to be a mobile phone; honestly, cows mooing, babies crying, birds tweeting – what kind of people embraced novelty ringtones?

I pressed the number again and as I did lovely Leonora came rushing in and picked up the handbag. I felt temporarily guilty. Birdsong was probably a less intrusive ringtone than most in a place like this, although

I seemed to remember there being a ban on mobiles altogether on the course.

Seeing I was on the phone, Leonora gave me an apologetic smile and I reciprocated, a shared ironic moment.

'Hello?'

'Hello?'

Our eyes met as we stood not ten feet away from each other, both frozen with horrified shock.

I tried to keep my face impassive while my mind flailed around in the enormity of this coincidence. Annoyingly, my first thought was that Jack's new woman was an inside-out gorgeous 'enlightened' yogi and not the innocent weak ditherer I had invented in my mind. Although after a few moments of my impassive silent treatment she did, gratifyingly, crack.

'Oh, Grace. Goodness, this is awkward – em, what can I say?'

For once, I was not the undignified gibberer. I raised my eyebrows a fraction and prepared to watch her squirm.

'You know we just thought, that is Jack and I, that this could be sort of an opportunity for us all to – well, I guess that's kind of backfired – which is a shame because Sita said—'

'Sita?'

It just came out, a knee-jerk shocked reaction, and it shifted the balance immediately.

'Oh yes,' Leonora said, her face brightening into an enormous smile, 'Sita has always spoken so fondly of you, Grace. To be honest Sita said she really felt we could be friends and despite this' – she gave a little shrug

to indicate the insignificance of our telephonic awkwardness – 'I really think we clicked.'

My lips must have been grazing the floor because
she looked at me, her large brown eyes full of genuine
concern, and said, 'Grace? Are you OK?'

It was in that moment that I had my true spiritual
awakening about the divorce.

'I am so OK, Leonora, and you know what?' I gave
her my widest and sincerest smile, 'I think Sita was right.
I am delighted, *thrilled* to finally meet you. Wow! This
has just worked out so well!'

After yoga, we spent time catching up on all sorts of
stuff. I asked her about the island and she said that,
believe it or not, it was Sita who had first e-mailed her
about this place when they were brainstorming this
workshop. It was the safest place on earth, she said. One
of the last places in the Western world where there was
no need to lock doors or hide handbags. It was all about
trust. The boatkeeper was an *amazing* spirit – he lived
alone in the old boathouse. There was nobody else living
on the island full-time except for him. Of course we
quickly got on to the common ground of Jack and his
ways, which was very 'affirming' for Leonora to connect
with another woman on. And our mutual friendship
with Sita, who we agreed was terrific. Leonora had only
met Sita in the flesh once before, when she had trained
in reiki with her on the trip to England where she had
met Jack. Had he not been in touch with me at that
time? Strange, because he had been here for about six
months and that was when he had got back in touch
with Sita. Actually, Jack had introduced Leonora to Sita
and – well – they had become instant friends and had

stayed in e-mail contact since. Sita often mentioned Grace because, of course, she thought Grace was *amazing*. Well, I agreed, I thought Sita was really amazing too. Really, *really* amazing. Then Leonora had an idea! Jack was flying up tomorrow evening and she was going to collect him from the airport. Why didn't I come with her? The Jeep was really comfortable and it would be company for her on the four-hour round trip. Actually, the Jeep was a gift from Jack's mother and they were planning to sell it before they returned to Australia for the wedding. She kind of grimaced the words 'divorce papers' and I laughed. Ha, ha. In the days before we were friends, eh? The money from the Jeep would upgrade them to business class on the way back because, to be honest, this was kind of a honeymoon-before-the-wedding for them. Jack's mum had helped pay for it. She was such an *amazing* woman. Wow. It must have been kind of painful for me losing her as well as Jack? Oh, I agreed, it *was* hard, but – genuinely? – it was my deepest wish that Leonora would bond with Jack's *amazing* mother and that the three of them would live happily ever after. Leonora was deeply moved, she said, and we hugged warmly before going to bed.

I did not sleep.

At 3 a.m., I took my bag and tiptoed down to the kitchen, where I foraged around for food. In a plastic bag, I packed half a loaf of bread, a bottle of water, some fruit and a packet of smoked-mackerel pâté. As I had suspected, the keys to the Jeep were in the ignition and it purred expensively out of the drive and left down the narrow road. As for directions, adrenalin sharpens the brain – and in any case there was only one road on the island and it led to the boathouse. Leonora was right about one thing – the ferryman was 'amazing'. When I told him that my father had just been involved in a near-fatal car accident and that it was imperative that I get off the island at once, he jumped to it. When we got to the other side, he kindly wrote down detailed instructions on how to get to the airport. For the next two hours, I listened to early-morning radio, the miscellany of eighties ballads and pre-recorded words-of-wisdom titbits aimed at turbulent souls who are crazy or unlucky enough to be tuning in at 4 a.m. I pulled in to the airport car park at around six. There would surely be a business flight leaving soon, and I didn't want to be hanging around. Leonora would be starting pre-breakfast yoga shortly so it would probably be an hour or so before she noticed that the car and I were missing. Now that I was back in civilization, I cleared out what was left of my food bag into a nearby dustbin, aside from the packet of mackerel pâté. This I opened, then, peeling back the carpet under the glove compartment on the passenger side, I smeared it generously over the rubber backing. Every time the heat came on, the stench would get worse. That was what two hours of early-morning radio had achieved with an already slightly twisted mind. I left the keys in the ignition, walked into the airport and booked myself on to the seven-thirty flight.

A few minutes after taking off, I looked down and saw the sea with a cluster of tiny islands, like God's afterthoughts, at its edge. I wondered how it was possible that I had driven for hours away from them and yet was looking down at them again in a matter of minutes. I thought about how time and technology conspire to create miracles we take for granted because they are man-made. And in the act of having had an intelligent thought, I suddenly felt confident enough to check in with myself about where I was with Jack. I was profoundly tired and expected to be more emotional as a result. I rummaged around in my head, waiting for the right question to hit the right answer and circuit my heart. Jack and Leonora. Leonora – young, beautiful, getting married to Jack? Nothing. A yogi, Jack's mother loves her, having a baby? Nothing. Jack – improved-with-age handsome, successful, having a baby? Nothing. OK, I said, let's tune in and have a pity party. Grace. Forty, divorced, no children. Nothing. Wow, I thought, I *must* be overtired. I didn't want to carry this shit back home with me and I knew that there was something I needed to get in touch with. So I closed my eyes and drew up a picture of sad, angry, resentful Grace in her yoga sweats and expensive heavy winter-weekend jacket smearing smoked mackerel on the undercarpet of her ex-husband's car. Was she pitiful? Shameful? Actually no, she wasn't. As a surge of encouragement and joy came over me, I laughed out loud at myself and thought how very glad I was to have the chutzpah to steal and then vandalize a car at gone forty. Jack and I always had great communication in our marriage, I concluded, and this had been the perfect way to end it because, after all, actions speak so much louder than words. I laughed again. I opened my eyes and the woman sitting next to me gave me a small smile in exchange for bearing witness to my sudden outbursts.

'I just hid smoked mackerel in my bastard ex-husband's car,' I said by way of explanation.

'Good for you,' she said, and we both started to laugh.

We talked for the remaining hour of the journey, and exchanged numbers at the baggage carousel. She was an artist in her late fifties, divorced with grown-up children, and lived not too far from me. We said we would definitely keep in touch, even though I knew we probably wouldn't.

In the taxi home, I thought of my old friend Sita, and wondered how I had forgotten that she was the only real source of sadness to come out of this. She had betrayed me; but mostly I had betrayed myself by believing in her as much as I had. I had imputed to her a wisdom and status that weren't truly hers. And in losing her, I realized that the loves we choose, our friends, our life partners, are subject to the vagaries of choice and change. The love of family, I thought, may not be any kinder but by its nature it is more certain.

As I put the key into my own front door, I felt that the only comfort I wanted was my mother. I had forgotten that, when life let me down, she was the only person I could turn to.

fourteen

Eileen

I did not tell anybody I was pregnant. Not my family, nor my friends in Dublin. I knew before I went to the doctor what was wrong with me, but was still hoping he would tell me otherwise. Any disease would have been better than an unwanted pregnancy.

The doctor who examined me was kind and concerned. Would I like him to refer me to an agency who could help? There were places that were set up to deal with this sort of thing. The Catholic Church made very good provision for girls in my condition. I wasn't alone; he saw a lot of girls like me.

I couldn't take it in. I wasn't 'a lot of girls', I was a good respectable person. I knew young women who thought nothing of going all the way with their boyfriends and this hadn't happened to them. The first time I had given in, I had got pregnant. All I could feel was a burning, overwhelming shame that this doctor knew what I had done. He could see the dirty state of me, the 'type' of girl I was. I knew I had to get away – from his surgery, from the city, from Ireland. I had to go to a place where nobody knew me.

When my next pay cheque came through I booked myself on an Aer Lingus flight to England. My only preparation for the trip was to tear an advertisement page out of *Ireland's Own* magazine that had the name and address of a cheap, safe place to board in central London. I told my workmates that I was going to stay with relatives and that I would see them in a week or so. I knew I wasn't going back; by walking away from my responsibilities, without giving notice to my flatmates or my job, I was effectively burning my bridges; leaving behind the life I loved in Dublin for ever. I had told my parents that Aer Lingus were transferring me to their London office and that I would not have time to come home beforehand but that I would write when I was settled. I could hear the worry and hurt in my mother's voice and was only slightly consoled by how much worse it would be for them if they knew the truth.

The bus journey into central London was longer than I had been expecting. After half an hour of straining to read street signs, I asked the driver to let me know when we had reached Kensington High Street. 'You got on the wrong bus if you're in a hurry, love. Kensington's the end of the line; it'll be another hour at least – goes through the middle and stops everywhere, this one.'

For the rest of the journey I gazed out from the top floor of the chubby red bus and found myself both amazed and afraid of this messy, vast sprawl of buildings, motorways, churches, synagogues, shops and stations. Could all this diverse life possibly be a part of the same place? This was the city where men from

Ireland came to make money and send it home; the land of opportunity where the streets were lined with gold. It was also the place where people came when they were in trouble and wanted to hide. There must be a lot of people hiding here, I thought, if it takes an hour to get to the centre of it by bus. For a time I was so enthralled with the sights – Marble Arch, Buckingham Palace, Big Ben, the gothic mansion of Westminster, places I had heard of on BBC Radio, landmarks I had seen in British movies or on the front of the English newspapers – that I forgot why I was here. When I remembered again, the excitement deepened into dread and I felt lost in the hugeness of this unfamiliar, terrifying universe of strangers. I got off the bus at Kensington High Street and asked a man for directions to St Bernadette's Catholic Girls' Hostel. He looked at me as if I were mad, until I showed him the newspaper cutting which gave the full address. He said that luckily for me he was able to direct me, but that it was at least a twenty-minute walk. When he did not offer to take me there or carry my bag, I felt my first pang of homesickness.

The hostel was a similar set-up to the one in Dublin, except the building was red-brick Victorian instead of Georgian. The door was open and I put my small suitcase down in the hallway and walked up to the half-moon desk. The sister on duty had a large impassive face with skin the colour and consistency of dough. I looked her directly in the eye and said matter-of-factly, 'I'm pregnant, sister.' There was no point in trying to explain myself, the damage was done and I just had to get through it as quickly and as cleanly as I could. The nun's lack of expression, one way or the other, confirmed what I had thought. London, the nun's face seemed to suggest, was heaving with immoral Irish girls, and the Church was nothing if not equipped to deal with them. I was given a bed in a room with four other girls and £5 to last me until such time as I got a job and could start paying rent. I stopped myself from telling the sister that I already had my last pay cheque. I would take all the help that I could and save my money for when I really needed it, which would surely be soon enough. Although frightened to find myself taking charity, I took some comfort from the fact that my life for the next few months would be organized for me. I neither wanted not expected sympathy, but was relieved that somebody else was taking care of what I should do next, that the Church was taking responsibility for my sins.

I worked for the next two months as a waitress in Lyon's Corner House at Marble Arch, and wore a cheap gold band on my wedding-ring finger to stop the world from seeing what I was. I slipped it into my coat pocket in the evenings as I had seen a bitchy nun berate another girl for wearing a wedding ring. She had said that we girls should not try to hide our shame, for being a public spectacle was part of our penance.

The baby came a month early and the birth was rushed and traumatic. The pain had woken me up and I had gone downstairs so as not to wake the other girls. Sister Bernardine was on duty that night and she was kind, the best of them. But I had said I was fine to go to the hospital on my own. I did not want a cloaked virgin as company during my ordeal. I felt humiliated enough.

I felt my bad labour was retribution for the sex act.

Blood, cramping, legs parted, grinding humiliation. The baby was taken away and put into an incubator and for the few hours before I held him, I felt hollow and exhausted. When I held him for the first time I felt reborn. The fact of him, his breathing, moving, warm tiny body, seemed extraordinary to me. That he was neither a doll, nor the tragic figment he had been in pregnancy, but a small, speechless, whole person. I called him Michael and he lit me up from the inside.

I loved my baby boy as every woman loves her first-born child: with pride, with wonder. For three months I fed him, held him, marvelled at his tiny fingers. I woke with him; slept with him; felt him as another limb, stuck to my breast, a small, sucking miracle. I was sent to a special house to recover and wean the child. Because Michael was premature, it was important that he had the care of his own mother before he was given up for adoption. There was great camaraderie in the mother-and-baby unit where I spent the next three months. We compared bottles and breasts and bellies; cooed over each other's babies, all of us still young enough to live in each day. We didn't focus on the future or think about the moment when we would have to give our children away.

I knew the instant I learned I was pregnant, from the moment of his conception, my child's future was away from me. I had to take my punishment. Keeping the child was not an option; not for respectable girls who understood that it was in the child's interests to be raised by a good Catholic family. I did not want to give my child away but I had no choice. The ability to measure 'morality' against my own right to happiness did not come until it was too late.

I took the train to St Albans on the day I was to hand Michael over. In my purse I had a postal order for six shillings to pay the foster-parents until a permanent home was found for him. I carried a small knitted bag with Michael's belongings in it. Four white vests, three pairs of nappy pants, five nappies, a romper suit, two pairs of tights, a wooden rattle, a tiny blue rabbit, a dummy and two bottles.

Michael was wearing a brand-new outfit, a two-piece sailor suit with matching hat and mittens which I had bought in British Home Stores. It was a little too big for him but would be good for another few weeks. He was wrapped in a soft wool blanket which one of the girls leaving the house had given to me. As the train clacked past the outskirts of the city, I held my baby in a protective cocoon and thought vaguely of what I might do and where I would go when he was gone. We passed stations with pretty names: Cricklewood, Hendon, Mill Hill – London offered endless places to hide and explore; life here was an adventure waiting to happen, I told myself. Despite that, up until the moment we were separated, I did not fully believe I would have to give Michael away. It didn't seem real – possible, even. It was as alien to me as the awful fact of pregnancy had been from the joyful reality of Michael when he was born. I was like a child playing on the train tracks, never really believing the train would hit me until it was too late.

I took a taxi to the orphanage, introduced myself at

the office, signed the release papers, explained the contents of the bag and handed over the postal order without fully taking it in. When the woman smiled and reached out her arms, I did what I had always done when someone in authority asked me for something; I conceded.

As I handed Michael over, I lifted my son's head to my face and breathed in the sweet scent of him for the last time. This was love, as certain a love as I knew I would ever find. There was nothing grey here, but a bright white certainty; love that came with no price, no duty, no questions. I breathed in on my tears, kissed him a silent goodbye, then breathed out bravely and placed him in the arms of the worker. I held the edge of the blanket for a few seconds, realizing that I wanted to keep it as a memento. When it came loose, the worker looked at me quizzically. I said, 'Sorry,' then tucked it back into the crook of the stranger's arm which now held my son. I did not touch Michael one last time. I loved him so much I was able to give him away. He would be taken into a good family who would give him a good life. I could not keep him because I had nothing to offer him. All I had was a mother's love. It was hard giving him up, but the past few months had taught me that sometimes life required you to do hard things.

At twenty, I could not possibly have known that it would be the hardest thing I would ever have to do in my life.

fifteen

Eileen

A year after I had given Michael away, John came looking for me in London. I had built myself a life of sorts in the suburbs, working nights in a pub in Hendon where I had lodgings upstairs with the landlord and his wife. They were from Kiltimagh, another Mayo town, so I trusted them and they knew I was respectable. I took a bus to Burnt Oak every morning, where I worked in a shop selling ladies' underwear. In the evenings I worked in the bar to pay for my keep, but I had every Sunday off. My local church was mostly frequented by English parishioners, and I found them stuffy and unfriendly, so I used to travel to the Catholic church in Cricklewood. There was an Irish social club attached to it and they had dances every month that I helped organize. Sometimes it was my job to book in the entertainment, bands from back home, and I had to arrange their transport and accommodation. When I did that, I remembered my previous, comparatively glamorous job working for Aer Lingus and I wondered if I wasn't wasting my life, drifting. But I didn't like to think about anything too much in the three years after Michael was born. Most of the time I was just relieved to be living an anonymous life where nobody knew what had happened to me or the terrible things I had done. I had enough money to pay for nice clothes, and managed to save quite a lot too. I had an idea that I would like to return home some day, but there was no rush. In the mean time, there was a telephone in the pub and I spoke to my mother once a week. She rarely asked when I was coming home; every Irish mother had a child in England or America in those days.

Because it was St Patrick's Day, I was working a daytime shift in the pub. By mid-afternoon, the King George was a sea of flat-headed, badly dressed drunkards. John parted them, gliding elegantly through our middle in a long coat, thick dark hair peppered prematurely grey at the temples, his light blue eyes lit from inside with glassy spangles, sober but intoxicated with passion. My stomach lurched with the excited dread which I thought was love.

John said he had searched all over Europe to find me. His heart had broken for me daily, his beautiful Eileen, as he had sown his wild oats, only realizing afterwards that I was his one true love after all. He was sorry he had left me the way he had, but he was here now, come to claim me, to take me away from this life of drudgery and hardship and back into his world of art and passion and culture.

In reality, John had abandoned his studies and squandered so much of his allowance on prostitutes and drugs that his parents had washed their hands of him. He owed everyone in Dublin money and had come to England to escape. He had arrived two weeks before and was staying in a small hotel in central London, with no money to settle the bill. He had remembered hearing from somebody that I was living there now, and had called my parents' house to get my details. He had been amazed to discover that these simple country people owned a telephone. That, he decided, was fate and helped him to concoct enough of a fantasy to convince himself he was still in love with me.

I paid his hotel bill, and the O'Gradys let him sleep on a couch in the bar as I promised he would help around the place. Mary O'Grady took an instant dislike to him after she noticed that he had helped himself to drinks from the bar a couple of nights after they had gone to bed, and not even had the manners to wash the glass after himself. She took me aside to tell me that the only reason he was still there was because I was such a good girl she wouldn't see me out on the street. I was embarrassed but justified it in my own mind: perhaps other people did not always see the John I saw.

After a month, our luck seemed to change as John got a small advance from a publishing company on his first book. I took the money and matched it with my own savings so that we were able to put down the deposit on a small house in Burnt Oak, a short walk from my day job. Because the house was near the tube station, I was also able to keep up my hours in the pub, getting a taxi home in the evenings. John stayed at home and wrote his books. After a morning writing, he spent his afternoons in the pub and was usually a little dozy with drink when I got home from work. It didn't worry me. John was a brilliant writer and that was what brilliant Irish writers did: they drank.

It was me who insisted we get married. John didn't want to, but I put my foot down and I said that I could not continue living in sin. Because he didn't think marriage was that important, John agreed, provided I kept the whole thing low-key. I bought a new suit and phoned my parents, who were disappointed it was happening in London and assumed I must be pregnant. The service was held at the side chapel of a small church in Camden Town, where the priest specialized in mixed-religion marriages. The marriage was witnessed by the O'Gradys. The only other guests were my parents, and their mood throughout was as muted as the beige fleck of my Jaeger suit. It was the only time they had ever travelled outside Ireland and they looked awkward and unhappy to be there, as if they might not be allowed to return home. John wore a suit and took us all for lunch afterwards to an Italian restaurant. In deference to my Pioneer family, he didn't drink that day. I glowed with pride as I drank my third glass of red wine and watched my sophisticated new husband order elegantly in Italian, ensuring that my parents were served with a plain meat-and-potatoes dish after they had expressed confusion at the foreign-sounding menu. For the first time in my life, I felt like a woman in all the right ways. The guilt of uncertain sex, the humiliation of my pregnancy, the punishing brutality of childbirth, all that was behind me now. I was a married woman, sacramented, secure, my life certain and mapped out.

Later that night, after we had made love, I could not

sleep. I lay awake staring at the naked shoulders of my new husband and thought about Michael. That scooped-out feeling came back in my stomach; guilt and fear blending everything away with its whispering truth until I felt hollow, void. I knew that I would have to tell John; I could not carry shame around with me. John was an educated, intelligent man. He was open-minded, a beatnik; he didn't judge people, he would understand. John woke up seconds after I had made the decision to tell him. He kissed me gently and called me Mrs Blake, then pulled on his dressing gown and went into the kitchen, calling out to ask if I wanted anything. It seemed like the right moment so when he came back in I just said it out: 'When you went to Paris, John, I was pregnant.' My voice faltered as I saw his face darken but I continued, 'It was a boy.'

John stood frozen in shock. He didn't need to hear any more, I could tell he knew instantly what had happened. I had given his child up for adoption, his child, his own flesh and blood. A son, doubtless blessed with his intelligence, his family's breeding. You didn't give the sons of people like him up for adoption; I realized that now, but it was too late.

As he struck the first blow, John started shouting – and his words hurt more than the physical shock of being hit. Bruises heal, but the hatred in his words never really left me. He said I was a witch, a weeping sham who had stolen a son off him, that I had tricked him into marriage in order to punish him.

As John beat me, raining down blow after blow, I could feel him willing the witch to retreat and bring things back to the way they were. He picked me up by the collar of my flimsy nightgown and shook me, but my limp body weighed it down and it tore, letting me fall to the side of the bed, where I banged my head. For a second he panicked, thinking I was dead, but then I moved a hand to cover my face. He lifted his arm to hit me again, then seemed to think better of it. In all probability he had remembered that he was sober, and that facing me afterwards would be easier if he went out and got drunk.

I stood up shortly after he left, cleaned myself up as best I could and got back into bed. Shock and shame buried my tears.

John stayed out all night and when he came home the following morning he was very sorry. He seemed shocked by my bruises; he gently touched the cut on the side of my lip, as if it would heal to his touch as easily as it had broken under it the night before. I flinched, and as I did I looked into his cowed eyes and saw a deep sorrow and shame; and fear.

'You have a terrible power over me, Eileen, to make me do such a thing.'

What was love, I thought back then, but a calling to deep emotion? And my husband was a passionate and emotional man. It was, he implied, my Catholic witch-craft that could reduce an intelligent, educated gentle-man to savagery.

As the months and years passed, I learned how to avoid being beaten by not doing or saying certain things, and that in itself was enough proof to me of my own responsibility. If I could avoid a beating, then surely there must be something I was doing, or not doing, to earn it. I never spoke about Michael again, and soon enough John stopped bringing the subject up. Either he had buried his pain or stopped caring. Nevertheless I carried the guilt. I had given away his son. I also believed that John loved me so much that when I disappointed him, he felt compelled to hit me. John was not a wife beater. He was an intelligent man, becoming recognized as a talented writer. Although his books did not earn us a great deal of money, they were well reviewed and important people had started to believe in him. While he could be surly at home, in public he was always affable, liberal and kind. Nobody would have believed that the bruises I claimed were from taking a tumble were caused by my husband smashing my face into a kitchen cupboard; I scarcely believed it of him myself. It was a shock each time it happened, a freakish occurrence. There was no routine to it, and it didn't happen frequently enough for me to ever get used to it. That was how I knew it must be something I was doing. It wasn't in my husband's nature to hit women. You only had to look at him to see that.

sixteen

Grace

'There is nothing to fear but fear itself.' I always loved that expression. It was one of those throwaway wisdoms that was none the less true. In therapy, I had pretty much learned to embrace the kaleidoscope of human emotions: envy, anger, joy, excitement, lust, resentment. They all had their place. Fear, from all I had read and been told, was the most important human emotion. Most other feelings had a relationship with fear. As a driving force to push something positive forward, as fuel for negativity or an excuse for standing still, fear was lurking about somewhere at almost every stage of emotional development. Recognize and manage your relationship with fear and you more or less have life licked. I knew that. The problem was, and it *was* a problem, I never really 'did' fear. I found it a terribly unattractive emotion. Although I tried not to, I found myself distinguishing between 'justified' and 'fake' fear, between the genuine arachnophobics to the silly squealing girls who were so 'scared of spiders' they needed a handsome fireman to clear one out of the bath for them.

I found that brand of affected female vulnerability high-pitched and annoying. Essentially, I was always more afraid of appearing like a squeaking attention seeker than I was of burying my fear and becoming a controlled tight-arse, with the result that, whilst no one would have described me as cold and unfeeling, I had always tended towards the stoic. By the time I reached adult life 'Feel the fear and do it anyway' was just plain 'Do it anyway,' and the fear bit was more or less dispensed with. It was a problem but, frankly, a problem which I was happy to live with.

Until my mother got terminal cancer.

I knew this was a huge and terrible thing that was happening and I knew that I was afraid of her dying. But I just couldn't let myself feel it.

I decided not to tell Mum anything about what had gone on with Jack. So when I returned home from my yoga trip, I wasted no time whatsoever in burying any suggestion of fear and getting on with the business of dealing practically and optimistically with the new situation in front of me. I went straight into my office, turned on my Apple Mac and Googled 'ovarian cancer'.

At the computer I entered a parallel universe which gave me a disassociated sensation. As if, when I saw something written on a computer screen, I knew it existed, but only as words and images on a plastic canvas. In that sense, none of it felt real. I loved the internet. It was an acceptable addiction for anal retentives like me. Here was something that enabled me to escape whilst giving me the excuse that I was informing myself – like the sixties poets expanding their minds with hallucinogens, but without the loon pants and the craziness.

Three hours later, I got up to go to the toilet and realized that I had not even taken my coat off. By that time I had compiled over a hundred pages of positive testimonials, affirmations and cures for various kinds of cancers. I was on a roll. Famished, I got into the car, drove to a local twenty-four-hour McDonald's, bought a big bag of carbs, then rushed home. I made myself a pot of coffee and settled down for the night. I felt like one of those rookie lawyers in a movie who stays up all night preparing for the Big Case. This was the biggest case I had ever had to prepare for, but I was detemined I could do it. The more information I gathered, the more in control I felt. Each new page was like a paving stone on my yellow brick road out of there – a sunny slab of hope. There was a way around this and I was going to find it. There was no need for my mother to die; I just had to stay positive. We could work through this. Intelligent, determined people always win out in the end. Mind and spirit can cure the body of anything. It was a Hollywood moment: if I worked hard enough and wanted it badly enough, this story would have a happy ending.

I stayed up all night; researching, printing off, editing out the nutball testimonials, the fanatics and witch doctors, and filing the stories that were inspirational and offered real, workable solutions. The message that came through from all of the success stories was that you had to take control of your own medical treatment. My mother's operation would more than likely be happening the following week; we were on standby waiting for the call. Once they opened her up, the surgeon would be in a much better position to discuss all of the treatment options.

By 5 a.m., I had the makings of what I thought was a very convincing document detailing a plan for my mother's recovery. I divided it into four sections: testimonials – stories from women who had recovered from cancer; mental and spiritual – affirmations and positive-thinking workshops; physical – diet and alternative therapies; and medical – cancer drugs. I put all the print-outs into a beautiful gold-leaf file which I had found in a stationery shop in Florence years beforehand and had been saving for a special project. I slept on my couch with my arms wrapped around my wonderful file full of solutions. I woke up after five hours feeling groggy but knowing there there was no point in going to bed as I would not be able to sleep until I had this sorted.

Mum hadn't been up long. Her hair was brushed and she had already applied lipstick but she was still wearing her best dressing gown. She was preparing eggs and when I went over and kissed her I noticed that she smelled faintly of drink. That made me feel sad, for some reason. Mum didn't look ill. She looked healthy and normal, like the fresh-faced, happy, 'recovered' women on the internet.

'Mum, come and sit down. I did some research last night and I found loads and loads of stuff on ovarian cancer, and you know what, some of it is really positive. I want us to work on this together, Mum. Leave breakfast, come and sit down and have a look at this . . .'

I spread the file open and started pulling out sheets of paper and laying them across the kitchen table. There was a little voice in my head telling me that I was behaving like an insane person. I had had virtually no sleep in two days, during which time I had travelled the length of the country and back again, stopping only to sabotage my ex-husband's car. In the period when I should have been recovering from my ordeal, I had chosen to skull a mountain of sugary stimulants and engage in an internet marathon. My little voice of reason was there, all right, but it was quite faint.

'Look, Mum – this woman had Stage Three ovarian cancer back in 1996 – and she completely survived. And this one – she had cancer seven years ago, and she's just come back from climbing Everest!'

In the midst of my enthusiasm, I sensed that Mum was hovering. Not in an interested, what-you-are-doing? way, but more of a when-are-you-going-to-leave? way.

'Mum, I know this is hard for you but . . .'

'No, no dear. It's all very interesting – really, it's just . . . this isn't the right time.'

Clearly, this was hard for her. I stood up and took her hands. She looked away from me, agitated, twitchy.

'Mum, there is nothing to be afraid of. We can get through this. Just come over and have a look at some of this stuff – or, I'll tell you what I'll do, why don't I just leave it here with you and you can—'

'Hello there.'

A man had just walked into the kitchen. I nearly jumped out of my skin.

'Ooh, sorry, sorry, I suppose I should have knocked,'

he said before putting down my mother's spare key and a Bagel Bakery bag on the table.

He was middle-aged, maybe in his early fifties, bearded and not entirely unpleasant-looking. From the way Mum was shuffling and tittering behind him, I guessed he was what she meant by this being 'not a good time'.

I was horrified, but only briefly. Mostly I was pissed off. I had never been a prude. Mum had had a few boyfriends throughout my teens and early twenties, some of whom I liked and some of whom I wasn't crazy about. They were all fairly standard-issue slacks-wearing suburban types, older than her and mostly met through the church or Irish community functions. I don't know where she had picked this one up but he was a good bit younger than her and looked as if he had been around the block a few times. The smell of drink, the lipstick, the 'best' dressing gown were evidently down to him. I was supposed to be still away on my yoga weekend, so she had felt it was safe to have him stay the night. Eugh. He wasn't wasting any time and straightaway went about making himself right at home.

'Hey, someone's been busy,' he said, picking up one of my papers and starting to read it. 'This crowd are really good, actually.'

It was all I could do to restrain myself from leaping across the room and slapping him across the head. The cheek! The arrogance! A complete stranger!

'Please put those papers down.'

'Brian.'

A smart-arse too. 'Please put those papers down, Brian. They're private.'

'They're only internet print-outs, Grace.' 'Grace'? He knew my name? Jesus Christ.

'Well, put them down all the same please, Brian. They don't belong to you.'

'They don't belong to you.' Where did that come from? That pompous schoolmistress voice? This was all back to front. I was having an almost-argument in my mother's kitchen with a man I didn't know.

'It's OK, Grace,' said my mother, and then, by way of explanation, 'Brian's wife died of cancer five years ago.'

Oh well then, that's marvellous. That explains every-thing. Man's wife died of cancer. Well then sure, Brian, go ahead and sleep with my mother and rifle through our private business. If your wife died, well, that's as much as I need to know. Go ahead, make yourself at home. Be my guest, Mr Bad-mannered Widower.

'I am so sorry,' I said.

He put the papers down and said, 'Thank you.'

I *wasn't* sorry, but his return 'thank you' seemed heartfelt. That made me feel guilty, and that guilt made me feel annoyed because, I thought, I have got nothing, *nothing* to feel guilty about, and frankly, I have enough problems in my own life right now without having to feel bad about somebody else's life, or dead wife, or whatever. I hurriedly gathered up my night's work into a makeshift pile and stuffed it all back into the gold file.

'Well – it was nice meeting you, Brian . . .' and before either he or my mother could open their mouths to object, I was out of the door.

I drove away from the house and tried to cling on to my indignation. Mum and this Brian man in the house should have been annoying enough, outrageous enough or just curious enough to keep my mind busy for the time it would take me to get me home. But it wasn't.

'*Died of cancer . . .*' Those three words had sneaked into my head, got briefly stuck in my throat and were now tearing at my heart like ugly, destructive gremlins.

I pulled up outside the corner shop and began to weep in heavy, reluctant sobs. I gasped back the tears, but this time there was no relief as there usually was after a good cry. Just a tight, terrified grip – as if a petrified animal had lodged in my stomach. This was fear, finally having its wicked way with me.

seventeen

Eileen

Four years after we were married, our daughter Grace
was born and the beatings stopped. I found stability
and peace in the routine of managing my home and my
jobs. With a small child, the shop and pub work was
no longer an option, so I took on cleaning jobs in
places where I could bring Grace with me. The local
parish priest's housekeeper was very kind and gave me
additional hours cooking and baking for resident and
visiting clergy. The parochial house was only a few
doors down from my home and within weeks Bridie
and I had become friends. Bridie was middle-aged and
as she had no children herself she absolutely doted on
Grace, often taking her for overnight visits so I could
do the occasional late shift for the O'Gradys. I was so
busy making ends meet that I didn't have time to dwell
on any problems in my marriage. John's critical acclaim
as a writer had not translated into money and so I still
had to support us all. Every moment I was not working
was spent with Grace, and being with my beautiful,
perfect child brought me as much happiness as I could

handle. In the first few months of Grace's life I did look at her tiny fingers, the curve of her plump sucking pout, and feel a pang for Michael. But each time it happened I shoved the thought aside and reminded myself how lucky I was that God had given me a second chance.

It upset me that John did not embrace fatherhood more. A noisy baby was not conducive to his work, and once the initial infatuation had worn off he began to spend more and more time away from home. He said he needed the support and solace of his fellow creative artists – intellectuals, publishers and pop singers, people who understood the demands of his work in a way I could not. His agent, who I never met, gave him space in his office off Carnaby Street. It wan't that many stops on the Underground, but I am sure it was a million miles away from his Irish suburban life with me and Grace. I found a way of encouraging him to go, without seeming to reject him. I didn't ask about his 'other life' or how he spent his days and nights away from us, and he didn't volunteer much. I was not naive and I guessed that my husband was probably taking drugs and going with other women, but my Catholic morals had adapted to my circumstances. As long as my child and I were safe and able to go about our everyday routine in peace, I was content. When he did come home, John seemed grateful for the comfort and stability we provided. I didn't make any demands on him and felt lucky because he left me alone most of the time. It was no hardship cleaning his house, washing and ironing his clothes, caring for his child and cooking for him once we were able to maintain a civil relationship. I didn't covet passion or intimacy in my marriage any more; I just wanted a quiet life.

I discovered that life was simpler when I became sexless and frumpy to John, like a loyal Irish mammy, offering respite, clean clothes and home-cooked food when he'd come home scruffy and hungry after tomcatting around town for a few days. I knew that, whatever his sexual exploits, whatever depravity he was experiencing on his bouts in town, he felt he was a better person for having me in his life. My presence, the fact of a 'wife', gave him a respectability, a dimension of decency that helped him believe himself to be a better man than he was.

All that changed when he came home one night and announced he was 'in love'.

Persephone, or 'Percy', Jones was the magnificent actress daughter of an English aristocrat; John had fallen in love with her and she with him. The only problem was that Percy wanted to get married and John knew that I would never give him a divorce. Not because I loved him, but because of my religion.

He bought a bottle of red wine and some flowers, ringing ahead to check I wasn't working. As luck would have it, Grace was with Bridie at the priest's house so we had the place to ourselves. As soon as he walked in the door, I could see that something had changed. He was sober and had a look of intent, maturity even, which I had not noticed before. He gave me the flowers, kissed me and said he had a situation he wanted to discuss with me. Of late, he said, an extraordinary event had awakened in him a finer sensibility. Something wonderful had happened that had made him see the world in a different way and he hoped that I would appreciate and support him on his new path. It sounded to me as if he had found God, and in those opening lines I felt a surge of hope, as if some marvellous spiritual insight was going to drive him to apologize for being a bad and inadequate husband.

Then it all started to fall apart. He started by explaining that his feelings for Percy were beyond his control, then tried to describe her to me so that I would get the picture. Theirs was a true meeting of minds, he said, there was chemistry, sparks; Percy was a woman who challenged him intellectually and sexually. He described her as tall and beautiful, then seemed to realize that I looked hurt, and started to fumble around his words. Flustered, he closed his eyes and blurted out that she was from a very wealthy family, like him; then he started to stutter and stumble again and said that none of that mattered really and that he was just going to concentrate and say what was in his heart.

'I love this woman and you cannot choose who you fall in love with,' he said, 'it just happens. True love is like a compulsion, a disease. I couldn't help myself. When you fall in love,' he said, 'you have to get married. That's how I feel about Percy and I hope you understand.'

I was so taken aback that I didn't say anything. He took that as a cue to continue so he explained, in a more assertive tone, how he had respected my religion by allowing himself to be cajoled into marriage before he was ready and now I had to respect his beliefs and give him a divorce so that he was free to marry the one true love of his life. He understood how it must hurt me to hear this, but, he finished, love could also be cruel. He looked relieved when he had finished, like he had run the race and all that was left for him to do was pick up the medal.

So I said what was in *my* heart.

'You can leave if you want, but I won't give you a divorce.'

Then I stood up and walked over to the sink.

The anger must have shot through him like a bolt of electricity and propelled him across the room; he grabbed my hair in a tight fist and drove my face down into the sink. Briefly, we both caught sight of his face in the mirror on the windowsill; it was contorted, enraged, unrecognizable from the debonair author he thought he was. I could see that his own violence made John even angrier. That I could do this to him, could still evoke such passionate feelings in him when he belonged to another. That I still had the power to turn his love into hatred – because, for him, that was what our relation-ship had always been about: power.

I had not been expecting the attack. If I had, I would not have said what I did; I would have handled it better. I had been hurt and angry with his declaration and had foolishly allowed myself the luxury of reacting. In the shock of the moment when he grabbed me, I realized that the reason John had been quiet in the years since Grace's birth was not that he had changed or settled or become a father, but because his attention had been elsewhere. I could feel the strength of his grip pulling my head back then pounding it down against the cold metal of the draining board. I struggled to move my head to one side and heard my hair rip from its roots into his hand. He threw me down and as my shoulder hit the ground, I fell into a familiar surrender, that moment where I would make myself as small as I could, curl my body into a comma to lessen the impact of each blow, form a fist around my fear and humiliation so that the truth of what was happening to me could never truly take hold. Tomorrow, it would seem like I had slipped and banged my head on the sharp table, just like I would tell anyone who asked.

Then something happened to change everything. I saw John's leg lift to kick my stomach and at that exact moment I heard the letterbox banging and Grace calling through it as she usually did, 'Mummy, Mummy.' Grace and Bridie were both on their way in. I knew that I could not surrender; I could not let my child see me like this. I stretched my hands towards my husband's ankle, grabbed it and tugged it towards me as hard as I could. He crashed down on to his back and there was a loud crack as his skull hit the floor. I scrambled to my feet and had composed myself sufficiently by the time I got to the door. I told Grace to go straight upstairs because Daddy had had an accident in the kitchen.

Bridie knew instantly what had happened, but I said nothing. I casually tidied my hair back from my face, not realizing I had a gash on my forehead. Bridie called an ambulance. We both expressed great relief when John came round just as the ambulance arrived, although in honesty our relief was that he had not woken sooner. The ambulance-man thought that he had probably broken a rib, and they took him to the hospital to check him out thoroughly. He was certainly concussed and almost certainly suffering from severe shock, they said.

I agreed with the diagnosis. John was shocked all right: he had never suffered physically at the hands of anyone before. As they loaded him into the ambulance, he stared at me with a blank, disbelieving look in his eyes. However, I knew the hurt would not last long and that he would be back.

Bridie insisted that Grace and I spend the night with her and Father Price at the parochial house. Frank Price was relatively new to the parish, but he was young (for a parish priest, certainly no more than forty) and had a great sense of social justice. He had recently requested missionary work in Africa, but been promoted to a parish instead and sent from his home in Scotland to this quiet London suburb, where he was being pampered in a four-bedroomed house by a motherly Irish housekeeper. Bridie knew Father Price would get the measure of the situation in an instant, and he did. She also knew his missionary zeal would make him likely to get involved, and she was right about that too.

I told him everything, but only because he asked and because I could not lie to a priest. Frank forbade me to return to the house and sent Bridie to collect a bag of things for me and for Grace. I would stay with them until the situation was sorted, he said, and I had no choice but to comply.

Bridie rang the hospital to check on John's progress so that when he returned from the hospital two days later, bandaged and bruised and ready for a fight, John found the tall and forbiddingly masculine figure of a fully frocked priest standing in his kitchen. At first, he was more amused than annoyed, but less than an hour later he left, under no illusions whatsoever about what would happen to him if he returned. Father Price told him that he was prepared to put through a request for an annulment; he had contacts and would ensure it went through as quickly as possible although, he warned him, the process could take years. This was non-negotiable and was offered on the sole proviso that John left the house that day and pledged never to return. The priest nodded towards a suitcase which he had taken the liberty of packing for him. Father Price said that, having been raised in the slums of Glasgow, he would be happy to give John a savage beating if he ever returned, such a beating, the priest assured him, that John would soon be pleading for the day when his wee slip of a wife pulled him to the floor and broke two of his ribs.

Grace and I returned home that evening, although Frank insisted Bridie sleep there with us for the first week.

Two months later, Bridie had to return home to Ireland to nurse her sick mother, and I was offered the job as Father Price's housekeeper.

The next time I heard anything about John was five years later, when somebody sent me a newspaper clipping from the the *Irish Times* saying that the writer John Blake and his common-law wife, the actress Persephone Jones, had been killed in a car accident in St-Tropez. The post-mortem had shown that both were high on drugs at the time.

eighteen

Eileen

There could not have been a better job for me than working as housekeeper for Father Price. It was less than five minutes' walk from my house and he was a very accommodating boss, allowing me to drop Grace at school and pick her up during my working day.

Frank Price came from a large, working-class Scottish family and spoke with a broad Glaswegian accent that I struggled to understand for the first few weeks. He was tall and well built with the big square face you would expect to see on a docker rather than a priest. From the first day he insisted that I called him 'Frank', and winced every time I forgot and called him 'father'.

Frank had a strong social conscience and a modern outlook on life and religion. Pope John XXIII opened the Second Vatican Council during the time that Frank was in the seminary, and he was one of a new generation of modern, liberal priests. They believed that the principles debated by the world's bishops and cardinals during 'Vatican II' heralded a true movement towards change in the Catholic Church. There was a prevailing spirit of liberal optimism among Frank and his contemporaries; they believed that divorce, contraception and marriage for priests were inevitable, indeed imminent. Many of them would never have become priests had they thought otherwise. In the decades to come, many of them left the Church to get married. Frank's passion was for righting social injustices and making the word of God accessible to everyone, especially the underdog. When his request for missionary work had been denied, he had turned his attention to the needy closer to home. At his first parish in Fife, the old parish priest had complained that he was 'unmanageable' when his young charge started to bring drunks home from the park to feed them in the parochial house. The bishop did the smart thing and used Frank's pioneering spirit to give him a tough parish in the Gorbals, where he set up a hostel for young men with drug and alcohol problems. However, Frank's earnestness, coupled with his liberal ideals and good looks, meant he began to be known to local politicians and the media. And as Frank's views did not toe the party line, the bishops eventually arranged a transfer down to the suburbs of north-west London.

In the few years he had been our parish priest, he had started a youth club and turned one of the large parish buildings into a day-centre for a community programme helping unmarried mothers and unemployed youths. The younger families loved him for his practical manner and easy sermons, but some of the older folks were offended by his unconventional ways and his refusal to wear a collar. 'I'm not interested in all that pompous nonsense, Eileen. Jesus wore the ordinary garb of his day, and that's good enough for me.' I often heard him describe Jesus as the ultimate working-class hero, which I guessed was how he liked to see himself. For that reason, it embarrassed him to be living in a four-bedroomed house on his own with a housekeeper doing his cooking and cleaning for him. The only reason he had allowed Bridie to appoint me as successor was that I was a charity case: a battered wife, a single mother who needed the work. Of course, that only became clear to me after I got there and realized that I had taken a job looking after a man who was more than able and willing to look after himself.

We struggled in those early weeks. I would arrive in the morning to a spotless house – bed made, dishes washed, shoes polished – and absolutely nothing to do. The two of us danced around the kettle competing over who would make the tea; he blocked my path to the broom when I knew there wasn't a crumb on the floor to sweep anyway.

I called Bridie: she had had the same problem, she told me, but she soon put him in his place. 'You've got to be firm, Eileen. He let me boss him about. Mind you, that was because I reminded him of his mother, but you're younger, Eileen. It's different.'

'*It's different.*' Women like Bridie and my mother hid ominous meanings in ordinary sentences. I knew she meant something by it, but I was afraid to ask what it was. But there was the germ of a feeling when I sat Father Frank down for his morning coffee, forcing a home-made scone on him, and said very assertively:

'Father – Frank. There's no point in my working here if you don't give me something to do.'

He paused and looked down at his feet; he seemed to be considering something. The moment seemed endless and I felt I should say something just to break it. Then he lifted his head again, looked me straight in the eyes and said, 'There's something I'd like you to do all right. I just don't know if you'd do it for me.'

It seemed quite clear that he was asking me to sleep with him. As clear to me as if he had said it outright. I must have blushed bright red because he smiled, broad and shameless, and said brazenly:

'Will you give it a go?'

'Well – what is it?'

I knew well what it was, but I wanted to force him to say it. I was just forming the words around my indignant fury when he left the room and came back carrying two plastic shopping bags full of papers.

'I have all these papers that need filing for the youth programme, and I just can't get around to it.'

From that day on, I made it my business to seduce him. I could feel him watching me, considering. And as he considered I performed for him: made myself aware of my everyday movements so that each of them became infused with possibility. Standing at the kitchen sink, my back arched, shoulders caving in and out as I moved the dishes over and back; wearing my hair swept up so that its nape might call out to him, willing him to tender feelings; swaying my hips slightly as I walked; reaching my arm an inch further into the cupboard to show him the curve of my thighs. I never turned to greet him when he entered a room but went about my business imagining, hoping, secretly knowing that my every move was driving him mad with desire. After ignoring him most of the day, I would then soften my voice and smile as I brought him tea or food, willing him to acknowledge his feelings.

He finally cracked in the kitchen, in a frenzy of urgent desperation on a Sunday afternoon after Mass and before lunch. It was me who led him from kitchen table and upstairs to the parochial bedroom. It was me who willingly adopted the role of wicked temptress to allay his priestly guilt, who managed his manly emotions when he browbeat himself for having taken advantage of my vulnerability. It was me who dried his tears those first few months when he doubted his faith, and it was me who persuaded him not to give up his job for a woman. I set the ground rules of a ten-year affair with Father Price that would be the first relationship in which I felt truly loved and respected.

I did not want to get married again: I had married John for life, and although I did not love him and was happy to be away from him, he was still the father of my child and would always, in my mind, be my husband. Grace was my main concern, and I did not want my child's life interrupted or disrupted with the presence of another man. Truthfully, there was not a man on earth, and this included Father Price, whom I trusted enough to bring fully into my daughter's life. My child had come close enough to harm with her brutal father and I would not involve myself with another man unless I was sure. And the truth was, I didn't think I would ever be absolutely sure about a man again. The next best thing, I realized, was having an affair with someone whom I could never get openly involved with. That way I could be certain Grace – and I – wouldn't get hurt.

I was happy to cook and clean for him, but this time I was getting paid. I was determined I would never be another man's slave again.

I learned over the next ten years that love holds no such absolutes.

nineteen

Grace

My head was very sympathetic, and I was able to negotiate the rest of the summer term off work. Despite that, I didn't see Mum for almost a week. I just couldn't stomach it. I called her every day, just to assure myself that she was still alive, but the whole incident with her new friend Brian and my irrational craziness in putting that file together was making me feel physically sick. So I went to the cinema a couple of afternoons, and tried to keep myself busy so that I didn't have time to think about it. When I did think about it, I became one of two things; paralysed or confused.

The paralysis was worse of the two because it was just pure, undiluted fear. Nothing complicated about it, just the reality hitting home that my mother was going to die.

Being confused was marginally better than being in paralysis, but it was a close race. It came from the part of me that was determined not to give up on my mother: the survivor, the optimist. Why should she die just because she had cancer? People survived cancer.

There was no reason to give up hope yet. The biopsy had diagnosed Stage IV but the MRI scan was far from definitive and it was not until they operated that they would know how far the cancer had spread. Ovarian-cancer patients had a 35 per cent chance of survival and cell growth was slower the older you were. There were loads of survival stories on the net. Loads. Mum could easily be one of those women. Her treatment programme had not even been decided on yet; in fact the whole 'terminal' angle, when I stopped to think about it, was probably hyperbole that my mother had picked up from horrible Shirley. Mum needed positive energy around her and it was my job to provide her with it. We didn't know anything for certain yet, which was surely a good thing? Or not. It could, of course, be much worse than they thought and she could have only weeks left. So then the paralysing fear would kick in, and I would find myself having to force myself into the basic machinations of getting washed and dressed, as if I was running a marathon through treacle, until the activities and arrangements of my day took over and helped me temporarily forget.

On the sixth day, I called Mum's house a couple of times and there was no answer. When there was no reply by lunchtime, I managed to talk myself down from a state of panic, got in the car and drove over there. I let myself in and called out. No reply. I went straight to the kitchen, where I found a note which read 'Gone to post office then might pick up a few bits and bobs in town. Back 4-ish.'

It wasn't addressed to me specifically, and perhaps because it didn't contain any appalling, earth-shattering, devastating information I took it upon myself to have a rummage around in her kitchen drawers. Actually, I was half looking for a cigarette. Mum usually had a secret stash of year-old menthol cigarettes hidden in the back of a drawer behind the Sellotape and batteries and crumpled Christmas crackers. I hadn't had a cigarette in over ten years, and while the decision to smoke was far from made, it seemed like a good time to indulge myself in a little dysfunctional behaviour. The drawer was stuck so I reached in and tugged at a lump of paper napkins that were caught in the back. As I pulled my hand out, I grabbed a square box which felt like a cigarette pack, but wasn't. It was a cheap black gift box, the kind which usually contains jewellery. It looked out of place in the kitchen; this was the kind of trinket box she kept in her bedroom dressing table. Curious, I opened it, expecting to find a tacky brooch – an unworn gift from a work colleague. But nestling incongruously in the ruched royal-blue silk was a tiny hospital ID bracelet. I let out an involuntary cry. My mother had preserved this tiny circle of cardboard from the day I was born. I slipped the faded yellow ring on to my thumb and saw how small it was. My thumb was almost as big as my wrist had been then. I became enveloped in the miracle of my own existence; here was evidence of a time that I had lived and yet had no memory of. A time before I was aware – when I was totally vulnerable, dependent. A time when I was barely separated from my mother's womb, virtually still a part of her physically, completely attached emotionally. Suddenly, I wanted to be back there. The fear and confusion of the past few days melted and

I was just a child who didn't want my mother to leave me. All I could do was bawl.

Eventually, I went in search of a tissue. I couldn't find one so I went upstairs to the bathroom and attacked the toilet roll. On my way back down I heard movement in my mother's room. I stuck my head tentatively around the door saying, 'Hello?' while praying it wasn't an intruder, or worse: Brian in his underpants.

The room was dark with the curtains drawn and there was a lump in the bed the size and shape of my mother. The duvet was drawn up over her head.

'Mum? What are you doing? I didn't know you were in—'

'Fuck off.'

Whoah! It was muffled but unmistakable. My mother aggressively swearing was enough to scare the shit out of me. I stood for a moment and wondered what to do. Should I go? Part of me wanted to run out of the room, the house, this whole vile situation. But instead I walked across and sat on the opposite side of the bed and waited. Eventually, her head emerged from under the duvet. She had her back to me and her hair was matted. The air in the room was stuffy and stale, an intimate sleep smell so offensive in strangers, yet acceptable and comforting from those you love.

'Please go, Grace. I'm fine. I'll come downstairs in a minute.'

I didn't move. I just couldn't. Something was making me stay, some instinct that if I left now, I might as well leave for ever.

'Please, Grace. I don't want you to see me like this.'

I waited silently and I could feel her sighing, too tired to argue. She said, 'The hospital rang.'

'That's great news, Mum.' Actually, great news would be 'Hey! We made a mistake! You don't have cancer!' but you do what you can.

'When do they want you to go in?'

'This afternoon – but . . .'

I felt dread rise up in me.

'But I don't want to go, Grace.' Then my mother started to cry. Her shoulders were heaving and her voice sounded small and terrified as she said, 'I'm afraid. I don't want them to cut me open.'

All my life, I had hated to see my mother cry. She was my mother; she wasn't supposed to cry. It was her job to comfort and protect, not fall apart. Mum was supposed to be strong for me, not the other way around. And my mother used to cry a lot. At films, at state funerals: when Princess Diana died, my mother was hapless with grief even though she'd had virtually no interest in the pretty royal when she was alive. Where I always reined in my emotions, my mother was more emotionally expressive. It wasn't that she was desperately needy, it's just that she found it easy to cry. Mum openly weeping used to make me feel resentful; something inside would start wailing, 'What about me?'

I felt myself automatically starting to harden, then I noticed the baby bangle, which was still wrapped around my thumb. An obvious truth hit home that startled me, even though it was so glaringly simple. This woman had brought me into the world and looked after me since my life began. Now her life was coming to an end and it was time for me to look after her.

I held the bangle to my lips and put it carefully in my pocket. With that one action I said goodbye to the baby in me, reached my hand over and touched my mother's hair.

'Don't be scared, Mum. I'm here. I'll be with you every step of the way.'

Mum was in surgery for four hours. I kept myself busy rearranging my life so that I could move into her house the following day. I made lists and phone calls; I went to the gift shop and bought magazines and crisps; I had tea and a sausage roll in the café. I familiarized myself with the layout of the hospital, this mini-city with its rubber floor tiles and mint-green walls and vast wheel-chair-accessible toilets; the decor and smell combined to create an atmosphere of menace. I never understood the fashion for glamorizing hospitals on television hospital dramas.

Mum was in a room on her own. I don't know how these things are decided, but I suspected it was just because the room was available. I was pleased for the privacy. We had spent the night before together, watch-ing pictures flicking across the small TV high up on a wall bracket near the ceiling, neither of us truly concen-trating but pretending for the other. It was the closest I had ever felt to my mother, sitting quietly in that anony-mous room, both too afraid to talk. When they wheeled her back in after the operation, she was still unconscious and the consultant was with her. When I saw him, I knew he had news and I wasn't ready for it. I had not been expecting to receive the information he was about to impart in any particular way, but now that it was imminent I realized that I wanted a few days' notice, and to be wearing a suit, and for it to be in his office, and for my mother to be conscious and, of course, for it to be hopeful.

'It's very bad news, I'm afraid.'

Anything but that; anywhere but here; anytime but now.

'Can we do this another time, er . . .' was it Doctor or Mr? I'd forgotten how to address a surgeon.

'Mr Cartwright.'

Oh right, yeah, thanks for that. 'Can we do this some other time, Mr Cartwright? It's just that I'd like my mother . . .'

'I'm afraid not. I have another operation to perform, and I'm already very behind today.'

Oh. I am so very sorry that my mother's cancerous tumour threw you off your important schedule. Please accept my most sincere apologies on her behalf.

'Perhaps you'd like to sit down?'

I did not want to sit down, particularly not for this patronizing prick, but I did. Mr Cartwright wore the impervious expression of the hardened autocrat. My guess was he was excellent at removing cancerous tumours, but bad with people. I would have settled for the first, if it meant he had removed all of my mother's cancer and completely cured her.

'I won't give you the medical jargon because I find so many people ignorant as to what it means . . .' But in the absence of the first, a bit of charm would have been nice. 'So I'll just say it straight. Your mother's cancer has reached her liver. It is widespread, advanced and inoperable. Prognosis is two to three months, at best. I have debulked the existing tumour so she should be more comfortable . . .'

The shock had me standing at the sink vomiting up my tea and sausage roll.

'Oh dear – are you all right?' he said, hopelessly. I just wanted him to stop talking now. If there was anything else, I wanted it sugar-coated.

'Just please leave me alone,' I said, quietly but with conviction.

'I'll get my office to make an appointment for you and your mother.'

So vomit and tears gets you an appointment, otherwise we'll just slip you the bad news like a date-rape drug and hope you can handle it. That's great – good to know you guys have a system for imparting traumatic news. Funny how I had read internet accounts of this happening to people, and yet had been completely unprepared for it myself. Guess it's that old adage, 'It'll never happen to me.'

Schoolteachers and surgeons – no matter how clever some people are, sometimes they just never learn.

twenty

Eileen

I made sure Grace never saw Father Price as anything more than a kind priest and my employer. But over the decade of our illicit affair, Frank and I fell into a comfortable relationship that was stronger and more committed than my marriage had ever been. Frank was down-to-earth, warm and open. I felt able to confide in him as I would a close friend. I didn't want marriage, he didn't want to leave the priesthood, and those honesties helped the complication and pain of our initial passion change into a loving friendship. I created a home for him, complete with all the comforts including sex and female company. In turn, he was attentive and appreciative; he placed no demands on me and allowed me to take charge of his home, his heart and his libido. Our affair was set against the backdrop of the 1970s free-love revolution, so it was easy for both of us to salve our consciences. Frank had Vatican II to remind him that the Church was on the brink of much-needed openness and change, and I had *Cosmopolitan* to remind me it was my moral and social duty to have orgasms.

One afternoon, after we had been together for seven years and Grace was going through an exhausting, questioning puberty, I tried to end our relationship. We had just made love, something that had been happening less and less often of late. Frank had been working extremely hard setting up a project for runaway teen-agers in the city centre, as well as carrying out his pastoral duties. He was spending more and more time working, and I had begun to feel taken for granted. My paid hours as housekeeper had become extended to preparing late, hurriedly eaten meals. My careful prettifications of his house were going unnoticed and unappreciated. It felt as if the affair had run its course and I was keen to end it before it became tawdry and stale.

Frank pulled on his underpants, and I looked at the dark patch of hair in the small of his back and felt a small sadness for the days when the sight of it had made me drag him back down on to the bed.

'I think we should stop seeing each other, Frank.'

His actions slowed down, and I could tell he was shocked, although he did not turn to face me.

'We can't,' he said. 'I need you.'

'Oh.' I was genuinely taken aback. 'Well, I can stay on as your housekeeper. It's just that I think it's time . . .'

'No,' he said, still facing away from me, 'I mean as a woman. I need you as a woman.'

My stomach lurched with dreadful familiarity. It was a declaration of serious love and one I knew I could not turn away from. Frank Price was a good man doing God's work and he needed me. What frightened me though was the realization that I needed him too. Despite my prot-estations, my boundaries, my determination not to, I had become dependent on him emotionally, as well as financially and spiritually.

So I stayed three more years. In making the commitment to stay, I changed the terms of the relationship, which became more equal. I became involved with the running of his projects, helping him with paperwork and proposals. We both grew so used to each other, so comfortable with the naturalness and ease of our friendship, that we became sloppy about keeping our relationship a secret. It was not that we were physically demonstrative or obviously in love, more that it had become impossible for us to hide our close involvement. We had gradually acquired the unmistakable air of old-love: finishing each other's sentences and speaking to each other with an offhand, presuming intimacy that was eventually noticed.

Fifteen years after he had applied for an overseas mission, the bishop's office wrote to Frank to say they were pleased to inform him that his application had been successful. He was being sent to Guatemala to work in a mission in the highlands, despite the fact that he spoke no Spanish and was not familiar with the political and social unrest in this small Central American country. His missionary work in north-west London had come to an end, they informed him, but it would continue to be funded largely by the Church, although the day-to-day running of it was to be handed over to lay managers. It was obvious that some pious parishioner had informed on him. His replacement, Father Dickson, was coming from an established parish in south London and a condition of his moving was that he bring his own housekeeper with him. Could Father Price please give notice to his own housekeeper; the parish would provide her with one month's severance pay. That enraged me: even though Frank and I had taken pains never to spend a full night together in ten years under the same roof, this new priest was insisting on bringing his housekeeper to live with him. Obviously he was a better politician than my outspoken Frank.

Frank was incandescent with rage. This was a clear case of begrudgery and bigoted jealousy. The die-hard conservative parishioners were ganging up on him because he was trying to do something for the under-privileged youth of the area, telling scandalous tales to his superiors when really they hated him because he didn't wear his collar off duty. He swore, and said that he would leave the priesthood, that the Catholic Church wasn't worth this trouble and he had half a mind to convert to the Anglicans.

But we both knew that wouldn't happen. Deep down, we knew it was over. Frank was not going to leave the priesthood for me any more than I wanted him to.

We never really said goodbye, not properly. We had been given just one month's notice and we spent it dismantling, packing and preparing for our new lives. The informality of our relationship made it easy for us to slip into denial about how deeply we were attached and we prepared for our parting with a mutual and in-creasing coldness. We stopped sleeping together and slipped into the roles of parish priest and loyal house-keeper. On the day before he left for Central America, I went around to give the house a final once-over for the new priest. The two large suitcases in the hall contained all of Frank's possessions. I saw with a sudden, shocking clarity that this was not my lover's house. It had not been his crockery I was washing, his table linen I'd been ironing, his furniture I had been dusting or his bed I had been lying in. All of it belonged to the Church. Even him. Especially him. I had borrowed him for ten years and now it was time to give him back. I felt foolish for having given so much of my life to a man whose life could be held in two suitcases.

As I was leaving that day, Frank gave me a cheque for £5,000, an inheritance he had kept aside. He said that it was an injustice my losing my job in that way, and he wanted to find a way to thank me personally for all I had done for him. It was an awkward moment, strangely cold and businesslike. He was doing his 'moral duty' by me, and I felt a spike of anger that he was leaving; that I had wasted so much time loving him. The money seemed inappropriate but, with faith in his finer feelings for me, I took it. An hour later, when I had finished my work, I left the keys on the hall-stand and we embraced. Neither of us spoke any passionate words; neither expressed the regret or the loss we were both feeling. There seemed little point when they were bound to lead us only to the same place. Our parting had always been inevitable and if we were in pain that was our own responsibility.

'I don't know what I'll do without you,' he said to me.

I smiled and didn't reply. My heart had already hardened around the idea that he would find a willing young woman in Guatemala to take my place.

twenty-one

Eileen

It was a month after Frank had gone that the fear began to set in. The money he had left me with had cleared my mortgage but the month's redundancy money did not last long with bills to pay and a teenage daughter to support. Grace's needs had become more expensive as she was getting older; she had her heart set on a school trip to France that summer, she liked fashionable clothes and needed cash to go out to parties and discos with her friends. Many of Grace's friends worked their Saturdays in a nearby shopping centre, and she had begged me to allow her to get a job clearing tables in a café with one of her friends. But I had become angry with her when she had suggested that the bit of extra money would help.

'I will not send a child of mine out working,' I snapped, then reassured her: 'Don't worry, Grace, we have plenty of money.'

It was a question of pride more than anything else. In my generation, the poor kids left home at fourteen to take up trades or work the farm because their parents could not afford to keep them in school. My daughter's contemporaries were from middle-class homes and were working for cigarette and clothes money. I could see that Grace was taken aback at my not letting her work; she was so sensible I always let her do everything that she asked me. But then, she was smart enough to know it was a battle not worth fighting.

Looking back, I was sensitive about being a single mother. I kept my mind busy with the day-to-day worries of rearing an easy and well-behaved daughter, so I did not have to consider the irony of having given my son away in order to avoid rearing him alone. I told myself that I had deprived Grace of a father, and therefore would not deprive her of the privileges of childhood. I was determined that my daughter would complete her education and have a good career, that she would do all of the things that I had not done with my life. I wanted Grace to become successful and independent and for her success to be through choice. I felt I had been lucky to have enough strength to get me through; I wanted her to get more out of life than I had done. To travel, succeed, see the world, experience life at its best.

In my forties and with no formal qualifications, I became frightened that I wasn't going to be able to get another job. The more I began to picture a future with no work, the bigger my fear became. I would talk myself out of applying for any job that interested me because I was under-qualified. I did not want to get menial work as a night cleaner, which was all I believed I was fit for – because what kind of a message would that send to Grace? Over the few months after Frank left, I became disheartened and depressed, although I took great pains to hide it from Grace.

'How's the job hunting going, Mum?' Grace would ask brightly when she got in from school. I would want to cry – sometimes scream out in anger – but I kept it all to myself.

'Oh, nothing's come up yet, darling. Just getting all those little jobs done I haven't had time for.'

I would spend the following day in my spotless kitchen, my drawers organized, sitting at my kitchen table looking at the local paper's job section, petrified of the future. I sat for hours some days, staring out of the window and wondering how I was going to find the strength to keep holding up the wall, to stop life tumbling down on top of me and, more importantly, my daughter.

One day, while I was chopping vegetables for dinner, Grace came in from school and started babbling on with her day's news. I was beginning to worry that she had sensed something was wrong, as she seemed to be constantly trying to cheer me up. Teenagers were supposed to be surly and difficult; I was just looking for things to worry about.

'Anyway, Sandra, you know my friend that works in Café Third in Bailey Newton?'

'I've told you before, Grace, I don't want you . . .'

'No, no, no, Mum – listen!' I put down the knife and pretended to listen. Grace was already slightly taller than me. She had a kind, open face, speckled lightly with spots. Sometime I was taken aback, realizing my daughter was almost a woman.

'Anyway, Sandra's boss was this really awful woman

called Mrs Daly, who was always coming in late and was really stupid and always yelling at them for no reason – anyway, she got fired on Saturday.'

I turned back to chopping the vegetables. 'Grace, I don't have time for all this tittle-tattle – really—'

'No, Mum. God, are you stupid? I mean, I thought you should apply for the job. I know it's not much, but it would get you out of the house and it could tide you over until something better comes along.'

I felt the rage bubble up in me. Grace had this awful way of patronizing me and giving me advice like she was an adult: my equal. It was an annoying trait she'd had since she was a little girl. In a small child it had been precocious and sweet; now that she was getting older it was infuriating, especially as I was finding it harder to contradict her.

'Grace, I can't apply for that job, I'm not qualified.'

'What do you mean?'

Grace seemed genuinely puzzled, so I said, 'Manager. They want a manager. I've never managed anything in my life.'

'You managed Father Frank all right – and virtually ran that project for him.'

'Grace, just leave it, all right?'

But she wouldn't. She just carried on and on.

'Jesus, Mum, it's not like it's a football club or a newspaper they want you to manage. It's only a café.'

'I don't have the qualifications, Grace, and that's that.'

'And what qualifications would they be, Mum? "Café management"? Where do you learn that, then? There *are* no qualifications for running a café, Mum.

You just turn up and do the interview and if they like you you get the job. If you're rubbish at it, they fire you like Mrs Daly – simple as that.'

I was not in the mood for a fight; in the face of Grace's badgering, I was feeling weak and weepy rather than annoyed.

'I was only trying to help, Mum, that's all.'

I heard worry and disappointment in my daughter's voice so I said, 'OK, I'll call in there in the morning and get an application form or whatever.'

'Great,' Grace said, her face suddenly brightening. 'It's Saturday so I'll come with you.'

I was so terrified I did not sleep at all that night. Since I had left Aer Lingus at the age of nineteen, I had not had what I considered to be a proper, responsible job. Although I had always worked and knew I was a good worker, I had always felt my jobs were more down to the kindness of my bosses than any special talent I had. The O'Gradys had employed me out of kindness, and the ten years working for Frank had truly blurred the lines between personal and professional. I had no confidence in myself whatsoever. Regardless of whether I applied for this position or not, I knew I would have to find some kind of a job and soon. But I did not feel ready to step out there into the real world. I did not feel prepared.

By seven o'clock that Saturday morning, I had showered and washed my hair, and when Grace came down the stairs at ten I was still flustering over what to wear. I tried to wheedle my way out of going, but Grace made light of it and said we should go over to the centre and do some shopping, then just pop in to the information desk and enquire anyway. But she made me put on my smart black trouser suit and pretty green blouse, just in case.

As soon as we got inside the main doors of the shopping centre, Grace frog-marched me over to Bailey Newton, the big department store. I mean, she virtually dragged me by the arms until I could not object without looking like a tantrum-throwing child. As we reached the information desk, she pulled an envelope out of my pocket and thrust it into my bag.

'What's that?' I asked.

'Your CV,' Grace said. 'Your qualifications. I typed them out last night.'

The woman had already said 'Can I help you?' before I had the chance to get angry or upset by my daughter's presumptuous actions.

Before I was fully aware what was happening, I found myself sitting in a small office on the sixth floor of a department store I could barely afford to shop in facing the Human Resources Manager. To my own amazement, I flew through the interview. I was exactly what they were looking for, the woman said. A mature, responsible woman who could manage a young staff. I had no direct catering experience, but she did not think that would be a problem. I was on a three-month trial so we could both see how we got on. The salary was more than I had ever earned before and they wanted me to start work the following day.

Grace punched the air when I told her.

'We'll see how I get on,' was all I said. I didn't want her to think she had won, but I knew that she knew I was thrilled.

What Grace did not know was that this was the second time in my life she had given me the courage to change. The moment when I pulled her father to the ground being the first.

Later that evening, I read the CV she had written for me and I cried. It was painstakingly detailed and beautifully typed. It must have taken her hours.

'Aer Lingus ground hostess: responsibilities included booking corporate parties on international flights . . . Manageress of established licensed premises . . . Priest manager' (that one made me laugh): 'responsibilities included administration of Church Community Youth Project.'

No other daughter would have done that, and I remember worrying that she was taking too much responsibility too early in her life. That not having a father had done that to her, that she had taken over the role of mothering me. But mostly I was moved that she thought so highly of me; that in her eyes I became an upgraded, better version of myself.

twenty-two

Grace

When Mum came round from her operation she did not ask if I had spoken to the consultant and I did not bring up the subject of her prognosis. She had been so terrified that she would not recover from the general anaesthetic that, if anything, she seemed delighted to be alive at all. In fact, for those first few days, Mum was in better form than I had ever seen her. Immediately after her eyes opened, she groggily professed herself 'starving with the hunger'. Once she had polished off a substantial hospital meal (pudding and all; she never was a fussy eater), she perked up even more and was positively delighted to discover they were going to give her painkillers as well. She actually said to me, 'Oh, I love this, Grace, being waited on hand and foot – it's like being in a luxury hotel. I don't even have to get out of bed!' The nurses were over and back to her – clearly they were thrilled to have such an appreciative and sunny patient, especially one who had just had a ten-inch sarcoma removed from her ovaries and whose cancer was growing by the minute. Mum was a real example to the other women on the small ward she got moved on to. I found it freakish and profoundly depressing. The flowers were *beyond* beautiful, she declared – they must have cost me an absolute *fortune*; she had *never*, in all her *life*, tasted *anything* as wonderful as that ham sandwich from the canteen; she didn't suppose there was any chance at all of the nurse getting her an extra pillow for her back? There was? Oh, that was just a dream come true! Mum's good humour was, I assumed, a reaction to the anaesthetic and the pain-killers. But as twenty-four hours turned to forty-eight, her mood showed no sign of darkening. Mum dying of cancer was very bad indeed, but if she was going to do it in the manner of Julie Andrews in *The Sound of Music*, that really was insufferable altogether.

Her physical recovery was extraordinary, and it made me even more depressed thinking about the pain she must have been in beforehand, lugging that great tumour around with her. Perhaps that was the most frightening thing of all: finding that I knew my mother so little. I certainly had never had her pegged as the stoic, uncomplaining type. Apparently I was wrong and she was a tough, good-humoured, brave, admirable woman. The nurses who buzzed around her bed making jokes constantly reminded me. 'Your mother is such an extraordinary woman!' they kept saying to me. 'You are so lucky to have a mother like that.'

I felt like spitting back in their chirpy faces, 'Yes – but hey-ho she's not here for much longer so would you kindly please just fuck off. Take your weird isn't-death-normal-and-rather-jolly attitude out of my face!' But I didn't. It was too harsh, even for me.

Mum had not asked me about her prognosis and I was not about to volunteer the information. I just sat there and tried to smile.

Inside I was shit-scared-petrified-paralysed: locked up tight, like everything I had ever felt was trapped in an expanding balloon in my chest and could explode at any minute. With a great deal of effort, I could talk myself down and the balloon would deflate and the immediate panic would subside. But I knew what was going to happen. I was going to freak out at some stage, and I didn't do freaking out, not in public: not out there in the real world. My freak-outs happened years after the event and in therapy. My problem now was that there was nowhere deep or hidden enough for me to store the fact that Mum was dying. I had to face it. And I thought it might have helped if she could face it too, instead of skirting the issue and putting on this bizarre, happy-happy act.

I kept myself busy. Again. I was starting to annoy myself. 'Keeping busy' was what people did to distract themselves from the fact that they were miserable. Unhappy married people kept themselves busy with kids and golf and cookery courses, so they didn't notice how much they hated each other. People stayed in jobs they loathed because they were kept too busy to leave. *Being* busy meant that one was engaged in living a fulfilling life. *Keeping* busy was the opposite of that; it meant you were running away from something.

If it was as simple as being afraid to face my mother's condition, I might have been less hard on myself. But it wasn't. It was the supplementary, peripheral messiness that nudged around the edges of my relationship with my mother that was causing the real pain, issues that I had looked at in therapy over the years but had never successfully dealt with. My anger at not having had a father; insecurity about why I never fully trusted her love for me: the way that I could not separate myself from her sufficiently for her foibles not to drive me insane with irritation, and yet I never felt close enough to her. The fact that I could tell a friend that I loved them, yet I still had not achieved that kind of open, affectionate communication with my own mother. The desperate truth that I was in my early forties and yet still craved love from her. She had not given me all the love that I needed, and very soon it would be too late. How unattractive, how frightening – to have reached the place in my life that I had, and still be riddled with the same questions and insecurities I had had as a teenager. How callous and neurotic of me to be thinking of my own emotional well-being when my mother was the one dying of cancer. And so I kept myself busy.

Four days after the operation, they said she was ready to go home. It was on the day that we had an appointment with the surgeon. I wore a suit and I dressed my mother in a fuschia tracksuit which she had instructed me to bring in for her. It was hideous and I felt certain that the surgeon would find it distractingly so, but I told her she looked lovely. She was thrilled that I liked it and offered to buy me one too. I said that would be lovely, whilst falling so deeply into a pit of despair that my mind began ordering my causes of despair into a list:

1. I do *not* want a fuschia-pink tracksuit
2. My mother and I are so spiritually estranged that she thinks I would wear a fuschia tracksuit
3. My mother is about to be told she is going to die
4. I am going to be there and I will freak out
5. I cannot stop making lists like my mother
6. The items on this list are not ordered according to importance
7. Just like my mother's Shirley blouse/have cancer list

Mr Cartwright was charm personified, all hand-shakes and warm welcomes. It was a relief, but also annoying given my previous experience of him. I was in such a state of holding it all together that, in fact, everything was annoying me. Somewhere in the back of my mind I realized that it was true what the yogis said, that intolerant, angry types really were just people who were in a lot of pain. Although it also irritated me very much indeed that I was now falling into that category of person.

'I expect your daughter has spoken to you already about this.'

'No, actually she hasn't,' Mum said with an assertive tone I did not recognize. 'I really feel it is your job to tell me how long I have got to live, and I am very angry that you spoke to her about it first. Her silence speaks volumes.'

He was utterly taken aback. Mr Cartwright had clearly had my mother pegged as a deferential 'Yes, Your Eminence Mr Surgeon sir' type. Which frankly, up until that point, I had always thought she was. However, he had barely got his mouth open to defend himself when Mum launched into him.

'My daughter has been out of her mind for the last few days wondering what to say to me' – she put her hand up to quiet him – 'so before you tell me whatever it is you have to tell me, I would like you to apologize to Grace for any hurt you have caused her by thoughtlessly laying the responsibility on her shoulders.'

I was stunned. So was Mr Cartwright.

'I'm, I'm sorry,' he said falteringly.

'That's quite all right,' I said immediately, before he had even finished speaking.

'Now,' said Mum in a you-are-ten-years-old voice that made the surgeon visibly flinch, 'you can tell me whatever it is you have to tell me.'

My mother's choice of words threw the surgeon off guard. Here was a woman being incredibly pragmatic and unemotional about her condition, yet she did not use the word 'prognosis' or ask simply, 'How long have I got to live?' She threw the onus on him completely with 'whatever it is you have to tell me'. He could tell her where he bought his new fitted kitchen or how many letters he had after his name or what he had for breakfast that morning. Or he could tell her that she was going to die soon.

I could scarcely believe it but I suspected that my mother was deliberately trying to make this more difficult than it already was. It was a spectacularly awful thing to do; it certainly raised the bar on the term 'passive-aggressive'. If the guy was gauche to begin with, Mum sent him over the edge.

'Well you see, the em, thing . . .'

Cancer! Tumour!

'er, sarcoma has . . .'

Right – sarcoma. Use a word she might not know the meaning of.

'been removed but er, the thing is . . .'

I couldn't take it any longer.

'The cancer has spread to your liver, Mum. In fact, that's the good news. It's so far gone that they can't make it go away and they think you have . . .

I couldn't say it.

'Three to four months left.'

Thank you, Mr Cartwright. I wouldn't have said he was on a roll exactly, but he managed to finish the job off.

'The oncologist can see you immediately, and he has already drawn up a suggested programme of chemo-therapy to improve the quality of the time you have left.'

'Well,' said Mum, and she sat for a moment staring in front of her at nothing in particular before patting her handbag and saying, 'Thank you for being so – honest – Dr Carmichael.' He did not correct her. She went to stand up but struggled. As I moved to take her arm, I realized that my face was wet and that I had been crying. And knowing it now didn't stop it happening; I had no control over this water leaking out of me.

I wept silently and as demurely as I could (which was not very) all the way through the meeting with the oncologist. He was a very nice man and kept the meeting short. The treatment he recommended would not extend Mum's life or treat her cancer, but it would stem some of its more unpleasant symptoms so that the quality of her life would remain reasonable. There would be no hair loss or side-effects, and it could be taken in tablet form at home. Less than a half an hour later, we walked out into the damp anonymous sprawl of the hospital car park. A small woman in a brightly coloured tracksuit who seemed hunched and a little uncertain on her feet and her lumbering, weeping mess of an adult daughter. We were gripping on to each other's arms so tightly that it was not clear who was aiding whom.

When we got back to her house, we made tea and sat facing each other at the kitchen table.

'How do you feel, Mum?'

I used to ask her that all the time and she had always looked at me like she didn't understand the question.

As soon as I said it, I realized I was too emotionally and physically exhausted to cope with the answer, whatever it was. So, of course, for the first time in her life she decided to answer the question. She looked out of the window intensely and pondered while I closed my eyes and thought that all I wanted to do was crawl upstairs and sleep for about a fortnight.

'You know, Grace,' she said, as if she had been thinking about this all her life, 'I think I have always felt a little afraid – usually just of silly things like not wearing the right outfit to a wedding or forgetting to put the bins out.'

I groaned inwardly. I had always wanted to have a heart-to-heart with my mother and now that it was about to happen, I just wanted to curl up like a cat and sleep.

'And now, when I should be feeling afraid – well, it's odd: I really don't feel afraid at all. Isn't that strange?'

'No, Mum. Not really.'

Actually it was. Really strange and scary and bizarre, but I was past the point of caring.

'You're exhausted, love, you've had a terrible shock. You should go to bed.'

It seemed wrong, under the circumstances, that she should be giving me comfort. But it also felt right.

'Thanks, Mum.'

As I kissed her, I caught a slow and serene sadness in her eyes.

Then I trudged upstairs, loosened my bra and crawled into my old bed, still fully dressed, where I slept for eighteen hours.

twenty-three

Eileen

I loved everything about FreshWater Shopping Centre: the marble floors, the state-of-the-art glass lift, the escalators, the wealthy women with their immaculate hair and showy clothes, even the white balconies along the three-floor-high ceilings that heaved with ferns and ivy. I was working there a year before I found out the greenery in them was fake, but somehow it only added to the magic of the place. The trickery of things that present themselves as genuine, like 'natural' blonde highlights and 'designer' clothes. I became immersed in the world of the refined retail experience and discovered I had been born to it.

From my first day managing the Café Third on the third floor of Bailey Newton, I was injected with a confidence that was no less than miraculous. I just walked in there on day one and I thought, This is me. I'm going to make something of this place. I was not a sophisticated woman, I had no special knowledge of the 'eating out' experience, but I just decided to leap in. I knew I was at a turning point in my life and felt that if

I could inject glamour and excitement into this drab, ordinary café then perhaps I could do the same to myself.

Within two weeks, I had lobbied my department manager to allow me to make small changes: disposable paper tray-cloths, new tabards for the counter staff and table-clearing girls. I swept through the shabby kitchens and found that my instinct for cleanliness was greater than my desire to be liked. There was no compromise when it came to crumbs in corners, and after a brief revolution I established a hygiene tyranny that had the local health inspector in my pocket. I saw the potential in Café Third: FreshWater was inhabited by rich women spending a fortune, who would pay extra for a cappuccino and waitress service. I brought in hot food with a foreign twist: lasagne, coq au vin – meals with a classy, elegant ring to them. I changed 'chips' to 'pommes frites'. There was coleslaw garnish with everything and soon after that a self-service salad bar.

NEW JOB! NEW YOU! had been the headline in a *Woman's Own* makeover article I read the day before starting, and it had seemed like one of the messages from God I used to get as a child. I didn't have a new wardrobe or a new haircut like the ladies in the article, but I left my history behind when I walked in the door of Café Third and started my forties with a clean slate.

I did eventually get a new wardrobe and hairdo (although I was never entirely happy with either), but the greatest change that happened was in my social life. I had been guarded with people most of my adult life, protecting my pride during my marriage to John and then my secrets with Frank. My circle of friends had always been small and centred mainly around the church. Bailey Newton gave me a new lease of life. In the multi-cultural, fast-living consumer culture, I became a different person. I found a confidence and vivacity that I had forgotten I had. I rediscovered Eileen from the Aer Lingus days, who used to book businessmen on flights to America and wear suits and high heels and had a rare smile that some said lit me up from the inside. Before marriage and motherhood took over; before heartache and hardship. It felt as if the good times had caught up with me again and undoubtedly the greatest thing that I refound was my flair for friendship.

Geoff was around my age, perhaps a couple of years older, but it was hard to tell on account of his dyeing his hair. He was head of Haberdashery and Fabrics – 'Buttons and bouclé, darling – that's me' – and he was a real laugh. 'You're a *right* one, you are!' he was always saying to me, and 'I'm going to have to watch *you*!' We had this cheeky repartee, he was always flirting with me and could say terribly rude things without making me feel insulted. I loved bantering with Geoff; it made me feel clever and funny, and I had never felt like that with a man before, not even Frank. Geoff was gay but only told me this after I had repeatedly tried to set him up with Juliana from Soft Furnishings. 'I don't go on about it as a rule, honey, not my style. Well, people of our generation don't talk about these things, do we, dear?' I did not consider myself to be part of Geoff's generation – he seemed strangely old-fashioned – but I was flattered that he had confided in me and was secretly thrilled to know a homosexual.

Sangeeta became one of the best friends I ever had.

She was very demure, a real lady. She always wore a sari and a bindi. Some of the staff found her reserve and formal way of speaking off-putting (along with her ethnic dress, people could be very ignorant), but Sangeeta had a warmth about her that I found heartening. When she discovered that I had never eaten Indian cuisine, the very next day she brought me in a tray of home-made delicacies, fragrant and spicy. I saw that the gift had taken her hours to produce and recognized the gesture as a cultural as well as a personal generosity. It reminded me of growing up in Ireland, where strangers would be taken into our home and given tea and home-made scones at the drop of a hat. Sangeeta was married with three children, and while she worked the children were cared for by her mother-in-law, who lived with them. Her husband was a doctor: 'An educated man; he doesn't mind that I like to work.'

We rarely saw each other outside work but we spent most of our breaks together, running small errands, discussing work, sampling the food in the rival coffee shops and food outlets in the centre. We didn't talk in detail about our lives; we were both too reserved, so I suppose that drew us together too. In any case, I had few day-to-day problems outside work. Grace was a model young woman, who had worked hard and had earned a place at university to study English. She was still living at home and never gave me a moment's trouble. Sangeeta never complained about her husband and family, unlike the other women, who seemed to moan perpetually, about their husbands in particular. I got the feeling that Sangeeta was smart enough to realize that complaining only perpetuated unhappiness. If you

were unhappy at home and came to work complaining
about it, then you became unhappy at work too. In my
day it was called 'Put up and shut up', and the more
I listened to people moaning about lazy teenagers and
noisy neighbours and mothers-in-law – lives which contained, as far as I could see, very little real hardship –
the better a policy it seemed.

Apart from Geoff and Sangeeta, there were another
half-dozen people who, at any time, I could call on for a
chat. Florrie in Luggage was a divorced Limerick woman
who spent every penny on clothes and make-up, and
every spare moment dancing in the Irish clubs of north-
west London. She was great *craic* and I went through a
spate of Saturday nights at the National Ballroom, where
I met her gang of 'girls' who were my age, divorced and
on the prowl for men. It wasn't my scene, but Florrie
lured me there from time to time and I surprised myself
by having the odd 'fling' throughout my forties – enough
to remind me that I was still an attractive woman, but
not so much as to get involved in a relationship. One or
two men fell in love with me but I had no interest in
them. I loved the feeling of being wanted, but I had lost
the will to give back. I no longer believed it was worth
it.

After six years, I left the café because I was promoted
to Senior Customer Services Manager of the whole store.
This was the official term for what was known in-house
as the 'complaints department'. It was recognized as one
of the most difficult positions within the company, and
the salary reflected that, as did my status in the shop.
I wore a navy suit with shoulder pads and high court
shoes in which I marched determinedly around each

department. Bailey Newton became my empire; I came to know and love every inch of it. The fine profiles of the shop dummies draped in sequinned eveningwear, designer suitcases, rack upon rack of shiny ladies' footwear, cabinets of glittering jewellery: I knew the whereabouts of everything, from the centre-stage showiness of the cream leather reclining chairs in Office Furniture to the humble Thermos flask hidden away in a corner of Household Appliances. I loved them all, but I had my favourites. Every morning I went slightly out of my way coming up the East Car Park escalator so that I could enter the store at the perfume hall. The heady opulent scent of Poison, Chloe, Jazz and Chanel 19 started each working day on a high for me. Some days I needed that high more than others.

The great thing about my job was that for the eight hours I was in there I was full of confidence. I had to be. Grace always complained that I was flustery and indecisive, and it was true, most of the time. But at work I couldn't afford to be anything but on top form. Bailey Newton had an affluent, middle-class catchment area, and it seemed to me that the more you had, the more you complained. My wealthy clientele complained about everything, from a crack in a cup bought last week to wear and tear on a pair of boots purchased a year before. It was a rare day when I did not have to deal with at least one complainant face to face, and some of them were heavy-going. The woman who sat down in Nursery Equipment and refused to budge until they had replaced her faulty three-year-old buggy with a brand new one. The man who vomited over Wilma on the Information Desk when I brushed off his food-poisoning story. There were the people who were just trying it on, looking for compensation that I knew they were not entitled to. There were the 'dripping taps' – those people who thought they could wear you down if they came back often enough; I listened and repeated my statement without becoming riled. To the shouters – the aggressive, bullying types – I kept my own voice low and calm until eventually they became embarrassed by the noise they were making. Then there were the serial complainers: lonely people who wanted to know why the bathmats had been moved, or why there were no purple umbrellas, or why we were selling a painting of a woman with a bare buttock in full view of passers-by, or why we didn't have any satsumas this week in the fruit basket at Café Third when they had been there last week. People complained about rude staff or the colour of the carpets, they brought back items with no receipts, wedding gifts on their fifth anniversary, shoes with torn laces, dry-clean-only blouses that had clearly shrunk in the wash, traumatized handwash-only sweaters. Very occasionally I exchanged a faulty, shedding duvet for an apologetic customer, or saw a child's face light up when I replaced a broken Barbie for their grateful mum, but most of the time I was defending the staff and reputation of Bailey Newton from the grasping clutches of a handful of greedy, angry opportunists who would lie through their teeth – bury their own mothers probably – for a refund voucher double the value of what they had spent. My two greatest weapons in doing this were a good suit and a serene but assertive smile. I developed an ability to listen and a demeanour of almost imperceptible haughtiness that could rise above the most aggressive complainant and make them think twice about abusing me.

My boss once told me that my most powerful weapon at work was my ability to make myself liked. In all the years I worked for Bailey Newton, not one complaint was ever levelled against me personally. I used to think that being likeable and not being complained about was a great thing.

twenty-four

Grace

In the first few days after Mum came home from the hospital, there was surprisingly little to do. Mum could not stay in bed and be waited on by me (although she had no problem letting the nurses in the hospital do so). By the second day home, she was back up pottering: making herself nasty instant-soup drinks, spraying the toilet with toxic air freshener and hauling herself up and down from the sofa to change the television channel because she had still not figured out how to operate the remote control.

'Honestly, Grace, this is a terrible waste of your time being here. I can manage fine.' Which was barely disguised code for 'Please go away and let me enjoy my eccentric home comforts without your critical eye following me around.'

At least I now could see how judgemental I was – even if it had taken a life-expectancy countdown to get me there. In any case, it didn't stop me being irritated by my mother's household habits; it just added an extra dollop of guilt into the mix.

Then there was the whole 'tragedy' element that I am pretty certain got to her, too. It can't be much fun watching your adult child's familiar critical face suddenly dissolve with mournful anguish as they remember that they should not be mean to you because, after all, you are shortly going to die.

So I moved back to my own home for a few days, but it just didn't feel right. I saw some friends, but could not bring myself to talk about what was happening with Mum and yet did not find myself sufficiently distracted by their news. I was teary and emotional and the only place I wanted to be was with Mum in her house. So I kept calling in: at breakfast-time with a bag of her favourite pastries from the Bagel Bakery; then I would go shopping and pick up some lunch; I would have found something for dinner too, and then when the evening meal was finished there would be something on TV I wanted to watch. By the time that was over, it would be so late that I might as well stay the night. The guilt of knowing she did not want me there compelled me to encourage even her worst habits. I uncomplainingly made her mug after mug of foul-smelling instant soup; poisoned the air with lavender aerosol spray; fetched her flammable nylon dressing gown and allowed her to wear it whilst warming her toes on the electric fire so she could save putting on the central heating. Now that my mother was dying of cancer, I was beatifically transformed into a tolerant saint who realized that all of these annoying foibles did not really matter. After years of complaining that eating all these salt-laden soups and sitting in front of an electric fire were highly precarious activities, my sudden turn-around meant that

Mum, quite naturally, thought I was trying to enact some form of euthanasia on her. Or perhaps I was just really getting on *her* nerves for a change.

'Grace. There's no need for you to keep coming around.'

'It's fine, Mum. Really. I just want to be here. To help you.'

'I know that, love, and I really appreciate it, but you must have things to do.'

'Really, Mum, there's nothing I need to do that's as important as being here with you.'

'But your work?'

'It's all sorted, Mum. Don't worry.'

'Have you not got friends you need to see? What about – what's his name again?'

'No, Mum. This is where I need to be right now.'

That was the truth of it really. It was what *I* needed, not what my mother needed. I took her hand and I looked into her eyes, and even as I did I could sense that I was wearing the expression of a crazed martyr.

It gave her whatever courage she needed to stop dressing it up for me.

'The thing is, Grace, I need some time on my own.' I knew that. And she was right. But it still felt like I had been kicked in the stomach. 'I'll be all right, Grace. The hospital called and they're sending somebody around tomorrow.' She touched my arm and smiled tenderly, maternally. 'Why don't you head off somewhere for a couple of days? You need a break too.'

'I'm sorry Mum – I'm crowding you. It's just that . . .'

I trailed it off, kissed her quickly and finished the

sentence off in my head on the way back to my flat. It's just that I'm afraid you're going to die too soon. Before we get the chance to do all of the things we haven't done yet. Before I give you a grandchild; before you visit Sangeeta in India, or drive through Paris in a sports car like the Marianne Faithfull song you love; before I believe I've really made you proud; before you fit into that size-twelve dress your Weightwatchers leader encouraged you to buy five years ago; before you trust me enough to tell me about my father; before I take you to Florence like I always said I would; before I can see the funny side of turning into you; before you try going blonde like you're always threatening; before I have learned everything I need to learn from you; before I'm ready.

And I knew, with certainty, what I had always known: that I would never be ready. That there would always be things undone, and words unsaid.

Uncharacteristically, I took my mother's advice and went away for a couple of days, to a spa hotel in Bath that one of my girlfriends had recommended.

After all the 'healing weekends' and 'spiritual retreats' I had been on before, this was by far the most enlightening experience. I wandered aimlessly around that beautiful, ancient city. I got lost down cobbled streets, sent postcards to friends I hadn't seen in a while, had a facial and a pedicure, took saunas and swims and time to just relax. I became acquainted again with Grace. Not the daughter or the teacher, the friend, ex-wife or lover – just me. I got back in touch with what I knew to be my core self: the strong, nurturing woman who would help me, and Mum, find our way through the next few weeks, months, however long it took for her to move from this realm into the next. I remembered that I believed in my own version of God and I prayed to that higher power that I would find the strength to not lose myself again, and I asked for answers. They came, as they always did when I took the time to meditate and be still in myself.

I wrote a list of things that I could do for Mum before she died. I kept the list short and do-able. It felt so right to put a small, modest order on our remaining time together. There was something healing too about writing it as a list.

After careful thought, much editing and several pots of room-service herbal tea it finally read:

1. Go to Paris, hire sports car
2. Long weekend Florence
3. Holiday in Ireland
4. Bath – pampering spa
5. Send Sangeeta a ticket to come here

Already I had achieved one thing from my earlier list – and that was the warm feeling I got when I realized that I didn't mind that I was writing a list, and was therefore turning into Mum. Actually, it felt good.

I rang Mum after I got back and she sounded in great form. I didn't question her too much – she said she was being 'looked after', which I wondered about but decided to let go. I said I would call in on Saturday for lunch, which made it a full five days since we had seen each other – a mountain of 'space' when one of you is dying.

Before I turned the corner to Mum's street, I took a walk around the block to the local park. I sat on a bench at the top of the big hill and looked at the familiar stretch of green as it rolled out in front of me down to the tennis courts and the swings. I had been coming to this park all my life and it always seemed the same. Although I supposed much had changed: shrubs must have been dug up, the tennis courts revamped, trees felled and replaced and flowerbeds moved, these all went unnoticed by me. The only thing I ever saw when I came here was the firm expanse of hilly lawn. As a small child, it had seemed to stretch for miles and miles with the nirvana of the swing park at the other end of it. I used to literally roll myself down the hill with Mum trotting after me fretting about grass stains. On the way home it had always seemed steeper than it was going down, and the sight of the ice-cream van at the park gates was often the only motivation to get me back up the hill again. That park was as familiar to me as our own small garden. I had experienced so much of my early life there. Scuffed my knees by jumping off the roundabout too early; tried to touch the sky with my toes on the swings; got into a hair-pulling fist fight with a bullying boy – and won. I had had my first fumbling kiss behind the bushes at the back of the tennis courts and smoked cigarettes in the dank, forbidden glamour of the ladies' toilets. As an adult, whenever I went to my mother's house looking for comfort, I made a detour here first. When Jack left for Australia, when I decided to move jobs, I came here before I broke the news to Eileen. I wondered was this a gift my mother had given me; staying in the same place all of my life? Never moving from this area, from our house so that I would always have this place to come back to? Or was it just an accident or laziness, that kept her here in this unremarkable suburb for most of her life?

'Most of her life'; the everyday phrase became a mental tripwire, a reminder that Mum's life was coming to an end. Behind it was the backed-up pile of questions I had never thought to ask: had she ever considered returning to Ireland? How long did she work in Aer Lingus? How had she met my father? I felt them tumble out of me and scatter away in different directions. So many questions, so little time. Unsaid, unlived, unexplored. It felt suddenly dangerous to be sitting on my own contemplating. I needed to be with Mum. To spend as much time with her as I could.

I walked quickly back to the house and felt strangely elated. My head was clear. The next few months belonged to my mother. We were going to do things together, make memories. 'Travel,' my mother had always said to me when I was a young woman. 'See the world! Go to all of the places I never got the chance to.' Every time I came back from holiday, Mum sat and pored over my photographs and drank in every detail. She had been on package holidays to Spain a couple of times with her work buddies, but had always made a face when I suggested going further afield. I always guessed that she wanted to, but felt it was too late. Perhaps she was just afraid of the unknown. Here was a chance for me to help her adventure. I knew this was what I wanted to do now: make sure that my mother tasted as much life as she could for the time she had left.

As soon as I opened the front door, I could hear that

she was not alone. There were voices coming from the kitchen and the door was closed. I opened it on to a tableau which was both bizarre and shocking.

My mother was leaning into the kitchen sink – I knew it was my mother because she was wearing her grotty green dressing gown – where it seemed she was being held forcibly by a skinny young man I had never seen before. Sitting at the kitchen table, leafing through a magazine was another, strikingly handsome young man of around the same age.

'Oi!' I shouted out instinctively, moving towards them.

'Grace!' a voice shouted from behind me, making me nearly jump out of my skin. It was Brian.

'Grumpflp,' my mother's voice said as the young man holding her head in the sink said, 'Hold on there, Eileen love. Just rinsing out the conditioner, then we're all done – quick with the towel, Dad!'

Brian politely pushed past me with a towel and handed it to his son, who then gently wrapped my mother's head, unfurled her tenderly from her uncomfortable crouch and led her by the arm over to the kitchen table, where the other young hunk stood up and gave her his seat.

'How are you, Grace?' Brian said. I was speechless. I studied his face for a hint of – I didn't know what, maybe embarrassment? Explanation? He gave me an innocent, open smile.

'Fine,' I said, and then I could not resist adding in a pointed tone, 'So what's going on here then?'

Mum, who I noticed was positively glowing with all the male attention, started talking nineteen to the dozen.

'Guess who the hospice sent me as my volunteer? Brian! Can you believe it! And these are his sons, Daniel,' she waved above her head at the skinny bloke, 'who's a hairdresser, and this is David,' she leaned across and took the handsome boy's hand, 'his brother, who is at college studying Music and guess what, Grace? We're organizing a fashion show to raise money for the hospice and I am going to model in it. Oh, and I've gone blonde! How do I look? I'm so excited, I haven't seen it yet!'

'It looks great, Eileen,' said Brian before I had the chance to comment on the wormy yellow highlights in my mother's tangled head. 'Will I put the kettle on? Grace – tea or coffee?'

This was the second time this had happened to me since I had learned of Mum's cancer, where I had gone away to clear my head and come back thinking I had everything worked out, only to discover:

1. my efforts disregarded
2. my mother in a semi-clothed state
3. Brian making himself at home

A definition of insanity that I favoured was when someone does the same thing over and over again, but expects a different result. In which case my mother and her friend Brian were, quite literally, driving me insane. The only thing I could do to claw back some control was end this situation differently from the last time. Dearly though I wanted to run screaming from the house, I didn't.

'Coffee please, Brian,' I said just as he was unscrewing the lid of the Nescafé, '*fresh* coffee.'

'Oh,' he said, 'I don't know where that is.'

'Don't you?' I replied.

The one Mum called Daniel clicked on his hairdryer and I had to ask Brian to repeat what he said next. I wished I hadn't.

'I said I'm sorry if I've crossed over any boundaries, Grace.' He waved me out of the kitchen into the hall. 'When Angela died the boys were young and – we were lost really. We went and stayed with friends a lot and there were people in and out to us all the time. We sort of got used to making ourselves at home anywhere, and well – sometimes we forget our manners. I'm sorry if we've overstepped the mark.'

I knew I should have been gracious and insisted, in that hospitable humble Irish way of my mother's, that there was nothing to be sorry for. But I just couldn't put my own needs aside; they seemed too vast, too unmet.

'Well, thank you for your honesty, Brian, but as I'm sure you can appreciate this is a very difficult time for me and my mother and actually, we do need our privacy.'

'Absolutely,' he said, and before I had time to add my postscript he was back in the kitchen, where he had opened the fridge door and triumphantly located 'Fresh coffee!'

Mum was still sitting at the table with the boys. She was asking the handsome David if he had a girlfriend and he was laughing flirtatiously. I felt a pang of petulant, lip-curling jealousy and cruelly imagined that he thought he had found a new mother.

Mum had a relaxed way with strangers, a way of welcoming people, making them feel at ease. I had seen taxi drivers get out of their cab after taking her on long journeys to give her a hug. She was lovable, with a combination of innocence and maturity that made people feel safe around her but protective of her at the same time. It was a happy knack, and had worked to my advantage over the years as Mum's busy social life and wide circle of friends meant that I had never felt the parental dependency I had seen other only-children, especially those with single parents, experience. I could see that the two boys were as smitten as their father and I knew that the 'privacy' I had asked Brian for was all too obviously redundant. Mum was clearly trying to distract herself from her illness although, selfishly, I felt as if she was trying to distract herself from me.

I let Brian make coffee and take me out to the garden while Mum's hair was being finished.

'Are you sleeping with my mother?'

He looked shocked, then laughed, smiled broadly and said, 'Is it any of your business?'

I felt as if the last drop of what little control I had had over my life in the past few weeks was disappearing down the drain. My face crumpled, clinging helplessly to the last scrap of my dignity.

He saw that and kindly answered quickly. 'No. I am not sleeping with your mother.'

'Good,' I said, gathering the ammunition and loading it quickly before he changed his mind, 'because she is very sick and I think it would be – inappropriate for her to be getting too . . . involved, with anyone at this time.'

'Oh I see,' he said, still smiling. Then added, 'Well, I'm not.' And he continued smiling, then took a sip of coffee and kept looking at me over the top of the coffee cup. Alarmingly I noticed that he had the same deep-set twinkling eyes of a television gardener I had a silly crush on. Then, even more alarmingly, I realized that he was flirting with me. How revolting! How inappropriate, and yet how oddly thrilling.

I gave him a withering look, but he didn't seem convinced, which was annoying but, I had to admit, very flattering.

'Da-daah!'

The boy hairdresser gave a little curtsy and introduced the 'new-look Eileen' to us. I had to admit, the blonde feathered cut he had given her was the best she had ever had.

'You look fantastic, Mum; you should have had it done years ago.'

I flinched at my faux pas but Mum didn't even notice. She was too busy fluttering around the three men, twirling and flirting and thanking them and asking them if they wanted to stay for a barbecue.

'Grace will pop down to Tesco and pick up some steaks and salad, won't you, love?'

It was going to be a long afternoon.

twenty-five

Eileen

Grace was twenty-three when she left home. We both knew it was time, but that didn't make it any easier when it happened.

Most of her friends had gone away to college, but Grace had chosen to do her degree and teacher training in London, so it made sense for her to stay at home. Or possibly she chose a university she could commute to so she could stay at home. Neither I nor Grace was quite certain which one it was, but lived in happy independence of each other as if it were the former.

I dispensed with all curfews the summer after Grace finished her A-levels, so my eighteen-year-old was allowed to come and go as she pleased. Another teenager might have abused the freedom, but Grace was meticulous about letting me know where she was and with whom, a trait that I attributed to my own habit of always leaving notes detailing my whereabouts. After a few weeks in university, Grace got weekend and evening work waitressing in wine bars and became virtually self-supporting. She redecorated her own room and bought her own food and, when she brought friends back, they were polite and respectable. As Grace got older, her diligence and maturity often unsettled me. As colleagues complained about their wild offspring, I wondered what unnatural impulse had made my daughter so sensible. I had worked hard to ensure that my daughter had enjoyed a carefree childhood but, far from being relieved by Grace's alert sense of responsibility, I felt it as a failure on my part.

Shortly after she started university, I came in from work one day and was shocked to discover that Grace had bought a new television for the house. She was just nineteen years old and it felt wrong, her making that kind of purchase. There was a strange young man in my living room installing a huge, brand-new television set and a video recorder.

'This is Dave, Mum.' Grace had chased in from the kitchen with two cups of tea. 'He's in uni with me but works part-time for Vision TV, so I got a great discount on these!'

I could see she was excited with her purchase and quite possibly with Dave. But I was angry; not at Dave's intrusion, but at my daughter's presumptuousness.

'We already have a television, Grace.'

'But I thought we needed a new one.'

'The one we have is perfectly good,' I said, smiling at Dave so that he wouldn't think I was mean. 'And in actual fact I have a video recorder on order at Bailey Newton.' It was a lie, but I was damned if I was going to live by my daughter's rules, however well-meaning they were. Grace was confused and in turn hurt at the rejection, and that hurt me, but we never discussed it further. Grace moved the television and video into the guest bedroom, where she also put a futon. We both forgot the argument and the revamped guest room became the early incarnation of Grace's own 'chill-out room' where she could entertain boyfriends and enjoy an independent student life.

I tried to make life at home as comfortable and easy for Grace as possible, so I could keep her with me that bit longer. It was selfish but I didn't want her to leave, because that would have meant I would be alone. I didn't have a husband to fall back on; there was only her. Because of that, I did not think about the sacrifices I made in my own life to keep her there. Only after she finally left did I look back wistfully at my forties and wish that I had enjoyed myself more: enjoyed a few more wild nights of drunken passion, stayed on for another week in Spain and smoked pot with that gorgeous young waiter who worked in the hotel bar. But while Grace was there I always felt I had to live by the conventions of motherhood. Respectability, responsibility, stability.

When Grace got her first job, as a primary-school teacher in south London, she rented a flat near to the school and finally left home. I was bereft. 'What's the point in giving rent to a landlord when you can stay here for free?'

She worried about leaving me on my own. I knew that, and her worry upset me more than loneliness ever could.

The day Grace finally left was a revelation in itself.

Grace and Dave packed his van and left at four. She kissed me goodbye and said tenderly, 'Will you be OK, Mum?'

I bristled and said, 'Of course. Don't be silly – go.'

I went upstairs and lay down on the single bed where my daughter had slept for the whole of her life; the mattress was bare but still musty with the smell of her, and I wept.

At six o'clock the doorbell rang. I wasn't going to answer it until I heard Geoff call through the letterbox.

'Bang, bang, only meeee!'

I got a bit of a fright. Geoff was one of my closest friends, but had only ever been to my house once before, when he'd come in for a cup of coffee after dropping me back home from the garden centre. Normally I went to his place. Geoff and his partner Barry were fantastic hosts and I had enjoyed their hospitality over the years, drinking and eating and laughing late into the night.

'Is she gone?' he said dramatically after I had straightened myself up and opened the door.

'Is who gone?'

'The girl, your daughter – Grace!'

'Oh yes, she left this aftern—'

'Excellent,' he said, pulling two bottles of sparkling wine from underneath his coat and pushing past me into the hallway, 'then let's get this party started!'

Sangeeta arrived shortly afterwards with her doctor husband, politely unloading trays of food from the boot of his car, then Florrie, Sharon, Barry and another dozen of my favourite people from Bailey Newton staff. All of my friends came in and took over my house, putting their bottles in the half-empty fridge, their coats on

Grace's redundant bed, piling their music tapes up next to the boogie box in the kitchen which my daughter had forgotten to pack.

By ten o'clock, my house was buzzing with laughter and music.

'You'll be lonely now,' Sangeeta said, giving me a squeeze.

'I can't believe you are doing all this,' I replied, 'it's all such a surprise.'

'Here's the surprise, ducks.' Geoff was slightly drunk. 'That you let that dull daughter of yours rule the roost for the last ten years when you should have been having fun!'

'Geoffrey!'

But it was Sangeeta that reprimanded him, not me.

With the support of my peers, I was finally able to let Grace go, secure that I had my own life to enjoy. These were to be my freedom years. Liberated from my personal responsibilities, I started to focus on myself. Through my friendships I began to decide what I liked – Lipfinity lipstick by Max Factor, Chardonnay, Indian food, pashminas, men with old-fashioned manners; and what I didn't like – waterproof mascara, pizza, racist attitudes, platform shoes, ex-husbands. Through these details, big and small, I started to forge an identity of a woman who was not just liked by others, but who liked herself. A middle-aged woman who was approachable and liberal and kind; still reasonably well preserved and who – if not groomed to perfection – at least evidently made an effort with her appearance. I sometimes felt sad that the years had sucked the confidence out of me, instead of making me stronger. I heard myself constantly fishing for compliments from my friends: 'Your hair *is* lovely, Eileen,' 'That bag *does* match those shoes,' 'You *do not* have too many cushions, your living room is perfect, you have great taste!'

I had always sought Grace's approval, but my daughter had just told me to 'have more confidence', as if you could walk into a shop and buy it. Most of the time I thought it was nicer to be the way I was, with a bit of humility. I couldn't stand those smug women with perfect hair and trimmed lawns who were always bragging about their high-achieving children and their lovely husbands and their holiday homes in Spain. Not being perfect made people like me, and I liked being liked.

For some years I had been a member of the 'Bailey Newton First Wives' Club'. We were a gang of 'girls', all divorced or separated, who pooled £5 a week then splashed out once a month on wine and a takeaway in each other's houses. Sometimes it got a bit raucous, especially if Sharon from Hosiery was there – she had a very bad mouth – or Florrie, who always tried to persuade us to go out dancing, with varied success. Mostly, though, we just sat around laughing. Sometimes we would have fresh stories of our husbands' new families or divorce proceedings that were still going on. Often there were new boyfriends to be discussed, or intriguing bits of gossip from work, but really it was just an outlet for us women to get things off our chests and have a few drinks without fear of humiliating ourselves in public.

When Grace left home I started, for the first time, to

host these evenings in my house. With the prospect of having visitors to impress, I acquired a whole new interest in my home. I fancied the place up with exotic cushions, throws and scented candles. I found I was a natural hostess, and really enjoyed spreading my soon-legendary cheese boards with fancy biscuits. Comments like 'Eileen, I don't know what you've done to this ham sandwich but it's divine!' and 'These paper napkins are gorgeous, where did you get them?' gave me an inordinate amount of pleasure. Perhaps it was because the early years of my marriage – when I might have been hosting dinner parties – had been so fraught that being concerned with fripperies like matching napkins and tablecloths seemed like a luxury to me. The nights that I hosted these clubs became the best ones, everyone agreed. And in my own home, with trusted women friends around me, I discovered the value of talking openly. The first time I talked about the violence in my marriage to John, I realized there was no big secret worth holding on to. The other women all chorused, 'The bastard!' and that encouraged me to finally confess my ten-year affair with Father Frank, which they really lapped up. In telling my stories and seeing the interest they elicited in my peers, I began to understand that my life as I had lived it so far was not as boring or as tragic as I had believed. It felt good to unravel the intensity of my past by talking, to loosen sad memories with laughter.

However, the single most important detail of my past remained unspoken: I could still not talk about having given Michael away. Then Melissa from the Wedding List desk got divorced, joined the First Wives' Club and brought me face to face with my past.

twenty-six

Grace

I had never felt more alone than I did during those few weeks after Mum discovered she was dying. She started to surround herself with an ever-growing entourage of old friends and new admirers. It was like she had rung up everyone she knew and said, 'Hey – great news, I have cancer and I'm having a party! Oh, and bring a friend along too!'

She was out almost every night, going to the Irish clubs in Kilburn with old work chums Sharon and Florrie. Geoff and Barry came down from their new home in Bath for a week's holiday and virtually redecorated the house, poignantly (and insensitively I thought) doing a major replant of the patio pots which my mother would probably not see come to fruition the following year.

As Geoff was leaving, I cornered him to get Sangeeta's details in India so I could call and tell her about Mum.

'I'm so glad we made it down,' he said tearfully. 'We needed some quality time with Eileen – it's been too long.'

'You lucky bastard,' I felt like saying, 'because I have hardly seen her this past month.'

I could understand Mum seeing old friends and more or less taking me for granted, but I found myself very hurt by the time she spent with Brian and his sons organizing the hospice fashion show. It upset me that she could put so much into consolidating this new friendship and throwing herself into their project at the expense of her relationship with me.

I had taken time off from my life and my job to be with her, and yet she was not making any room in her life for me. All I could do was tag along in the background as an accessory and sometimes facilitator to her frantic activity. I became taxi driver to and from social engagements; tea maker and biscuit buyer for the constant stream of visitors; and fashion eye as she fussed over the new look Daniel had given her. I made sure she took her medication; nagged her about drinking and smoking (two bad habits she had taken up with gusto); cooked sensible meals for her which she refused to eat; and tried to get her to take vitamins and early nights. I became parent to an insubordinate teenager who thought she knew better than me. It would have been a role reversal if I had not been such an impeccable, boring teenager myself. It was a dynamic I had always feared was there, but Mum's dying had given her the courage to bring it to the fore.

On more than one occasion, I had to get out of my bed and come downstairs to ask her and her friends to keep the noise down. I was glad that she was having fun, but I was also depressed that she was having fun. My sense of humour had gone on a sabbatical, and had

not told me when it was coming back. To add insult
to injury, it had called up my sense of self, and that
had gone along too without informing me. So when I
tried to meditate, instead of being able to reach down
into my core and find what I was searching for I just
drew a blank and ended up deciding that what I
needed was a cup of tea and half a packet of chocolate
biscuits. Although what I felt I truly needed was a
half-quart of whisky and lashings of sex with a complete stranger. If my mother had decided to spend her
final months on earth in quiet reflection, I might have
been able to get away with a bit of both, but one of us
had to remain sensible. In any case, if she had gone
the contemplative, dignified route, I would have doubtless been more centred in myself and better able to
help her – and me. As it was, I felt painfully ill-
equipped and frustrated just tagging along in the back-
draught of her social chaos; like the put-upon secretary
of some monstrously demanding boss. Basically, Mum
seemed to stop caring what I thought of her. For the
first time in our relationship, I felt her true power and
authority over me and I was unable to stand my
ground. Although perhaps I would have been better
able to do so if the ground under me had been steadier
and surer. She was crazy, overdoing it, and I sensed
fear in her shrill insistence on keeping moving all the
time. But she did seem certain in her actions – and I
wasn't. I didn't know whether to stay where I was and
run around after her just to spend as much time with
her as I could, or go on a grief-workshop weekend
myself. My uncertainty really bothered me because, of
course, I liked to be right. Knowledge of her impend-

ing death seemed to be giving her something whilst sucking it out of me.

Four days before the fashion show, Mum decided to host a barbecue for the 'committee'.

'How many sausages is that, Mum?' I said, trying to temper my sarcasm with humour.

She closed her eyes and mouthed over a few names. It was taking her quite a long time and I lost patience:

'Come on, Mum . . .'

'I'm working it out. About five sausages a head – not counting the vegetarians – I'd say about two hundred . . .'

'Christ, Mum . . .'

She raised her eyebrows at me defiantly and smiled.

'How many people are on this bloody committee?'

'Just us four . . .' ('us' was now her Brian, and his boys), 'but we wanted' ('we') 'to invite some of the women who'll be modelling.' Now I raised my eyebrows. 'And some of their husbands – and then I mentioned it to the girls . . .'

I put my head in my hands.

'Oh come on, Grace . . . it'll be fun!'

This was what Mum wanted, but I just couldn't hack it. I thought I wanted my mother to spend the last remaining months of her life doing what she wanted to do. But really I just wanted her to spend them with me, doing madcap things like driving through Paris in a sports car, not buying catering packs of frozen sausages and potato salad and fretting over gingham paper napkins. If I had never been through the 'home entertaining' experience with my mother before, I might have thought this was a touching idea, a chance to say goodbye to her friends, a kind of living funeral. But I knew my mother better than that. She threw a big party almost every year. She would invite everyone she knew and several people she didn't, then nearly give herself a nervous breakdown for weeks beforehand, obsessively scouring cookbooks for ideas then eventually settling for her old favourites: 'creative cheese boards', unusual food combinations on cocktail sticks and bucketfuls of carbohydrate-loaded potato and pasta salads that would be sitting in our fridge for weeks afterwards. There would be paper bunting hanging off the washing line which would invariably be set alight by one of the many thousand scented candles she would have lit hours before anyone arrived so that the house smelled like a brothel when they got there. At seven – an hour before anyone was due to come – she would be in tears, proclaiming that nobody had arrived and the evening was ruined. When people did start to arrive, she would fretfully force them into the kitchen to eat and watch their faces for signs of approval.

It would take a week in bed for her to recover from the stress and she would say 'never again'. Until next year.

And this time there would be no next year, so I said, 'Mum, why don't you let me organize this party for you?' And instead of her usual response, which was 'No, Grace – I couldn't possibly put you to all that trouble,' but actually translated into 'Back off with your fancy sun-dried-tomato mini-bruschetta and leave me to my cheese plate,' she exclaimed, 'That would be wonderful! Thank you, Grace!' Which I took to mean 'The invite list is already out of hand, I've taken on too much and now it's all yours.' A cruel opinion, but one which neither the preparation nor the party itself did anything to repudiate.

The 'models' Mum spoke of were volunteers who were either in treatment for cancer or in remission. Several of them had special dietary requirements which they rang to inform me about. Over the next few days they kept ringing me on my mobile.

'Larry Fink here – just to let you know that Marjorie can't eat red meat. Or chicken. Or fish.'

'So she's a vegetarian, then.'

'No – she can eat tofu.'

'Tofu isn't meat. It's a plant.'

'Is it?'

My charm bracelet fell into the pesto I was stirring with one hand. 'Look, I've made a note of that, I've got to go.'

I was up to my eyes organizing this feast, this celebration of my mother's life – ordering in specialist Irish cheeses and actual (off-season) shamrocks for my own 'creative cheese board'; taking delivery of fabulous French wines; chopping and skewering peppers for vegetarian kebabs; up and down, up and down to Tesco looking for extra mascarpone for dessert, more burgers, Quorn fillets, wheat-free pitta – when the mobile would ring, again, with some bizarre request.

Gloria was lactose-intolerant, but she loved cheesecake. She only had a few months left; would I be able to do a special dessert using soya? Christine could only eat raw food and *no fruit*! Would I be able to do her a vegetable platter? Sushi was a favourite if it wasn't too much trouble.

I was so frantic, mutating into my mother with my floating-water-lily-candle centrepieces and fleur-de-lis napkins, that I barely noticed how insane it was that these people were all calling me until my mother wandered into the kitchen, put the phone back in its cradle and gave me one of her apologetic 'Oh-dear' smiles that indicated she was about to say something ghastly.

'That was Larry Fink. He said you were very rude to him. He wasn't going to ring me, but he said he felt duty-bound.'

'Rude? What did he say? What did I say?' After all, I didn't want to upset a man whose wife had cancer.

'He said it was your manner more than anything else.'

'Oh my God, Mum. I am so sorry.'

'Yes, well, he said you weren't very professional.'

' "Professional"?'

It all came tumbling out. Mum had been talking to Larry's wife, Marjorie, who was very well-to-do and a bit of a know-it-all and she had said, 'Why not get in a caterer, Eileen? I mean, you can't take your money with you . . .' Seemingly, she had said it in such a patronizing way that Mum had told her that she had already employed a wonderful caterer who specialized in cooking healthy organic food for very sick people.

'You said WHAT?!'

'And when she rang looking for the woman's phone number, I had to give it to her. Then of course she told everybody – I think she was trying to catch me out.'

I was almost speechless. 'Why didn't you tell me? Were you not worried I might say something?'

'Oh no, dear. Sure, I don't really know these people. What do I care what they think?'

The barbecue went off like all of Mum's parties. There was dancing, drunkenness and a decimated cheese board – the guests had a fabulous time and the hostess was left shredded with exhaustion, head in hands, saying, 'Never again.' Except that the hostess this time was me and not Mum and that there was no 'again' to worry about.

Mum seemed to really enjoy herself, but I felt it was a wasted opportunity. I would have liked a ritual of some kind, for there to have been some acknowledgement of Mum's life. A sentimental moment, I suppose, where all of her friends old and new might have bonded. Geoff was supposed to say a few words, but he got drunk early and in the end I was too busy pretending to be Mum's posh organic caterer to get the chance.

The fashion show was being held in a characterless modern conference hotel next to the hospital.

I drove there directly with Sangeeta, whom I had picked up from the airport less than a hour beforehand as her flight had been delayed. It was such a rush that I barely spoke to the poor woman all the way there. Sangeeta was the only one of Mum's friends that I didn't feel I had to make small-talk with. She had a calmness that made me feel close to her, even though I didn't know her very well.

The reception room was in the basement; there were no windows, horrible carpets and a few hundred blue office chairs in lines around a makeshift catwalk. To the left of the stage was a DJ station where Brian's son David was fussing about with another couple of impressively hip-looking twenty-somethings. He gave me a friendly wave, but I replied with a cursory smile. I didn't want to go into the whole story of Brian and his sons with Sangeeta. I needn't have worried because Brian came out on to the catwalk from 'backstage' a few seconds after we sat down and made a beeline for us both. He hugged me, which was entirely inappropriate and for Sangeeta's benefit, then warmly greeted her with the usual 'I've heard so much about you'. Creep.

'Can we go backstage and see Mum?' I demanded, standing up.

'Best not,' he said, 'I think she'd rather you got the full impact of her performance on stage, and if you see her now it will spoil the surprise.' What 'surprise'? A blow dry, bit of lipstick and a frock? Did he really think I had never seen my own mother dressed up before? I really needed to have words with this guy. This was not the time nor place, but this hijacking of my mother was going to have to stop – and soon.

The room filled up quickly and we were handed programmes, which were nothing more than typed lists of the clothes and the shops that they came from: all local boutiques and one major chain store. It was all rather shabby and I had this terrible feeling that this was going to be a disaster. It could be the most excruciating, embarassing moment of my life and hers and if this was a screw-up, if that man Brian and his sons made my mother look foolish, there would be hell to pay.

Eventually the lights dimmed and suddenly when the stagelights and music started up, the empty amateurism of the makeshift setting was gone and the place was transformed into a proper theatre. David and his chums, it seemed, knew what they were doing, as did Brian, who appeared on stage in a tuxedo, thanked everyone, then spoke movingly for a refreshingly short time about the cause of hospice care, managing to name-check his wife without seeming sentimental, and gave a short eulogy to the 'star of the show, an extraordinary woman without whose help and motivation tonight would not be happening – Eileen Blake'.

I was thrilled for her. Mum deserved that kind of recognition and applause.

The lights went down suddenly, there was a thundering drumbeat that made the legs of my chair vibrate, then Tina Turner started belting out 'Simply the Best' at full volume. A spotlight came on at the back of the stage, then from beyond a screen of dry-ice came a middle-aged woman wearing a full-length red evening dress and matching jacket. My stomach lurched with nerves when I noticed it was Mum and that she was faltering slightly. She was afraid she'd fall off her high heels; she was too nervous. She had helped with the Bailey Newton fashion shows, but always backstage. She was socially gregarious but she didn't really have the confidence for this. For the first time since all this had been happening, I realized that this was Mum's big night. This was important to her and I didn't want her to fail. Sangeeta reached over, took my hand and gave it an excited squeeze. I tried to smile back, but I was petrified for Mum. I took a deep breath and willed her to move. As I breathed out, she came striding down the stage, her hand on one hip, swinging them both in an exaggerated swagger. The room erupted as she reached the end of the catwalk and gave her audience a two-handed Marilyn Monroe kiss. She stood there for ages, grinning and sparkling, drinking in their adulation, then turned on her heels and danced back up the catwalk. I was shocked, not by how confident she appeared, nor by how many people in the crowd were there to support her, nor by how glittering and glamorous she looked under David's expert lighting. I was shocked at how well she looked: how uncompromisingly, energetically alive.

After her came another dozen or so women, most of them around Mum's age, one or two heart-rendingly younger and wearing funky hats and scarves to cover their chemotherapy hair loss. What they all had in common was their defiant alive expressions; NOT DEAD YET! wore a young – no more than twenty – bald punk on her T-shirt as she dragged Mum up to the end of the catwalk to do a little jig during 'Come On Eileen'.

It was not like I was seeing who my mother was for the first time, but I was finally allowing myself to admit who she was. Mum's identity had always been about other people: where she stood in the community, the parish, her job, not in her status, but in how much she was able to give to other people, and how much love and respect she got in return.

The night of the fashion show epitomized that. I had

dreamed of sports cars, pampering spa-facials, and Mum seeing the world. But she had lived the best years of her life as part of a community. And that was how she wanted to die.

twenty-seven

Eileen

It was a small group that night. Just me, party-mad Florrie, Sharon from Hosiery and Melissa, a pretty mixed-race girl from the Wedding List desk. Melissa was quite newly separated and we all liked her. She had been to a couple of First Wives' nights before her marriage finally hit the rocks. I had given the evening a French-bistro theme, with red candles stuck into empty wine bottles, a two-litre winebox of red, my new Edith Piaf tape and a large French cheese board. I had even made Grace dig out an ashtray with a picture of the Eiffel Tower on it that she'd brought back from a trip to Paris. I didn't go mad, but I did roll out the red gingham tablecloth and 'For once,' Grace had said grudgingly as she dropped off the ashtray, 'it actually looks appropriate.'

Several people had called to cancel but I didn't panic; all the more important to make sure that the three guests who did come had a good time. In any case, these small gatherings had an intimacy that the larger groups some-times lacked. In a bigger group, there was always the occasional prude who tended to steer the conversation towards safe subjects like well-priced garden furniture and wouldn't get what Florrie called 'down and dirty' about the torrid details of her private life. Secrets were what made the First Wives' Club tick. I had a feeling that that night was going to be a good one, and for the first three hours it was, until Melissa, out of the blue, suddenly said, 'I'm adopted.'

Florrie and Sharon had demolished the first winebox and were into the real plonk.

'Bernard from Household Appliances is adopted . . .'

'Really? I always thought he was from East Grinstead?'

'And I've found my birth mother, but I don't know if I want to meet her,' Melissa continued.

I felt my body lock. It was not as if I had never met anyone who was adopted before, Bernard from Household Appliances for one, it was just that this was one of my circle of confidantes, and this conversation was taking place in my home.

Florrie and Sharon were not interested in talk moving away from their favourite subject – men.

'He *is* from East Grinstead – but what's that got to do with his being adopted?'

'He once told me he was *born* there. People normally move after they've been adopted, don't they?'

'I think Bernard's a bit creative with the truth sometimes . . .'

'He's creative somewhere else too . . .'

'How do you know?' Gasp! 'You didn't?!'

Melissa seemed exasperated more than upset by them ignoring her. I hoped that that would be it, but then she turned to me and said:

'Eileen – what do *you* think I should do?'

I did what I always did when somebody had said something that upset or offended me: I smiled and changed the subject – 'Would you like some toast with that Brie?' – then I shot up from the table and started rummaging in the bread bin.

But Melissa was too drunk to notice the social subtlety of having upset the hostess and carried on. 'The thing about being adopted is, no one really understands what it feels like. Apart from other adopted people. I mean, it's a whole identity thing, you know?'

I nodded and tried not to listen. I felt sick. Like I'd been punched.

'I mean, my adopted parents are black, so I was raised black. That means something, yeah? To be a black woman raised in south London – that's my iden-tity, right? All right, I'm born "mixed"-race, but my parents are West Indian and I'm raised in Brixton and I get my hair braided and my parents push me to study hard in school so I can make them proud and be a credit to my culture, my race. *Then*, I find out that my mother is white. She's a white Irishwoman. Like you, Eileen! How weird is that?'

I felt faint now. I was a little light-headed myself and my thoughts became confused. Was this girl accusing me of being her mother? No, no. I had a son. Melissa was half black. She wasn't my child. That wasn't what she was saying.

'Would you like one slice or two, Melissa . . .?'

'So my father was black, but that's not the same thing really, is it? I mean I never really thought about it before? But since I turned thirty, I can't stop thinking about it. That's how intense it is being adopted, yeah?'

'You know, I think I'll have some, too. Florrie? Sharon? Would you like some toast with your Brie?'

Melissa covered her face with her hands and scraped them down her pretty coffee-coloured features in a gesture of stress.

'I'm making you uncomfortable, Eileen. I'm sorry . . .'

'No, no Melissa – really I . . .'

'No, Eileen. I'm sorry – I'm a bit drunk, I think, and I'm bringing the mood down. I'm gonna drop the subject now; could you call me a taxi?'

When the taxi arrived twenty minutes later, the two older women clambered in first, all handbags and gussets and giggling. Melissa held back and said to me, 'I don't really feel like going dancing with those two madwomen, but I suppose I better had . . .'

I felt bad. I knew she wanted to stay and confide in me. Instinct more than will made me say, 'Stay on for a coffee; they won't even notice you're not there.'

We talked for a few minutes about the others, silly gossip, then Melissa said, 'I'm sorry about going on about the adoption stuff earlier. It's just that—'

'I gave a child up for adoption when I was nineteen.'

It just came out. Melissa looked taken aback, but I didn't care. Once the first line was out, the first and highest hurdle jumped, my terrible secret came rushing out. Words I did not dare think because they were too harsh softened in the telling. The relief of the revelation pushed me into emptying myself of all of it: the forgotten details of the birth; his delicious smell; the guileless, innocent tears giving him away; the injustice of times changing, so that before my son would have been three years old I realized that I could have kept him. I only started to cry when the story took me to the recent years, the years when I should have forgotten, but would suddenly see what might have been for me: a friend's son graduating from university, a young neighbour helping his elderly mother into a car.

'I want to show you something,' I said.

I went to the kitchen and found the small jewellery box that contained his hospital baby bangle, and rummaged at the back of my bureau for the copy of his birth certificate. I hadn't looked at it in years, since just after Grace had been born, but I knew it was there. I handed it to Melissa.

'It's the biggest regret of my life, Melissa, but I have learned to live with it.'

Even as I said the words, I realized that I had not learned to live with Michael's adoption at all. I had learned to forget, which I now knew was not the same thing.

'I'm telling you all this because I want you to know how it might have been for your mother. Times were very different then.'

Melissa had tears in her eyes but she smiled, got up from her chair and gave me a warm hug. I think we both knew that I had not told Melissa about Michael to help her, but to unburden myself.

I did not sleep that night.

I was haunted; my love for Michael had been hidden in a safe in my heart for all these years and the confession had decoded the lock and flung open the door on all the grief and shame. The obsession I had been hiding from for most of my adult life was sitting looking at me.

Where was he now? What did he look like? Who were his 'parents'? What did they call him? I turned off the lights and lay down to sleep but my head kept asking questions, drawing pictures of this faceless child, boy, man. My love for Michael had grown alongside him, except I did not know where he was, what he looked like, or even if he was alive or dead.

The next morning I could not face work and rang in sick. I sat and watched television, flicking channels, wondering if the news presenters and gardening experts and soap-opera actors were my son. By the end of the day, I knew that I would have to find a way to package these feelings away again before I went crazy. Sangeeta called in on her way home from work, to check I was all right and give me the day's gossip.

'Oh my goodness, Eileen, you look terrible.'

Whatever capacity I had once had for hiding my feelings appeared to have gone from me. I felt raw and vulnerable and collapsed into tears as soon as I saw my good friend.

I told Sangeeta everything in the urgent confession of a child. The Indian woman held my hand wordlessly throughout and squeezed it firmly to let me know she did not judge me. Sangeeta understood what it was to make sacrifices.

'What shall I do, Sangeeta? I'm going out of my mind.'

'Maybe you should try to find him?' she said.

'No.'

I said it so suddenly and so surely that I shocked myself. In that one word, that less-than-one-second instant, I felt completely certain. Not that I had done the right thing in giving my son away, not that I could return his love to that empty cave in my heart, but simply that there was nothing I could do to change the past. He had lived his life with another family – good or bad. That I was not a part of his life was *my* cross to bear, not his.

In the coming weeks, I learned from Melissa that she had found her mother through contacting the Catholic Society, the organization through which I had arranged Michael's adoption. I contacted their office and put my name down on a register to say I would be happy to co-operate if Michael ever wanted to contact me.

Melissa met her birth mother and told me all about it.

'She wasn't what I was expecting, Eileen. She was cold – not motherly at all. Not like my own mum, or you. I don't think I'll bother meeting her again.'

'I'm so sorry,' I said.

'Don't be.' Melissa seemed genuinely pragmatic. 'To be honest, I think the best thing I got out of the whole thing was my friendship with you.'

I agreed. The experience with Melissa, painful though it had been, had brought my secret out of hiding. There was nothing for me to be ashamed of, no taboos any more, I was finally free to really be myself with my friends and workmates. I no longer had to protect myself from the truth of my past, although I still felt I had to protect the person closest to me – Grace.

As for the wound itself, the loss, the grief of having given my son away, that was just something I would have to learn to live with, properly this time. Because I now knew that I would never try to forget Michael again. He was more than the baby bangle and the birth certificate in a hidden box. He was my son, not with me, but my son none the less. I had known and loved him, and for those few brief weeks he had known and loved me. It wasn't as much as I would have hoped for, but it was something. And sometimes you just have to accept as much as God will give you and be grateful for that.

twenty-eight

Grace

I started to notice a gradual deterioration in Mum's condition in the weeks following the fashion show. I think she was hiding a lot from me before then. She lost her appetite and had less energy, though there were days when she got out of bed, washed, dressed and arrived down the stairs like a miracle. 'I feel great today!' she would announce, and we would head off to the garden centre for coffee and a potter around the plants. Then suddenly she would turn to me and say, 'I'm tired, Grace, let's go home,' and there was an urgency in her voice. Sure enough, the moment we got back to the house, she would head straight up to her room. The first time I saw her stop halfway up the stairs to rest from the effort I caught my own breath with panic before taking her arm and gently leading her up to bed.

For three days she said she just felt like resting in bed, and I brought her meals up to her. She reacted as she had to the nurses in the hospital, calling the experience 'a luxury lie-in', rubbing her hands together in delight and saying, 'This looks delicious – you're an angel!' When I went back up to collect her plate, the food would have been pushed around but hardly eaten. When I objected she smiled at me, her eyes detached and faraway.

'I've gone off salmon,' she'd say. 'Maybe a bit of chicken would be nice?'

Then for a while we played this game where the chicken was too spicy, or not salty enough, or the potatoes were overcooked, the vegetables raw. I ran up and down the stairs pandering to the tastes of a woman who I knew would normally eat her own arm if she was hungry enough, both of us pretending that the problem was my cooking and not the cancer kicking in. One day, halfway up the stairs with a poached egg – medium – on a lightly toasted – no butter – granary roll, it hit me, hard and sharp in the centre of my chest. I breathed in, went into her room, laid the poached-egg meal she didn't want on the dressing table, and sat down on her bed.

'Mum,' I said, 'are you in pain?'

'Oh, Grace, I hate it when you do this big "Let's sit down and talk" thing. No, I am not in pain – if I was I would tell you. Now for God's sake, please can I have something decent to eat . . .'

She was in pain. I could see it as clearly in her face as if she was screaming for the morphine pump.

'I'm calling the doctor.'

'What for?'

'You're in pain, Mum, I can tell.'

'I told you I wasn't in any pain, Grace.'

'Well, you're lying.'

'Don't be so stupid, why would I do that?'

'I don't know. For the same reason you made me

poach an egg when I know you hate eggs. To annoy me? To protect me? How the hell should I—'

She flinched. Her nose wrinkled, her eyes closed and her mouth opened on an aborted shout. It was an expression I had never seen on my mother's face before; I had witnessed sadness and fear, even petulant anger, but never true physical pain. It was as shocking as if I had felt it myself. It made me feel very young and very small, and very aware that I was neither of those things and so had to look a lot stronger than I felt.

I bit my lip and steadied my voice over the words: 'How long has this been going on?'

She looked at me and I realized that she was studying my face for cracks before she decided to tell me the truth.

'A few days.'

'Where does it hurt?' Why did I ask her that question? What difference did it make? What, did I think I was her doctor? I was trying to sound like I was in control. Like I knew what to do. 'Will you let me call the doctor, Mum? They'll give you something . . .'

'I want to stay at home.'

It could have been me saying it: not wanting to go on the school trip to France, not wanting to leave home and go to university. I grew up and got married, separated, mortgaged, and thought I had moved on. Now here I was again, at home, with my mother. I felt like I wanted to stay at home too. Not this home, where I was running up and down the stairs trying to coax food into my dying mother, but the home of my childhood, which was full of familiar colours and smells, the place where

I felt safe, and comforted, and as if nothing could ever change.

The doctor was nice. He joked with Mum and gave her Fentanyl morphine patches, which would slow-release the painkiller into her system throughout the day.

'No smoking now, Eileen!' he said, but she didn't respond. In movies, dying people remain plucky and brave, joking with doctors and comforting their grief-stricken loved ones. Mum gave the doctor a watery smile, then turned her body to the wall as he was leaving. My stomach sank. She didn't want me to see the terror and depression written in her face, and I didn't want to see it either.

'I'll call in two days to see how she's getting on,' he said to me as he was leaving. 'Let me know if there is any change before then.'

He didn't have to say it out loud: 'This is it starting – prepare yourself.'

There is nothing heartening or interesting I can say about the physical symptoms of my mother's death. The unthinkable became the everyday; I learned that I was a kinder, stronger person than I thought I was and got no comfort from knowing it. I got to know Mum's body: the folds of her flesh, the new frailty of her bones, the delicate intelligence of her fingers as I rubbed oil into her hands and nails, willing the purple veins to spring to life behind her transparent skin. I bathed her and was shocked, not by her nakedness but by the fact that her body had remained hidden to me all of her life. She didn't need coaxing and there was no awkwardness on my part; my ministering to her was always a silent, seamless act of love. She relaxed when I touched her and there was relief but also responsibility in that.

The most upsetting thing was seeing her lapse into a depression. She stopped wanting visitors; I kept in touch with her friends but did not encourage them to visit. I knew that Mum would not want them to see her that low, and they respected my wishes and kept away. The only person who called in every day, who would not be put off, was Brian. Surprisingly, I was grateful for his pushiness. He always brought groceries with him, things we needed, and sometimes thoughtful, useful stuff like home-cooked lasagne or scented candles. Sometimes he sat in the house and let me fly down to the shops, get out for an hour or so. Brian seemed to know what to do and say. People were so polite about Mum dying; perhaps because he had been through it himself, Brian understood that I was never going to ask and so wasn't afraid to give help even when it wasn't requested. Yet he never crossed the line between privacy and propriety, and sometimes didn't go up and see Mum at all but just sat there with me. We became friends. I needed someone new to talk to; I felt estranged from my old friends, because I knew them too well and had expectations of them. When they didn't take my pain away or distract me, I felt angry with them. With Brian, I had no expectation and no emotional investment. I could afford to be bitchy, or angry, or upset. And because I felt free to be those things with him, I rarely was. My initial hostility and resentment towards him disappeared.

Those days passed in a haze of Mum's declining health and increasing needs. That I had nursing skills at all was an ordinary miracle, but I finally had to admit to my limitations. After almost six weeks, I felt it was time. I knew the names and effects of too many drugs: Fentanyl, Codalax, Oxycontin, Temazepam. Apart from her daily chemotherapy dose, I was administering pain relief, laxatives and sleeping tablets. I kept having to call the doctor to increase the morphine. All the time in those last few days, I knew she was in a lot of pain, deteriorating faster than I could cope with.

Mum wanted to die at home. She did not want to go into the hospice but she did it for me. I objected, but we both knew I couldn't cope any more.

'I wish you had a brother or sister to share this with,' she said as they were wheeling her into the ambulance. But the doctor had just administered a large dose of morphine, so she didn't really know what she was saying.

I followed in my own car. When I arrived, Mum was being 'set up' and I was told by a pretty, plump-faced woman on the reception desk to take a look round and make myself at home. 'There's a family room upstairs, Grace. Help yourself to tea or coffee.' It was a smallish, modern building with bright, airy rooms. There were flowers everywhere, the heady scent of lilies and roses wafting from every windowsill. The family room had a brand-new navy three-piece suite, a cabinet with videos and DVDs next to a large television set, and a small kitchenette that was packed with biscuits and cakes bought by generous visitors. Most of them spilled from a big basket with a 'Help Yourself' tag written in the confident round writing of a schoolteacher. There was a play corner with toys and children's books that made me feel guilty that some poor child was about to lose a parent or grandparent or, God forbid, sibling. Horribly, it also made me anxious that my mother's last few days might be disturbed by the sound of screaming kids. All along the broad bay window was an array of huge indoor plants, flourishing in the warm, sunny environment; the living embodiment of life after death.

I should have been happy and relieved that my mother was in such a nice place, but I wasn't. I went to the canteen and gulped down a hot sausage roll and a cup of tea. I was surprised to find I was hungry. Then I went back up to the family room and launched into the 'Help Yourself' basket, willing myself not to bullishly go and find where they had taken her but to wait until somebody came to get me. Several copies of *Hello!* magazine later, a nurse in her mid-thirties came in and said, 'Grace?'

A shot of anger came out of nowhere. What was this? Had I been transported to the planet Kindandfriendly where everybody knows your name?

'Yes,' I said, standing up. Except I said it in a way that compelled her to signal me to sit back down.

'Your mother is very depressed,' she said.

Hello? News flash! She's dying of cancer! Slightly depressing state of affairs, wouldn't you say?

'Really?' was the best I could manage. But it was a good 'Really?' A sarcastic one.

'She's sleeping now, Grace.' No need to keep using my name – it's really annoying me.

'I'd like to have a talk with you about maybe getting you both some counselling. It's of great concern to us that our patients are allowed to make their transition in peace.' Her tiny eyes blinked quickly under the weight of heavy bars of clumpy mascara.

'It's of great concern to me too – ' I pointedly checked her name tag – 'Tamara. But I am sure Mum will be fine after a couple of hours' rest. She is a very resilient and cheerful person.'

Resilient and cheerful – it made her sound like a kitchen accessory. But I was not about to be told about my own mother by some nurse. I stood up and slung my bag over my shoulder.

'Do you want to see her before you go?'

OF COURSE I WANT TO SEE HER. SHE'S MY BLOODY MOTHER!

'Lead the way, *Tamara*.'

Mum was lying back, with her mouth open and her eyes closed. She had a drip in her arm. In this context, she suddenly looked truly ill and very frail to me. Even though I had seen her less than two hours beforehand, it must have been the defeat of being in hospital. I should never have let her come in here. Nice as it was, I should have kept her at home. I must have cried because Tamara touched my arm and said, 'Are you OK, Grace?'

I reacted with my instinctive cure for any pain that was coming up: instant denial, instant burial. 'I'll be back in a few hours,' I said sharply and left.

I called in to the shopping centre on the way back to Mum's house to buy her some new nightclothes. It felt strange to be back out in the real world where there was life and everything was normal. I felt like I had hardly taken a breath for twenty-four hours; as if a part of me had ground to a halt, shocked by the reality of my mother's condition. The hospice was where people went to die; and where their loved ones went to watch them die. Being out of there was, in itself, a diversion.

By the time I got back to Mum's house, went into the kitchen and opened the fridge, my mind had kicked into the detail-driven, neurotic, indecisive, low-grade-panic mode that was so familiar to me from my mother. Should I have lunch here, or go back to my own flat? I hadn't been there for a few days and perhaps I needed to pick up some things. In fact, there was probably food rotting in my fridge that I should clear out. After all, that was my real home. Perhaps I should take my stuff out of Mum's house now and move back into my own place? Then again, I had gathered far too much stuff over here; I only had a two-seater car and there were at least two carloads what with all my books and shoes. Why *did* I bring all that rubbish with me? But then, suppose they let her home? The nurses had said they might; they said they were going to see how Mum progressed and that if there was a respite they might let her home. And if she came back home and I had moved out, I'd only have to move back in again and that would be a nightmare; having to pack it all up again. Then I remembered that the nightmare was not having to move my stuff but the fact that Mum was dying. And that instead of being in the hospice with her, I was standing at her fridge checking yogurt sell-by dates and worrying about how I was going to fit all my shoes into the boot of my MG. I could not get what the nurse had said about Mum being depressed out of my head; it floated to the top of my consciousness like a bloated body in a bog. I felt nauseous, rushed to the toilet and threw up, but I didn't feel better afterwards. The anxiety started to escalate, pumping me up. So I paced, in and out of rooms, desperately trying to find something to focus on outside of myself.

In the dining room, I walked over and drummed my palms on the ridges of the rolltop desk. It was reproduction 'antique' and my mother's pride and joy, the most expensive thing she had ever bought; she said it made her feel 'posh and important' every time she looked at it. She had had a small party to celebrate its arrival in the house, and Geoff officiated over the 'official opening' by cutting Bailey Newton ribbon which they had wrapped around it, then swigging back half a bottle of sparkling wine in ten minutes. I had thought the whole thing tacky beyond belief at the time, but now it seemed curiously moving that so much of Mum's happiness could be tied up in an inanimate object that would outlive her to become a genuine antique. As I clicked my nails along the polished mahogany slats, it suddenly occurred to me that Mum probably had a stash of cigarettes hidden in there. That was exactly what I needed. I would start smoking again. It was the perfect antidote to Mum's cancer, a delightfully inappropriate attention-seeking act of self-destruction. There was a slight feeling of *déjà vu*, but nothing like what was to come.

Within weeks of arriving in the house, the desk had become a receptacle for all the miscellaneous rubbish that wouldn't fit into the already bursting kitchen drawers. The lid was permanently down except for when Mum would ease it up an inch and shove in those things she didn't need but wanted to keep: hotel sewing kits, paid bills, 'On Sale' pamphlets, unsent postcards. On the outside it was always polished and perfect, then under the lid – chaos. Every couple of years, Mum would become gripped with dread and procrastinate vaguely for a few weeks before 'taking the plunge' and launching into it for a big 'sort-out'. Within days it would be scattered and scrappy again and down the lid would come. I opened it slowly to protect the chaos from tumbling down on to the floor.

I needn't have bothered, as the desk was tidy, gleaming like the day it had arrived. In the centre of it was a carved wooden box I had never seen before, and on the top of that a letter addressed to me. I opened it even though the sight of it made me feel sick again.

Dear Grace,
Enclosed are my solicitor's details, all my affairs are sorted. The box contains a few things I have kept for you over the years.
     Love, Mum.

It was the shortest note she had ever left me. Straight to the point, no frills, no lists. I suppose she didn't know what to say.

The box was largeish. Part of me didn't want to look inside but another felt compelled. I rummaged quickly, knowing that this was not the time for reminiscing; it was too early yet. There was an old school copybook with an English essay in it; a diary from my French exchange trip; a bracelet I had made for her from wooden beads. Then I spotted the small black box that contained my baby bangle. She must have found it where I left it back in the kitchen. Except that when I picked it up, the box was not black, but navy – and smaller than before. It was a different box. I opened it and took out the bangle. A few seconds passed before I realized that this was a different baby bangle from the one I had found in the kitchen. I looked at it closely: 'Baby Blake' it said, and then my date of birth. I ran into the kitchen and tore open the drawer where I had left the original box. My heart jumped when I saw it was still where I had left it. Not stopping to think, I opened the box and looked at the name and date on the bracelet. 'Baby Gardner, 2/7/1961'. My mother's maiden name, six years before I was born.

I couldn't make sense of it at first. Baby Blake, Baby Gardner. My mother's married name, my mother's maiden name. There were two babies on two different dates. Did this mean I had a brother or a sister? Is that what it meant? My face burned as I felt the blood rush to my head. I was shocked and shaking. It was obvious the answer was yes, but I could not believe it. I went over to my laptop, which was 'sleeping' on the kitchen table. I paused, breathed deeply and then Googled 'adopted siblings'. Without stopping to think, my fingers scrabbled across the keyboard and registered on the first site that came up. I gave my own details and my mother's maiden name. I sent the form off, then sat staring at the screen as if waiting for a reply. And I was just chastising myself for being so ridiculous and desperate when my inbox pinged.

Within ten minutes of opening my mother's box, I had a brother. His name was Michael Phillips. He was forty-six and married with two young children.

twenty-nine

Eileen

I would have stayed working for another five years at least, but they retired me at sixty. Geoff said it was illegal, but I knew myself that it wasn't. Big companies like that know what they're doing. It was all because of Sandra Jones. She had come to work in Customer Services three years previously and had made my life a living hell. She was a young, pretty thing, only in her mid-twenties, and she seemed very nice to begin with. 'Excellent presentation – oh yes, the PR department's in full swing there, dear' had been Geoff's comment. He hadn't liked her from the start.

There were six customer services managers in total, four part-timers and one other full-timer like me. At any given time, there were three of us on duty. Even though we were all more or less equal, there was an understanding that, as the eldest member of the team, and the person who had been there the longest, I was 'the boss'. I had 'Senior' before my title, was paid more than the others and attended the weekly management meetings on my department's behalf. I had often been told by my immediate boss that they would have promoted me years ago if I hadn't been so good at dealing with the customers. 'We need your hands-on experience, Eileen, you're irreplaceable out there on the floor,' he used to say. I was a good boss, never nasty or pushy but firm; I knew what I was doing. My age and experience gave me a natural authority which I admit I enjoyed. I liked showing the younger staff members the ropes, and I loved it when they deferred to me with their problems. Most of them couldn't hack the pressure and moved on after a couple of years, but the challenge of new staff coming in, showing them the ropes, bringing them along, was one that I had enjoyed. I felt it kept me young myself, kept me challenged and alive. Sandra Jones put a stop to all that. She was the other full-timer and at first seemed full of excitement about working in her favourite store, getting worked up by the new fashions and perfumes. 'How do you cope with all this temptation, Eileen?'

'You get used to it,' I said. 'The novelty soon wears off.'

'I hope so,' she said, 'or I'll be broke before too long.'

I knew it was a hint to start discussing salaries. I had a way of avoiding those conversations, which were unnecessary and inappropriate. Young people seemed obsessed with how much money they were earning, rarely focused on doing the job for the sake of it. They all seemed to wish they were doing something else, something silly like being a model, an actress or a pop singer. 'Customer Services Manager' didn't seem good enough for most of them, which hurt and puzzled me.

Sandra was different. She seemed to really enjoy her job, and she won me over with that.

Sandra had studied Retail Management at college, but I only discovered that after she had been working with us for a few months. One of the other women had mentioned it to me and I had thought it was nice that she hadn't bragged about it. It turned out that Sandra had been keeping her fancy qualifications to herself because she had other plans. One day three of us, Sandra, myself and one of the other managers, Alison, were on a coffee break.

'You'll be coming up for retirement soon, Eileen, won't you?' Alison asked.

'Sixty next month,' I said. 'I can't wait.'

I didn't mean it – it was a hot day and I was feeling grumpy. In fact, I had hardly thought about my retirement at all. I knew I could carry on until I was sixty-five – maybe they would even let me do some part-time work after that. I felt young. I couldn't imagine being a 'retired' person. I didn't think anything more about it, until the management meeting the following week when I walked into the room and saw Sandra sitting at the round table. Mr Bertram, the Managing Director, was sitting right next to her and they seemed to be sharing a joke as I walked in. Before I had even sat down, Mr Bertram said, 'Eileen, I've got some exciting news. Sandra is the new Head of Customer Services.'

He said all sorts of stuff after that: restructuring departments, times changing, all the usual nonsense about computers that he had been going on about to me for months. What it boiled down to was that I was no longer needed.

'We still need you, Eileen, out there on the floor.'

'Oh yes, Eileen, your experience is invaluable,' said the two-faced little cow.

I lasted three months. Sandra badgered me into early retirement so that she could replace me with one of her college friends. I couldn't get to grips with the new computer systems and I didn't even want to try. It was the worst three months of my life. For the first time in almost twenty years, I dreaded going in to work. They put in a call centre and every complaint had to be fed through these new grey machines that terrified me. I had loved my job because I knew what I was doing and everybody respected me. Now everything was changing and I didn't want to learn how to do new things. I wanted to carry on doing the things I knew how to do, the things I was good at. I became so stressed out with it all that I got snappy with a couple of customers and one of them sent in a complaint about me by 'e-mail'. Sandra took me off the floor straight away, so that I was in the computer centre with her all day, every day. After a week, I resigned. Mr Bertram said he was very disappointed and that as a mark of his respect for all the work I had done for Bailey Newton down through the years, he would give me a retirement package, including a lump sum of £10,000 and my full pension.

Geoff said that was a sure sign of guilt. 'You should sue, Eileen, my love. That's unfair dismissal.'

Geoff was still there, pottering about in Haberdashery well into his seventies. But then, as he said himself, 'People don't sue the buttons department, darling, but they do sue Complaints.' So even he agreed that times had changed. 'We're dinosaurs, Eileen – from a different age, when manners mattered. Now it's all dirty track-suits and wanting to get your bits out on the telly.'

Geoff was always blaming young people for every-thing, but I didn't agree with him. I loved young people; I thought these 'Spice Girl' types were great, showing themselves off in their skimpy outfits, all cheek and back-chat; they seemed so full of confidence, and I wished I had been more like that when I was young. I loved the new pop music and reading about all the latest fashions and fads. I considered myself modern in my outlook, and people often said I was more like Grace's sister than her mother. I was not just young at heart; I felt young in my body and my mind, too. I just didn't like computers, and it seemed unfair that everything in my life had to change just because of that.

It took me a long time to accept my retirement. Bailey Newton wanted to have a big party for me, but I refused. I felt it was just another way of trying to put a happy face on the terrible thing they had done; Mr Bertram tried to persuade me but I was tight-lipped in the meeting. I didn't tell him what I thought of him, but I was very quiet and I could tell he was hurt. I didn't care because I was hurt, too. Sangeeta had gone back to live in India the year before and the only person left there from the old days was Geoff. I was sorry after-wards that I hadn't let them give me a proper send-off, because it was ages before it felt like I had actually left. It was like when somebody dies and you don't go to the funeral: some part of you believes that they are still alive.

For the first few weeks, it was like I was on holiday. 'I'm loving the break,' I remember saying to Sangeeta when she telephoned from India after she'd had heard the news: 'getting on with all those little jobs, shopping – I'm having a great time!'

But after a while, I realized I wasn't on a 'break'. This was my new life: doing little jobs and mooching around the shops. I wasn't Eileen Blake, Senior Customer Services Manager at Bailey Newton Department Store, I was just plain Eileen Blake again, ordinary and old. I had no plans, no hobbies, no other ambitions for myself apart from that job, which I had loved. Added to that, I had never sat still in my life, and I didn't know how to do it. To begin with, while I was distracting myself by filing photographs and cleaning out cupboards, I recalled the days after Frank had left. This time, my energy was fuelled not by fear that my life would fall apart, but by a determination to prove that it was not over just because I had finished working. However, when the photographs were filed and the cupboards cleared, I realized that there was nothing else for me. My life had truly been filled with Grace, then work. Friends were important, but they had their own lives. Retirement began to seem like a kind of purgatory; an empty void of boredom and loneliness stretched out in front of me. It put me at a complete loss.

Struggling to fill my days, a routine evolved around the television schedules. I had two TVs in the house and had never watched them much before then, but in those early months it became a kind of an addiction. In the morning, I would make myself a cup of tea downstairs, then go back up to bed with it and watch breakfast television. At around ten, I would shower and dress, then eat my cereal in front of a gardening programme.

Sometimes I would sit there until lunchtime and go to the shops for my groceries in the afternoon. Other days, I would shop in the mornings and then fill the afternoons with programmes about shopping, decorating, cooking, having affairs, rearing difficult children; other people doing things. I lost interest in doing anything myself. There didn't seem any point.

Some days, I didn't leave the house at all. I telephoned Grace every day, as I always had, but I didn't want to trouble her with my loneliness. It wasn't fair to put pressure on her; she had her own friends, job and social life. Because she was an only-child, I had always taken great care to make sure that Grace never worried about me. Annoyed by me? Yes. Irritated? Almost constantly. But I never let her know about anything that would make her worry about me. I took pride in that.

It seemed that my life had changed overnight from that of a successful, popular woman to that of a nobody. A few weeks after I had retired, Geoff's partner Barry was offered a new job in Bath, and so the two of them rented out their apartment and moved away. Sangeeta was living back in India, and although we wrote and telephoned each other regularly, it wasn't the same as seeing her every day. Everybody else – Florrie, Sharon, Melissa – I had lost touch with, in that careless way that people do in large cities. It is easy to make friends, but not so easy to keep them in the long term. You cancel a couple of arrangements because you are tired, or it seems too far to travel in traffic, and then next thing you know you have not seen somebody you considered a close friend in over a year. In the small town where I grew up, you saw the same people day in and day out for years.

My mother was friends with the girls she went to school with until the day she died. I enjoyed the anonymous freedoms of the city, but now I wondered if I had enjoyed them enough to justify being lonely in my latter years. I missed seeing people every day, meeting old friends and making new ones.

I was doing so little during the day that I found it difficult to sleep at night, until I found unexpected solace in a Martini bottle. I don't know what made me fix myself a tumbler of the stuff one night, except that I found a bottle of it in my drinks cabinet left over from one of my First Wives' nights. The alcohol made the low hum of anxiety, the empty sad feeling I had had since my retirement, evaporate, and helped me slide easily into a deep sleep. Night-time drinking became a habit for me after that – a secret indulgence that carried on right up until Grace started nursing me towards the end. I looked forward to my bedtime Martini or two, and saw them as an advantage of living on my own. I could do as I pleased, with nobody to judge or criticize me. Often I would bring my dinner upstairs on a tray as early as eight o'clock, have a few drinks afterwards and next thing I would be asleep. Sometimes I woke up in the morning in the same position, with the dinner things spilled around me on the bed and the television still on. Most of the time, though, I got up later to switch off the TV and bring the dirty dishes downstairs, although usually I couldn't remember having done it the next day.

My drinking didn't affect anybody else, and all it did really was help me to sleep. I never saw the harm in it, except when I started to get the bloating around my stomach. I thought it was probably something to do with drinking and eating late at night. In the end it was the weight gain, which I thought was caused by my new bad habits, that sent me to Curves gym – and that was where I met Shirley.

thirty

Grace

The picture on the computer screen was a male version of me. I had thought I looked like my mother, but I realized now that I didn't look like her at all. My broad brow, my chin, my thick dark hair – they were shared by this stranger. I sat and stared at it for several minutes in a state of suspended shock. After what might have been five seconds or an hour, I moved my eyes down to his profile. The two paragraphs were short and chatty. No tortured pleadings from an abandoned child; his adoptive mother had died the previous year, and for the first time he felt curious enough about his birth parents to want to contact one or the other of them. 'I've no desire to disrupt anyone's life, I'm just interested in learning more about the circumstances of my birth.'

There was an e-mail address. Bristling with a combination of fear and curiosity, I typed in, 'I think I'm your sister.' I pressed the Send button without allowing myself time to decide. I had followed this whole chain without stopping to think. I knew if I thought about what I was doing it would be too huge, and I was already overwhelmed by what was happening with Mum. What was the next step?

I nearly swallowed my tongue when not five seconds later my inbox flashed: 'Blimey! Send me your mother's name and details.'

'I've checked on your page. They're the same,' I replied.

'Can I have your name? Phone number?'

'Send me yours first.'

'They're on the web page.'

The tears were streaming down my face. Here I was in the middle of a strangely intimate correspondence with a man whose blunt, matter-of-fact e-mail tone was already causing the kind of low-level irrritation I had seen other people have with their siblings. He felt like my brother, even though I had never met him, even though he didn't know my name.

I could not bear to ring him. I was afraid of the sound of his voice. I typed in; 'Where are you?'

'At work.'

'I mean, where? London?'

'NW6.'

Oh my God. He was less than half an hour away. It seemed so unlikely.

'Want to meet up?' I typed slowly, still unsure that this was what I wanted, but compelled none the less by a sense of urgency. A lack of time; Mum's impending death?

'Hendon Station, half-six?'

'Great.'

Two hours away. I was terrified to meet him, and

yet some part of me wanted to get into a taxi and tear straight round to his workplace.

'What do you look like?' he asked.

I smiled to myself, glad to have one up on him.

'You,' I typed.

Meeting my brother was the single most incredible, wonderful event that had happened to me in my life up to that point. I was shaking so much leaving the house that I couldn't drive and had to go back inside and telephone for a taxi.

'I'm going to meet my brother,' I said to the taxi driver, just to see how it sounded. Just for the novelty of saying out loud the words 'my brother' for the first time. He was uninterested, and it thrilled me that the extraordinary thing I was experiencing seemed to be so ordinary to an outsider.

Michael was a hugger, one of these big bear-like men, tall and broad. We looked almost identical and the mirrored delight and surprise in each other's faces drew us into each other's arms. Everything after that initial hug was a bonus. I felt as if I knew him and he knew me in a way that was beyond description. We had both been reared as only-children, so the sibling bond was as extraordinary for him as it was for me.

'This is weird,' he said. 'I don't know anything about you and yet you are *most certainly* my sister.'

He said 'most certainly' in this pompous public-schoolboy voice that irritated me in a glorious, sisterly way.

'Yes, I *most certainly* am,' I said.

He laughed, and I realized that I had known that he would. It seemed miraculous, unreal, that I had instincts about him.

We talked for three hours. He had enjoyed a wonderful childhood in north-west London, and although his adoptive father had died when he was in his late teens, he had been close to his mother. She had lived with him and his wife Katy and two kids: Molly, six, and Paddy, four, until she died the previous year. 'Katy only has one brother and he lives in Australia, so the troops have been depleted somewhat.'

He had married late in life ('I was a bit of a mummy's boy, to be honest'), but that hadn't frightened Katy. She was a nurse (divorced, 'a complete bastard, but that's another story'), a few years younger than him, and he met her through a woman at work who kept fixing him up. He was an insurance assessor. He had always known that he was adopted, that he had been named 'Michael' by his birth mother. His adoptive parents had liked the name and never changed it. His mother had given him the exact location of his birth and Mum's name shortly before she died, along with details of the Catholic Society, where he could apply for his adoption file any time. He had objected, insisting she was his 'real' mother, but she had said she wanted him to have them anyway. He had never bothered to follow through on the adoption file, so he didn't know who his father was. 'Registering with the site was a kind of an impulse thing I did at work one day. I never really thought it would come to anything.' He had been astonished to get a response, but now that I had turned up,·

he was delighted. He left it right to the end before mentioning our mother.

'Do I look like her?' he asked. He didn't; he looked like a slightly older, male version of me. The thought flashed into my head that we must have had the same father, but I didn't have room to accommodate it.

I told him she was in a hospice and very ill. His face dropped, became solemn; I wanted him to be jolly and smiling again. He was the first person I had met since all this had begun who I felt had truly cheered me up, made me forget.

'Did she ever tell you about me?'

'No,' I said.

He didn't look hurt or upset by that, but I still felt disappointed for him. I told him about finding the baby bangle but as I was talking I felt a stab of dread, as I realized I had to face all that later. Her having not told me . . . should I tell her that I knew? Was there any point now that she was . . .

'Would she like to meet me, do you think?'

Whoah!

I could have flailed around trying to put sugar on it, but in the end I just opened my mouth and told him the truth: 'I have no idea, Michael. Finding out about you has made me realize that I don't know my mother as well as I thought I did.'

I didn't want to go home, and although I hadn't said anything Michael invited me back to his house for dinner.

'Would your wife not be freaked out, you suddenly arriving home with a sister?'

'You're joking! She'd be delighted. So would the kids: an auntie to hassle for sweets!'

It sounded idyllic. Katy was obviously as delightfully emotionally unfettered and open as my brother. '*My brother*' – it was weird, and yet I *wanted* to go back to his house with him. I felt like sending for my things and walking into a new life where everything was fresh and alive, as if the circumstances of how we arrived there could be wiped clean. I didn't know this man, I had never met his wife or his children, but any sense of propriety, caution, the natural hesitation of common sense was gone. Perhaps that was the next step after being overwhelmed, the desire to leap. To stand at the edge of a cliff and jump, not knowing or caring if you will be caught.

'I won't today, Michael. I have to get back to Mum in the hospice. I'll call you tomorrow, if that's OK? Maybe we can talk about what to do about Mum then.'

I was relieved to hear myself sounding sensible, even if I didn't feel it.

When I got back to Mum's house, it all started to crumble. This was too much. How had she kept this secret from me for all of my life? Why had she given Michael away? If we did share the same father, she had been married to him and yet Michael had been born years before me. Horribly, selfishly, I could not help thinking: All those years in therapy, all that money I spent, when I only ever had half the story of my life! And all the while I was also thinking, I don't have time for all this now, I should be with Mum at the hospice.

I was confused and desperate, and I did not know what to do for the best. Should I bring Michael to see

Mum, or would that be a really terrible thing to do at this stage? She had gone her whole life keeping the fact of his birth hidden from me, probably from herself. She had her reasons for doing that. Did I want to blow it all open and possibly cause her confusion and pain? Or was this the right time to help her lay the past to rest? I could not work it out on my own, so I rang Brian. Not because he was any kind of oracle or because I especially respected his opinion, but because he was the person I knew would understand my dilemma immediately, yet who didn't have enough of a history with my family to turn it into a drama. There was no the time for that, and much as I loved to analyse, this situation was so messed up, I just needed someone else to answer the question for me.

thirty-one

Eileen

If I had not started drinking late at night, I would never have joined Curves. And if I had not joined Curves, I would never have met Shirley. And if I had never met Shirley, I would not have gone to the hospital that day. And if I had not gone to the hospital that day, I would not have found out about the cancer until even later than I did – by which time it would have been too late to do all of the things I wanted to do before I died.

So sometimes things that seem to be bad for you, like drinking half a bottle of Martini before you go to sleep, can turn out to be the right thing. It all depends on how you look at your life; that was something that I learned shortly before I discovered I had cancer.

I had invited Shirley around for supper, and as it was the first time I was entertaining her 'formally' I wanted it to be special. I decided to do a simple steak and salad – Shirley didn't look like a big eater – but I went overboard cleaning the house and making it look nice. It felt good to be taking pride in it again, as if joining the gym and making this new friend had helped me turn a corner towards getting some of my old life back.

The weather had picked up and I thought we might have a drink in the garden first, so I went out to give the patio chairs a wipe with a damp cloth. My garden was small and nothing special: a modest patch of grass surrounded by shrubs and flowerbeds that had built up over the years to a reasonable state of maturity. In the full flower of summer it was pretty enough, but that was more by happy accident than design. A short drive away there was a garden centre with a lovely café where Grace sometimes used to take me. Over time I had picked up the odd plant, then plonked it into a spare patch of ground, usually just as it was about to die. There were clusters of blue and green ceramic pots – most of them empty, some with mossy, half-dead weeds. Gardening had always just seemed like too much hard work: mowing that patch of green was a chore that sometimes I let go until it was knee-high, then I'd get a handyman in to strim it down for me.

As I was wiping down the chairs, something colourful caught my eye. It was a huge, beautiful rose, with velvety candy-pink petals. From their centre outwards they were feathered a rich, purply red. I had never noticed anything like it before growing in my garden, and straight away it occurred to me that it would make a wonderful arrangement for my table that evening. Quick as a flash, I snipped it with a pair of sharp scissors, popped it into a single-bloom vase and put it in the centre of my kitchen table.

Shirley came and we both got quite drunk that night. She didn't comment on the food, and just hummed a vague note of approval when I pointed out the peony rose I had found in the garden. I put her in a taxi at about one o'clock, but when I went up to bed myself I couldn't sleep. I knew I had had too much to drink, so I lay down and napped fitfully until four when I gave up and went downstairs to make myself some tea. The kitchen was half lit from the beginning of the day, and in the grey light the peony seemed to glow like a withering ghost. It was drooping, with most of its petals fallen on to the table; I noticed that I hadn't put any water in the vase and for some reason this made me feel very sad, and I started to cry. Such a stupid thing, crying over a dead rose, although I knew there must have been more to it than that. After a few minutes I made myself tea, and as I was tipping in the milk I felt drawn out to the garden, perhaps by the strangeness of being up at that time of the morning and the novelty of hearing uninterrupted birdsong in the city. I brought a cushion out with me and did what I had done too rarely in my sixty years up to then: I sat and looked at my garden. In all those years living in that house, I had never put any effort, thought or care into my garden, and so I placed very little value on its importance or beauty. And yet, in the growing light that morning, it looked remarkably beautiful to me. There was a hedge in one corner with deep red flowers, opposite which another was flowering tiny lilac spears. Over a low wall, a blue weed-like plant was spreading into the lawn, and behind that was a pink flowering ivy creeping up the wall. I was surprised at how lush and alive it was. This beautiful garden had grown out of hurried purchases planted as guilty after-thoughts. It had never enjoyed anything more than my creative leftovers, had been maintained with no more than scraps of my care. And yet that morning it looked glorious, and I realized that it wasn't me that had made this garden – it was God. For once, that didn't make me feel guilty, it made me feel grateful. In that moment I got back a feeling of faith I did not know I had lost. It was stronger now because I knew that somehow, like my garden, it had been working, growing, changing, flourishing all the time, even when I didn't know it, even when I couldn't feel it.

I also thought, If God can make something this good grow out of so little, what could we make if we put in a little effort?

I ran into the house and quickly rummaged around in my bookshelves until I found the *Encyclopedia of Popular Garden Plants* that Geoff had bought for my birthday years ago and which I had never opened. Slowly I went around the garden and said out the vaguely familiar names of the plants: buddleia, clematis, campanula, lavatera, escallonia.

As I was going around checking the plant names, it began to rain gently; 'soft' rain, we used to call it in Ireland. I went back into the house, but as I went over to the patio chair to collect my cushion, something caught my eye. Soft pink peony petals bursting out of their bud; from the same plant I had butchered the day before. I could have sworn I saw them actually moving, growing out towards the light, and it reminded me of a miracle I had once seen.

That first day in the hospital with Shirley, when the doctor came to me and said, 'We have found a growth, Mrs Blake; we would like you to come back for more tests,' it was as if I was living in two worlds. One was the world which had been turned upside down, the place where I had gone from being a perfectly healthy sixty-something woman to someone who had terminal cancer. In that world I was distressed, shocked, depressed, afraid. I tried to be brave because that was the world that I lived in with Grace and my friends. But then there was this other sphere, the secret world of my heart that had remained hidden for so much of my life, even and often especially to myself. In there I had been living with the cancer growing in my body for a long time, and it was like the garden: I didn't know it was there until the doctors pointed it out to me, and then it seemed like I had known all along. I wasn't exactly happy or accepting of it, but it had the ring of the inevitable. As if someone I was very fond of was dying, but I knew it was God's will.

The big surprise was not that I had cancer, but that I could have such wildly contrasting feelings about it. That I could be completely shocked and terrified, and yet in another part of me completely calm, more concerned about how my friends and daughter would cope. But then I discovered first-hand that nothing heightens the senses and emotions more than death. In those last few months, I learned what an extraordinary, contradictory, strong, remarkable woman I was. Some of it through the eyes of other people, and some of it like facts of life that I had never had the will, or the courage, to look at before. Perhaps it was a shame that it took the process of dying to give me the confidence and self-belief that had always eluded me, or perhaps I could have died twenty years later as I had lived most of my life, believing myself to be an 'ordinary' woman, and I am not sure I would have traded with God on that. My friends and family would have traded, but me?

Even with all of that, it still took a few weeks for the news to settle in me. The hardest thing was going to be telling Grace, and to be honest I didn't want to tell her at all. Perhaps that was, in part, a selfish act. In not telling Grace, not saying the words 'I have cancer' out loud to the person closest to me, I was able to stop it from becoming real. Shirley knew, but that was different. Her histrionics would have been offensive if they didn't act as a sort of entertaining distraction for me. (Shirley reminded me of when I was a child in Ireland and used to marvel at the old women keening at wakes and funerals, weeping and wailing and wringing their hands inconsolably until the refreshments arrived and they would tuck into the tea and sandwiches as if nothing had happened. Professional mourners; Shirley was a professional hysteric.) I was managing my feelings, accommodating the cancer, but I knew that once I told Grace all that would change. Once Grace took it into her world, I had no say, no control over it any more. 'It', the cancer, the fact of my impending death would become a runaway train or, worse still, one of my daughter's 'projects'. Grace was such a strong character, I was afraid she would react by hijacking the situation, taking over.

I put off telling her for as long as I could, but then she found out anyway, which was annoying, especially as it was my fault. She found a list I had written for myself when she was snooping around my kitchen, as she always did. After she found the note, I still didn't want to tell her, I was afraid of hurting her. I was more afraid of what my death would do to her than I was of dying myself. I had always believed that loving Grace more than I loved myself meant that I was a good mother, but I came to wonder if I had been right about that. Perhaps I would have set her a better example if I had been more assertive and confident in myself, and perhaps it would have been better if I had worried less about disrupting her life and told her the truth about her father, and about Michael. But then we mothers always get it wrong.

Despite my stubborn refusal to talk to her about my cancer, Grace pushed and pushed. She didn't give up; she was dogged in her determination to get me to do the right thing. As she had done so many times before – when she almost caught me being beaten by her father, when she made me apply for the job at Bailey Newton – my bossy, pig-headed, marvellous, emotionally extravagant daughter dragged me kicking and screaming into my own life. In forcing me to face my situation head-on, she made me decide how I needed to spend those last few months.

I wanted to give my death a meaning, leave something behind. I wanted to get things in order. In her persistence, she also made me realize that the thing that bothered me most about dying was Grace herself. What would happen to her when I wasn't around? She wasn't as tough as she made herself out to be and she relied on me a lot more than either of us was prepared to admit. We spoke to each other almost every day, and even though she had always been bossy and capable, it was those very character traits that illustrated her vulnerability to me. Nobody else saw. If she had rebelled, or come back home looking for money or solace from time to time, I would have worried for her less. It was her very infallibility that frightened me, her seeming self-reliance. If Grace was in trouble, she would tell nobody and nobody would think to ask. There was no one to scoop her up and take care of her. Not that she had ever asked that, even of me, but she had always known that I was there for her. She had always known she had somebody to turn to, somebody who loved her enough to withstand any hardship, to carry her through any storm. Once I was gone, there would be nobody who cared for my Grace the way I had. So I made it my priority to set Grace's life up to be as easy as it could after I was gone.

thirty-two

Grace

'I can't tell you what to do about Michael, Grace. It's up to you.'

Brian was not his usual cocky self. The one time I needed to rely on the opinion of the most opinionated person I knew, he came over all wishy-washy.

'Do you want me to come over?'

'No, no, there isn't . . .'

. . . time. There was no time. None to even finish the sentence.

I had gone back to the house after my meeting with Michael, picked up my car and gone straight to the hospice. Mum had failed in less than twenty-four hours out of my care. Either the hospice was terrible – which it wasn't – or she had only kept herself alive these past few days for me. She didn't have long left, the sister in charge told me. She was asleep all the time now, so I sat with her for a while then wandered around the rooms of this miniature, intimate hospital, avoiding other grieving people, leaving untouched cups of tea behind me, half eating chocolate biscuits and thinking Will I, won't I ring Michael?

When I eventually snapped open my mobile phone and called Brian, the story exploded out of me so fast that I felt angry at myself for having wasted half a day sitting on it. So his understated response was a bitter disappointment to me. And there was something else.

'How did you know his name?' I asked.

'Whose name?'

'Michael. You said "Michael". My brother's name.'

'Did I? I don't think I did.'

Had I said his name when I was telling Brian the story? No – I was certain I hadn't. Was this some kind of freaky telepathic thing where, now that my mother was dying, the name of my brother was stretching through the boundaries of our known universe and implanting itself in the minds of other people, as if he had been there all along?

No. So what, then? Where my mother was concerned my mind had become used to pre-empting the unthinkable.

'Did I say Michael? Really? Is that his name?' Brian's words were runny and his voice weak. He was a terrible liar, really pathetic. I could hear that he was trying too hard, which meant my instincts were probably right.

'Brian, did you know about him? Did Mum tell you about Michael?'

There was a silence into which I wrote a yes, yet when he sheepishly admitted it – 'Yes, Eileen told me about your brother' – it still felt like a shock. It stung like I had been walloped across the face – a huge, black betrayal, a lie that had lasted a lifetime.

And then suddenly there it was, my answer. Shorter

than I had expected, easier, sweet and certain, my epiphany. The startling realization that none of it really mattered any more. I could be hurt or not hurt that Mum had told me about Michael. I could be angry about Brian, with Brian; none of that would change things. None of it meant anything. What did it mean that she hadn't told me about him all of my life? That she had felt able to tell Brian, and who knows who else, but not me? Was it that she loved me too much to tell me? That she was afraid of my reaction, or hers, or that I would try to find him? The point was that, whatever it meant, it didn't *matter*. I was at the edge of a precipice and I had two options, leap or turn back, risk or waiver, yes or no. Leaping is always saying yes. It wasn't in my nature to say no. So I dialled Michael's mobile number and arranged to meet him at the front door of the hospice in an hour's time. Then I went up to Mum's bedside and tried to tell her what I had done.

I told her everything else: all of the things you're supposed to say, and all of them true. That I loved her; that she had been a wonderful mother; that I was grateful to her for all the times she had been there for me; that I was proud to call such a strong, independent, beautiful woman my mother. I recalled good times that we'd had, laughter, and I told her that I didn't mind growing up without my dad, that she had been mother and father to me – and I was surprised at how much I meant it.

But for all that pouring out of me, I could not tell her about Michael. Even at this last-minute stage, even when all that mattered was the truth, I still couldn't tell her. I got a taste of how it must have been for her. Some things are too big to put into words; was it cowardice that stopped us both from telling the truth? Surely all secrets are better out in the open? Or perhaps, telling secrets is the sole prerogative of the people who own them. All I needed in that moment was for my mother to die in peace. I did not need Mum to know I had found Michael and I could not pretend that I knew what she needed, if it was right or wrong to bring him in to meet her. The only truth I had was the idea that my mother might have regretted giving her son away, missed him – the pain of having birthed him as a lonely, frightened, young Catholic girl was too terrible for me to think about, too painful a reality to contemplate, so I could only manage my own feelings about it. And in knowing that, I understood then why she had kept him a secret from me for all these years: to protect me. She had not needed me to know about him. But if keeping secrets is a weakness, I thought, it is a normal weakness. Like loving someone too much to let them go, like the savagery of physical illness and the ignobility of pain. My mother had the courage to walk down a catwalk, dying of cancer, in her early sixties. She didn't have the courage to tell me I had a brother. And did I have courage really – or was everything I had ever done an act of unthinking rashness? If I had ever bothered to look properly, would I have 'leaped' as often as I had?

Oh my God! I couldn't do this. I couldn't land this on my mother now. Jesus! What had I been thinking? I had to go downstairs and ring Michael straight away. I had to head him off.

I left Mum's hand gently by her side and went

downstairs to the reception area as quickly and demurely as I could. When I got there, Brian was sitting in an armchair engrossed in a women's magazine. I walked over and stood in front of him.

'Hi,' he said, 'I came anyway.'

I burst into tears. Messy, stupid, girlish tears. Like a plain girl being told she's pretty for the first time. I was about to dissolve into his arms and he was about to catch me when I heard Michael asking for me at the reception desk. I looked at Brian, and saw my terrified face reflected in his eyes.

'I don't know what to do,' I said.

'Sshhh . . .' he said, rubbing my arms like a comforting father. Then he wiped my eyes with his palms and said, 'Want me to take him in to Eileen?'

As soon as I saw Michael's concerned, serious face I knew instinctively that it was the right thing to do.

'Yes.' I barely whispered it.

They followed me up the stairs and Brian took Michael to see Mum.

There were words spoken; I heard mumbling and a high note that could have been my mother's last words. I don't know what went on between them for the time they were behind that curtain, but the miraculous thing was that I didn't care. It has not seemed important to me, then or now. It was their time and I was able to let them be.

After a few minutes Brian stuck his head through the curtain and signalled me. Mum was lying with her eyes closed and her hand curled limply in Michael's palm. I sat at her other side and took her other hand in both of mine. I could not keep my body still and silent like the men; I knitted her fingers into mine, squeezing them, stroking them, holding them to my mouth and kissing them, willing movement into them, trying to fuss and fiddle them back to life. Brian stood sentry at the end of the bed. Silently she left us; she was there and then she wasn't. We sat there, a peculiar trinity in the immediate wake of her: Brian, stern and serious, Michael in awkward disbelief and me dissolving into tears.

My soul scooped out and started chasing around the room searching for her, and what was left of me disappeared into a tunnel of loss.

thirty-three

Eileen

My final list

1. Go blonde
2. Finish the garden
3. Sangeeta – send her a ticket to London?
4. Stock up on *posh* scented candles
5. Solicitor! Solicitor!
6. Designer sponge bag & smellies for hosp.
7. Kitchen drawers – finally sort out!
8. Find husb. for G
9. Party – First Wives gang!
10. Geoff down to decorate living room

It's true that we are only given as much as we can handle in life. I always had enough: enough strength when I needed it; enough love, once I knew where to find it; enough faith to believe things would work out for the best – which they did. I knew that in the end, because I was looking back. For most of my life, though, I had looked forwards and I always wanted more for myself. More freedom, more fulfilment, to be leading a greater, better, more graceful life. But I never had the self-confidence, the get-up-and-go to achieve more than just enough. That's why I passed my dreams on to my daughter. I wanted her to have more. In those last few months of my life, I realized that I had succeeded on both counts, and had been holding on until I had truly seen all that I had achieved, both in my own life and in what I had been given with Grace.

Everything happens for a reason; I believed that then and I believe it now. In some ways dying was the most successful thing I ever did. During the fashion show I looked better than I had ever done, because the limited amount of time left gave me the confidence to do and say things I never had before. I redecorated my house, redesigned the garden, and I felt more loved and more alive than ever before. But the most important thing that dying did for me was making me finally realize what I had done with my life.

I had never thought that my life amounted to very much, not compared with what it might have been if . . . well, if I had ever completed the big things that were on the list I was always too afraid to write down: go to university, make Frank marry me, write a book, travel, find my son. I always kept my lists manageable, do-able. I never struck out too far for fear I would fall.

It was only when I found out I was dying that I made a conscious decision to truly live. Like most people, I realized, I had just been pottering along; now I was suddenly filled with this burst of energy to *get on with it!* I had a bit of money saved and I was going to blow every last penny of it doing the things I had never done. Would I splash out on designer clothes? Go shopping in New York? I sat down to write a list full of ambition; write down all the crazy things I ever wanted to do in my life and see how many I could get through. But then, as I started to write, the strangest thing happened. I realized that what I wanted to do now was just a version of what I had been doing all along. Have a party, go shopping for cosmetics and candles, visit friends or have them visit me. And I realized that all I wanted out of my life was more of the same. So all I had left to do was get the full value out of what I had. And the beautiful, amazing thing that I discovered was that through the prism of my impending death, the colours in my garden were brighter, the people in my kitchen were warmer, and I had some time to appreciate it all. How lucky, I felt every day then, that God didn't choose to just run me over by bus. But I was extra-careful crossing the road, just in case.

In those last few months, one way or another, I did everything that was on my list. Brian – well, he just fell into my lap. Literally. Shirley and I had gone out to the Irish Club, and Brian was in the dance hall with an Irish friend of his. With his two left feet, he fell over the edge of the carpet and sent his beer flying on top of me. Shirley was the worse for wear and attached herself to him – it was disgusting, actually, and put me right off her. Right away I could see what a nice sort of man Brian was and thought, Grace! Shirley asked the two men back for a party at my house, then she and his friend went off and we got talking about my cancer, his wife and the volunteer work at the hospital. He ended up staying the night on my sofa. I'm not sure why, except now I think he just thought I was nice and wanted to be my friend. Maybe I reminded him of an older version of his wife. After he met Grace the following morning, I didn't take any chances. I rang the out-patients unit at the hospital and put myself on a list for a home counsellor. I dropped his name and prayed.

There was no getting rid of him after that. I knew Grace, however objectionable she made herself at times, was no fool and would fall for him eventually.

If Brian was a gift out of the blue, the old reliables coming through for me was even more of a gift.

When I rang Geoff and told him the news, he didn't make a fuss, just said, 'Let me know if there's anything I can do.'

A month later, I rang and said I had a project I wanted his help with.

'I want Grace to be able to move in here after I've gone, but there's a few bits I need done.'

'She doesn't deserve you – besides, I thought you were leaving the house to me and Barry?'

'Will you come?'

'Of course.'

He came down and stayed for two weeks. During that time he redecorated the living room to beyond my wildest dreams, all shades of beige and brown and really classy. I could never have done it myself. Then he set to work on the garden, and the two of us wore a path to the garden centre, spending before and behind us on pots and plants. We both enjoyed ourselves immensely: 'You're quite a creative little woman really,' Geoff said, and it felt like a real compliment. Grace was so irritable with us both during those weeks that at times I felt like slapping her and saying, 'This is all for you, you selfish cow!', but I didn't. She'd find out soon enough when the solicitor read out my request that she live in the house after I was gone.

In any case, she more than made it up to me by organizing the most fantastic party of my life. Everything was perfect: the food, the lighting, the music – nothing, nothing about that night could have been more special. It felt like not my last party, but my first one. It was the only party I had ever felt completely relaxed at – and the first one I had ever fully enjoyed. There were no goodbyes. Rather, it felt like my chance to say hello properly for the first time to so many friends, old and new.

The missing link then was Sangeeta. I had spoken to her throughout, but did not have the courage to ask her to come and see me. I knew she was busy with her family, and her own mother was unwell so it didn't feel right to ask her to travel halfway around the world to see me. Grace bringing her along to the fashion show was one of the most extraordinary things that ever happened to me in my life, like a dream come true; neither of them will ever know how much it meant to me. It was through all of these things that I came to understand how much I had achieved in my sixty-odd years. I had created, found and held on to all of these wonderful people, all of this love. This was what my life had amounted to – and it was a lot. Too much to fit into a few short months.

Then, when I started to get very sick, everything

changed again. Knowing that you are going to die is one thing, but the actual process of dying is a terrifying one.

I became depressed. Afraid. My faith wavered and I started to hate God – to wonder if He existed at all, or if I was just going to be sucked down into a cold black hole. Death moved truly down from my head to my heart. The knowing I was going to die became seeing and feeling that I was dying. What I had experienced as a kind of terrible adventure had sunk. The glamour and excitement, the live-for-the-day attitude that had launched the *Titanic* of my terminal cancer now hit the iceberg and for those final weeks I shivered on a cold raft, knowing my fate.

I could not stop thinking about Michael. He haunted my drug-fuelled dreams. In my conscious moments I was torn, wondering whether I should tell Grace about him; fearing that I had confessed all to her in some morphine-induced moment of candour. My body began to shrink and gnarl; the humiliation of pain and the indignity of being dependent on drugs might have taken me over, broken my spirit completely, were it not for Grace. Because amongst all of the fear, the anger and the depression were those moments of warmth and closeness with her. Times when she would gently lift my body to one side when changing the bed, bring food to my mouth with tender confidence, and I would feel that the circle was nearing completion. That I had borne and reared this marvellous woman, who from her childhood had shown herself to be full of beauty and courage and humour, but who was now revealing herself to be so much more. She was not just my child any more, but for the first time ever perhaps I was forced to see her properly as a woman. Through her nursing me, I felt God was forcing me to understand fully what she was capable of; what a strong, special character she was. Sometimes I thought that was to torture me because I had to leave her, and other times I took it as reassurance that she could look after herself when I was gone.

A few days after the fashion show, I had decided to get my affairs in order, and I tackled the final clear-out of my office desk. I wanted to put together a box with a few things, memorabilia for Grace. It was a foolishly sentimental idea as the house was full of her stuff anyway, but I had found an ornamental box which Sangeeta had once brought me back from a trip to India and I thought that might be a nice use for it. While I was rummaging I found a dictionary and, for no particular reason, I looked up the word 'grace'. I made a note of what it meant. I thought it would be a nice gesture for Grace's box:

1. elegance of movement;
2. courteous good will;
3. the free and unearned favour of God;
4. a divinely given talent or blessing

Throughout her life she became all of those things to me, and towards the end it seemed to me that the miracle of Grace had stretched back to the moment when I had first seen the film star's name as a child.

My daughter became my Amazing Grace; God-given and human, Grace made it possible for me to hold on to life, and eventually Grace made it possible for me to let it go. Brian brought Michael in to me moments before I died, but I knew it had been Grace who had found him for me. His smile, the warmth of his hand over mine was my final miracle. I knew who he was and I said his name. 'Michael.' That was all.

I heard a priest once say at a funeral that when you die, you are like a tree in winter. The leaves have fallen: the possessions, the foreign holidays, the passionate romances, the lost jobs, the petty fights and jealousies are all gone. What is left are the bare branches: the essence of your life that will live on through the years, rooted, strong, standing sentry over what you have left behind.

I left this world with my two arms outstretched, the dead twigs of my fingers encased in the hands of my two children. How it came to be that way didn't matter, because I knew that holding them together in that moment meant I would never have to let either of them go again.

Epilogue

The morning of my mother's funeral, I found a bottle of Chanel No. 5 in an old black handbag she had once borrowed from me. It had leaked, staining the fake-satin lining. The scent was so familiar, so cloyingly real, the smell of my mother getting ready for a special occasion, that for a moment I believed she was there, but she wasn't. That is the worst kind of pain, when you can feel something but you know that it isn't real.

Perhaps that's why I started going to church again after she died: I needed to believe in something because my heart was full of her and my mind had to make sense of that fact, make my overwhelming feelings mean something tangible. So I turned to Mum's Catholic God. The man in the white beard put her in heaven and there were angels and the Virgin Mary and all that malarkey that she believed in. It comforted me and I knew she would have liked it – which is why I never did it when she was alive. That was another small miracle that I discovered: my relationship with her continues even though she is not physically here any more. I find things that remind me of her, I talk to her and I hear her talking to me. Her things are all around me: Mum is as much a part of my new family as I am.

I know that blood does not automatically guarantee an affinity, but for Michael and me it did. Perhaps it was losing our parents and the mutual need we had to extend our families that made us feel instantly close. Or perhaps Mum's Irish blood ran warm in us both, carrying her craving for people. We see each other once or twice every week and meet up for Sunday lunch. Katy is like a sister and his kids call me 'Auntie'. His daughter looks like me.

Then there is Brian. It's been a slow-grow love with its roots in our friendship. We disagree about everything that's not important, like politics and religion, but agree on everything that is important, like where the dustpan and brush should live, and his sons' girlfriends. He supports me; he let us move into Mum's house, he held me when I fell apart after she died. I tried to push him away so many times and he wouldn't go. He knew he could make me better with his love, and he has. Kindness in a lover, I have learned, is a much underrated quality, and I intend to be with Brian long enough to return the selfless kindness he has shown to me.

I thought I knew who I was before Mum died, but I didn't. Therapy doesn't teach you who you are; life does. And the only lessons I ever truly learned were through the hard things. You suspect you know yourself, but it is only when your back is against the wall that you will see what you are truly made of. Mum dying was the hardest thing that ever happened to me but through it I learned that I had strength and compassion. I was the same person I had always been, but I first experienced the depth of my own humanity through her death. It was a lesson I would have happily lived without if it meant keeping her with me. But she isn't with me, and I did learn it, and I'm grateful for that. I learned other stuff too.

1. That you can love someone and be irritated by them at the same time.
2. That nothing is ever absolute – not even a mother's love – but that doesn't mean it is compromised. It's still a lot.
3. That life can never be completely taken away. It lives on in the hearts and lives of those whom you have touched.
4. That finding the truth is not important – that there is only what is in front of you in each moment. Hold it, enjoy it, because soon it will be gone.
5. That there is no 'meaning' in life – nothing means anything.

It means nothing that Mum gave Michael away; it means nothing that I found him; all that's important is my friendship with him now.

I have changed. I'm less selfish now that I have other people to be responsible for. I lose myself in their lives, forget who I am and what I want and need. I am focused on them and I am happy with that. I live less in my own head and more in the distraction of doing. For years it was just Mum and me, and now I live within the community of an extended family. It seems bizarre and yet somehow she created this life for me.

This morning I tackled the garden for the first time. Mum is dead but her garden continues to flourish – growing wild like an unwatched child. Her lawn was a square patch of long grass and in the middle of it was a patch of blue forget-me-nots. I found a trowel, dug them out and replanted them in a small pot for the kitchen windowsill. My life and how I live it is her legacy.

Acknowledgements

For research, thanks to Mary Gillian,
Eammon O'Boyle and Nicky Molloy.

Special thanks to Mary Keane Dawson
and Grainne Casey.

Thanks to my agents for your ongoing support,
Marianne Gunn O'Conor and Vicky Satlow,
and
to my editors, Imogen Taylor and Kersten Dobschuetz,
for making it better.

Also Helen Falconer, Una Morris and Dee Hanna
for their invaluable input and advice.

To my mother, Moira, for inspiration and strength.

My husband Niall for being there.